MOVING ON

Rosie Harris

This first world edition published 2015
in Great Britain and the USA by
SEVERN HOUSE PUBLISHERS LTD of
19 Cedar Road, Sutton, Surrey, England, SM2 5DA.
Trade paperback edition first published
in Great Britain and the USA 2015 by
SEVERN HOUSE PUBLISHERS LTD.

British Library Cataloguing in Publication Data

Harris, Rosie, 1925- author.
Moving on.
1. Grandparent and child–Fiction. 2. Retirement
Communities–Fiction. 3. Liverpool (England)–Fiction.
I. Title
823.9'14-dc23

ISBN-13: 978-0-7278-8474-9 (cased)
ISBN-13: 978-1-84751-580-3 (trade paper)
ISBN-13: 978-1-78010-628-1 (e-book)

All Severn House titles are printed on acid-free paper.

Severn House Publishers support the Forest Stewardship Council™ [FSC™],
the leading international forest certification organisation. All our titles that
are printed on FSC certified paper carry the FSC logo.

Typeset by Palimpsest Book Production Ltd.,
Falkirk, Stirlingshire, Scotland.
Printed and bound in Great Britain by
TJ International, Padstow, Cornwall.

For Pat Gregory

Acknowledgements

With many thanks to my agent Caroline Sheldon and to the SEVERN HOUSE editorial team for all their help and support.

One

Jenny Langton sighed as she switched off the mower and flopped down on to the garden seat to take a short rest.

A trim woman of medium height, with dark brown hair and hazel eyes, wearing dark brown cotton trousers and a light blue linen top, she looked very capable and younger than her fifty-nine years.

It was almost the end of June 1973, a dull muggy day with a threat of rain in the air, which was why she had decided to cut the grass that afternoon.

Although it was only a week since she had last cut it, it had looked so long and unkempt she'd felt duty bound to do it.

She looked at the lawn critically, noting that the lines were slightly uneven, and sighed again. When Eddy had cut it the stripes had always been as straight as a dye. And when he'd finished mowing he had always trimmed around the edges afterwards with a strimmer so that they were sharply defined. Well, trimming them would have to wait for another day, she told herself; it would take all her energy to put the mower away in the garage.

She missed Eddy so much, she reflected, as she went indoors and made herself a cup of tea. You didn't expect your children to die before you did and Eddy had been only thirty-eight, exactly the same age as his father, William, had been when he had died in 1945.

Eddy had been only ten years old then and, as a result, Jenny reflected, they had become exceptionally dependent on each other, comforting each other in their grief. Even after he had grown up they still remained close.

It had been almost as much for Eddy's sake as her own that she had stayed in Warren Point, the house that William had bought and been so proud of owning.

It was a lovely house on a high promontory at the end of Warren Drive overlooking the point where the Mersey estuary joined the Irish Sea. In the far distance the Snowdonia range of mountains in North Wales were clearly visible.

William had been so proud of their achievement the day they

moved in there. Eddy had been a three-year-old toddler and he had carried him to the end of the garden so that they could look out across the Mersey to the Bar where liners waited their turn to come into Liverpool to dock and unload their passengers or cargo.

As soon as the tide was right for them to do so, a fleet of little tug boats would come out, attach their lines to the liner and guide it into port.

The house had cost far more than they could comfortably afford but William was confident that he could meet the overheads. He was halfway up the ladder of management at the Premium Printing Company based in Liverpool and he intended to get right to the very top; to one day become managing director of the company.

The early days really had been quite a struggle, and it had taken them several years to completely furnish the house in the way they wanted it. They'd chosen every item with care and always the very best they could afford. Jenny loved every inch of her home and still treasured all their possessions.

Eddy had grown up there enjoying a happy, healthy childhood, attending the nearby junior school in Wallasey Village and then advancing to Wallasey Grammar School. He had also had an active social life in the local community.

William's death when Eddy was only ten had been a terrible blow to him as well as to her, but with her encouragement Eddy had fulfilled all the plans his father had outlined for him; grammar school, university and then a position with Premium Printing.

He'd gone to a university in the south of England. It was there that he'd met and fallen madly in love with Fiona, a red-headed, feisty Londoner.

Deep down, from her very first meeting with Fiona, Jenny had thought their relationship a mistake. She was Eddy's first girlfriend and he was mesmerized by her. He had always been so sensible about everything that Jenny hesitated to intervene, afraid that it might be jealousy on her part that was making her feel that it was an unsuitable match.

It had been a whirlwind courtship and, not wanting to appear to be an overbearing or possessive mother, she relied on his good judgement, constantly assuring herself that he knew what he was doing. After all, she hardly knew the girl, and apparently Eddy had known her throughout the three years he'd been at university.

Eddy had joined the Premium Printing Company when he left university and the same year married Fiona. For economic reasons they had moved in with Jenny in Warren Point. In William's will the house had been left jointly to her and Eddy so it seemed to be the sensible solution. It was large enough for Eddy and Fiona to have their own set of rooms and live independently.

Like his father, Eddy was ambitious and settled in well at Premium Printing, but his home life was far from stable. Fiona was not domesticated; Jenny was proud of her home and Eddy found himself continually making peace between his wife and mother over domestic tiffs.

Fiona was a career girl and found work as a press relations officer for a shipping agency in Liverpool. Her hours were so erratic that within a very short time it was agreed between the three of them that the running of Warren Point would be left entirely to Jenny. They also agreed that they would all eat together and that Jenny would do the shopping and cooking.

When Fiona discovered she was pregnant she was far from pleased. From the moment Karen was born she resented having to give up her glamorous job. When Karen was a year old she insisted on going back to work and asked Jenny if she would look after Karen.

At first Jenny had refused. She was already kept busy running their home. But Fiona said that if she wouldn't do it then she would engage a full-time nanny. Jenny hadn't wanted to have another stranger in her home so she had given in and agreed to look after Karen.

Karen was an adorable baby and Jenny found she enjoyed looking after her and watching her grow into a bright toddler with a sunny smile and endearing ways and finally into an intelligent little girl. She often thought of her as the daughter she had always wanted.

Eddy idolized his little daughter but Fiona seemed to hardly notice the child. She didn't appear to have any maternal instincts whatsoever. She didn't even pick Karen up and kiss her or sit and cuddle her, and, as Karen grew older, it was always left to Eddy or Jenny to read her a story at bedtime.

When Fiona's job took her away from home for several days at a time she never enquired after Karen's welfare when she returned. The only time she seemed to notice the child was when they had visitors, and then she basked in their praises when they said what a lovely little girl Karen was becoming.

Fiona made no secret of the fact that she found living in the north of England very dull. It was the start of the swinging sixties and Fiona wanted to be in the thick of all the excitement. She was convinced that to do that it was imperative for her and Eddy to move to London.

For once Eddy dug his heels in and refused to listen to her. Shortly after Karen's fourth birthday Fiona told him that she couldn't stand being married to him any longer and that she was leaving him and wanted a divorce.

Nothing Eddy said or did could persuade her to change her mind. When Eddy finally agreed to a divorce she told him that she didn't intended taking Karen along with her.

'She's your responsibility. I never wanted a child,' she told him. 'Your mother has cared for her practically from the day she was born so she can carry on doing so.'

Eddy was a devoted father and worked hard to provide for Karen and his mother. Like his own father he was determined to become managing director of Premium Printing; but he died before achieving his goal.

As soon as he had known about his illness a few years earlier Eddy had set up a special fund to make sure that there was enough money for Karen to complete her education.

Jenny and Eddy had had great hopes for Karen's future. She was bright and intelligent and enjoyed school. They hoped that she would follow in his footsteps and work at Premium Printing. They had wanted her to go to university but Karen had dug her heels in and steadfastly refused.

'I want to leave school and start work the moment I am old enough to do so,' she insisted, her green eyes flashing as she pushed back her shock of dark blonde hair.

For the first time Jenny realized that there was a strong resemblance to Fiona, both in Karen's looks and manner, and it troubled her.

It was around this time that Karen suddenly started asking questions about her mother. She wanted to know what she had looked like, what she had done for a living, why she had left, where she was now and why she never wrote to them or came to see them.

Jenny left it to Eddy to fill in the details but she was aware that Karen was suddenly taking a great interest in her appearance and in what she wore. She changed out of her school uniform the minute she came home and deplored the fact that her clothes weren't the latest styles. Jenny insisted that she would have to wait until she was earning her own money before she could buy any new ones, so Karen wore frilled petticoats with her last year's cotton skirts to make them appear fuller and longer in keeping with the latest fashions.

When she left grammar school, nothing either Jenny or Eddy could say would make her change her mind about going to university. They did manage to persuade her to go to a secretarial training college in Liverpool.

'She can always go to university later on as a mature student if she wants to,' Eddy told Jenny. 'I'm pleased that she won't be leaving home. Anyway,' he added, 'it might even be better to let her start right away on the bottom rung of the ladder at Premium Printing and work her way up; that way she'll know what it's all about.'

Jenny had agreed with him, knowing that Karen was not only assured of a secretarial position when she had finished training but that Eddy would be there in the background and able to keep an eye on her progress.

Now with Eddy's recent death, everything had changed. Karen was nearly eighteen now and within a matter of weeks would be leaving college where she'd been studying English and secretarial skills.

She would certainly have to earn her own living, Jenny mused, because rises in the cost of living meant that the money Eddy had left would quickly be exhausted and her own income from the insurance William had taken out wouldn't keep them both. In fact it barely covered the expenses involved in running Warren Point.

She knew Karen had been promised a position as a secretary at Premium Printing but with Eddy no longer a director there Jenny wondered how well she would cope on her own.

In the last few months her personality seemed to have changed. She was far more demanding than she had been when Eddy was alive. Nowadays she was ready to argue about most things; certainly about everything she was asked to do. That sort of attitude wouldn't go down at all well in an office, Jenny thought worriedly.

It was no good dwelling on the problem Jenny reflected, but she suspected that Karen didn't really want to be a secretary, rather she would have liked to work in public relations, the same as her mother had done.

Two

Karen Langton, looking extremely efficient in her trim black suit and plain white blouse, picked up her notepad and newly sharpened pencil and made her way into John Williams's office.

It was her second week at Premium Printing and she was now becoming used to being summoned almost the moment she arrived at work to take down dictation by Mr Williams, a middle-aged balding man who was one of the directors.

Karen supposed that he must spend the previous evening thinking about all the things he had to do next day and started composing the letters on his way into work in the morning.

To her surprise, instead of leaning back in his black leather swivel chair, closing his eyes and beginning to dictate the moment she entered his office as he usually did, he was sorting through a pile of papers that almost completely covered the top of his desk.

'A reporter from the *Liverpool Gazette* is coming in late this morning for a story on the history of Premium Printing. You'll find all the details you need in these,' he said as he gathered the papers up into a single pile.

'Since your father was a director here you probably know most of the history of our company anyway,' he added as he handed them to her.

'You want me to put together a publicity story from these?' Karen frowned.

'That's right. About two thousand words,' he told her crisply.

'Surely it's up to the reporter to do that.'

He stared at her over the top of his gold-rimmed spectacles. 'I want you to do it. I want the article to be accurate, not some trumped up journalistic make-believe. If we hand it to him ready to set then we should get what we want.'

'Very well, but if he is a properly trained journalist then I'm afraid he will make changes because he will want to rewrite it in his own style,' Karen warned.

Mr Williams dismissed her with a wave of his hand, completely ignoring what she had said.

Returning to her own office, Karen devoted the next couple of hours to writing and rewriting her piece; polishing it until she felt it was not only a hundred per cent accurate but ready to be published exactly as it stood.

Mr Williams didn't even glance at it when she returned to his office and handed it to him.

'You'll find the reporter waiting in reception,' he told her. 'Give it to him and tell him not to change a word of it.'

'How do you know it's accurate?' Karen asked. 'You haven't even looked at it.'

He dismissed her with a wave of his hand. 'When you've done that, come back with your notebook; I have several letters to dictate.'

Feeling a little miffed, Karen went down to the reception area. Waiting there was a tall handsome man in his mid-twenties casually dressed in grey flannels and a dark green tweed sports coat. He was drumming impatiently with his fingers on the counter.

She looked at him speculatively. He didn't look like a reporter but there was no one else in sight. 'Are you from the *Liverpool Gazette*?' she asked.

'Depends who is asking,' he told her, his dark blue eyes twinkling.

'Have you come to collect some copy?' she asked primly, not responding to his teasing look.

'Is that all you have for me?' he asked, holding out his hand to take the typed sheets from her.

'Make sure that it goes in exactly as it stands with no alterations whatsoever,' she told him decisively.

He frowned. 'I can't promise you that; it's bound to need some editing.'

'No!' She clung on to the papers. 'It has to go in exactly as it is written. Those are Mr Williams's instructions.'

'Is he the chap I spoke to on the phone?'

'Yes. He's one of the directors here and his word is law.'

'So did he write this copy?'

'No, I did.'

'You did.' His blue eyes gleamed. 'Well, that certainly makes all the difference. If you did it Miss . . .?' He paused and looked at her enquiringly.

'Langton, Karen Langton.'

'Thank you, Miss Langton.' He reached out and took the typed sheets from her hand. "I'm sure it will be perfect and I'll see it is printed just as it stands,' he told her with a mocking little bow that brought a flush to her cheeks.

'Would you like to see an advanced copy so that you can check that I have kept my word?' he asked, turning to look at her as he headed for the door.

'That might be a good idea,' she countered. 'I was always told never to trust a newspaper reporter.'

'Touché! Well, in that case you'd better meet me tomorrow night at seven o'clock at the Odeon restaurant and check it over while you have dinner with me.'

He was gone before she could answer, and Karen went back up to her office with a half-smile on her face. He certainly had a nerve, she thought, wondering whether she ought to keep the date since he had not even told her his name.

She was still thinking about him as she collected her notebook and a couple of well-sharpened pencils and returned to Mr Williams's office.

For the next hour she was forced to concentrate on what he was dictating and put everything else out of her mind.

'Have you ever thought of using a dictating machine, Mr Williams?' she asked when finally she closed her notebook.

'I beg your pardon, Miss Langton?'

The thought had been in her mind for days but she inwardly choked as she heard herself saying it out loud and saw the startled look on his face. In many ways Premium Printing favoured old-fashioned methods and stuck to the traditional ways of running a business.

'You've only been here five minutes and already you're trying to change the way we do things,' he said tetchily.

'I was thinking that it would be time-saving and more economical,' Karen told him, her chin jutting defensively.

'Indeed! Well it might be more economical and certainly time-saving if you returned to your office and typed up the letters I have given you rather than sitting here debating about something that won't happen.'

Dismissed, her cheeks burning, Karen went back to her desk and tried to concentrate on what she had to do but Mr Williams's reaction infuriated her. He hadn't even asked her for details about how it might improve things, she thought rebelliously.

He certainly didn't have the company at heart; he hadn't even checked what she had written about its history, she thought, as she finished typing the letters, put them in a folder and returned them to his desk for signature.

She wondered if he would even bother to read it when it was finally in the newspaper. At least she would have prior knowledge that it was word perfect and unchanged, she thought, as she remembered the reporter's promise to let her see it before the paper went to press.

She switched her thoughts from work to what she would wear for her dinner date at the Odeon restaurant. She had never been there but she knew it was quite posh and she didn't really have anything in her wardrobe sophisticated enough for such a place.

Also, she still had to tell her gran where she was going. She was bound to want to know more about the young man she was going with, and Karen realized that she still didn't even know his name.

There was only one way to find out, she decided. She'd telephone the *Liverpool Gazette* and ask if she could speak to the reporter who had been sent to collect the material from them. She wouldn't give her own name, simply say she was Mr Williams's secretary.

Her ruse worked. The reporter's name she was told was Jimmy Martin.

'He's not here at the moment so shall I ask him to telephone you when he comes in?' the girl on the switchboard asked.

'No, that won't be necessary,' Karen told her, and she rang off quickly before the girl could ask any more questions. She hoped that the girl wouldn't tell Jimmy that someone from Premium Printing had phoned although even if she did he had no proof that it was her.

As Karen feared, Jenny was far from happy at the thought of her going out to dinner with a stranger.

'I really think it is irresponsible of Mr Williams to expect you to do something like that when you are so new to the job,' she remonstrated. 'Make sure you get a taxi to bring you home and charge it up to Premium Printing. It's not safe for a young girl to be on her own in Liverpool late in the evening – and certainly not when you have to get the ferry home. Perhaps I ought to come over and meet you.'

'Gran! I'm eighteen and I'm a working girl now. I can take care of myself, so don't worry.'

'I wouldn't worry if I knew this young man you are meeting there. Why on earth couldn't he bring the paper to the office; surely that would be a far more professional way to behave.'

'I think he thought he was doing me a favour by asking me out for a meal,' Karen said, her cheeks flushing slightly. 'Anyway, there's no need to worry, he wouldn't be working for the *Liverpool Gazette* if he wasn't respectable.'

'I'm not so sure,' Jenny said worriedly.

'I'll be all right. Far more important is what am I going to wear?'

They spent the next half hour deciding. In the end Karen settled for a plain green dress that reflected the green of her eyes. Jenny offered to loan her the double row of pearls she only wore on special occasions.

'I'm not sure they will look right on me,' Karen murmured, wrinkling her nose in disdain as she held them up against the dress. 'I was wondering if I could borrow your green pendant; that would really look stunning.'

'My pendant? Surely you don't mean the one that your father bought me! That's a real emerald and I would be heartbroken if you lost it.'

'Please, Gran, it is a special occasion,' Karen begged. 'I promise I'll take great care of it.'

Jenny went into her own bedroom and then brought back the pendant. She fastened it around Karen's neck and stood back, frowning.

Karen drew in her breath as she stared at her reflection. 'It really is beautiful, Gran.'

'Well make sure you take care of it, it means a great deal to me and I couldn't bear to lose it,' Jenny said smiling.

'It will be like having you there beside me all evening to make sure I behave myself,' Karen teased as she leaned forward and kissed her grandmother on the cheek.

Three

Jenny couldn't settle. She picked up her knitting, did a few stitches and then put it down again. She turned on the TV, watched for five minutes or so then switched it off and turned on the radio. That was even worse. She switched that off, got up and went into the kitchen to put the kettle on, hoping that perhaps a cup of tea would calm her jangling nerves.

She knew that it was ridiculous to feel so apprehensive simply because Karen had gone out to dinner at the Odeon restaurant with someone called Jimmy Martin, but she couldn't help it. She had never met him and she suspected that he might be a good deal older than Karen.

What was more, as he was a newspaper reporter, she imagined him as somebody rather brash; a man of the world. What on earth was he doing taking a young girl like Karen out to dinner? In her eyes it boded no good.

Frankly, she didn't trust his motives and, even though she looked older than eighteen, Karen was not very worldly wise, especially when it came to men. She was friendly with quite a number of boys who had been at college with her, or played tennis with her, but she had never had a serious boyfriend.

This was her first date and Jenny wished it was with one of the boys from the tennis club, someone she had met and knew.

The evening seemed endless. Finally, Jenny put on a coat and walked to the end of the garden. She stood there looking out across the Mersey to where she could see the lights of Liverpool twinkling against an inky black sky, inwardly praying that Karen was safe and that she would be home very soon.

Karen had jokingly said that if she could borrow the emerald pendant to wear that evening then it would be like having Jenny standing by her side keeping an eye on her; now Jenny hoped she still felt that way and that the pendant really was acting like a talisman, keeping her safe.

★ ★ ★

Karen Langton was enjoying herself. The Odeon restaurant was packed with couples and groups of three or four. They were all engrossed in each other's company and the delectable food and delicious wines being served there.

Jimmy had secured a table for two tucked away in a far corner of the room. From where she was sitting Karen could see all that was going on and revel in the luxurious surroundings.

She'd been so relieved to find that Jimmy was waiting outside when she'd arrived. He was smartly dressed in a dark grey suit, and a pale blue shirt set off by a blue and grey striped tie. The moment she saw him all the nervousness she had felt about the evening vanished.

'Wow! Do you look stunning,' he greeted her. 'Blondes should always wear green, especially when they have such lovely green eyes as you have.'

'You scrub up well, too,' she told him with a wide smile as he took her arm and guided her into the building.

The restaurant impressed her. It had seemed to be vast when they were led into the dining room. When they had taken their seats and she'd regained her composure she realized that one wall consisted entirely of mirror glass from ground to ceiling and had the effect of doubling the size of the room.

She left the ordering of the meal to Jimmy because she had no idea what to choose. She'd simply said she liked fish and chicken best and left it to him to do the rest. The result was the most wonderful food and wine she had ever tasted.

He chose a starter of deep fried Brie with cranberry jelly and salad and she found it delicious.

On her way over on the ferryboat Karen had been wondering what they would talk about. As a reporter he probably knew all that was going on and she was not sure that she would be able to keep up with him. The last thing she wanted him to think was that because she was younger than him and only just out of college, that meant she was ignorant of what went on in the world.

After a few false starts, however, she found talking to him was easy. He seemed to be really interested in why she was working for Premium Printing.

'I would have thought that someone as smart and pretty as you would have gone in for something more glamorous than being a secretary,' Jimmy commented.

'Really?' Karen was startled; she wondered if he was making fun of her or simply trying to make conversation and put her at her ease.

'My father was a director there and I more or less simply walked into the job when I left college,' she explained, as the waitress collected their plates after their first course and they waited for the main dish to be served.

'Ah, that accounts for it. You see I couldn't understand why with your looks and figure you weren't working as a model or something to do with fashion.'

Karen smiled at his flattery. Then, as they tucked into the pan-fried smoked haddock topped with a poached egg on a bed of delicately flavoured mash potatoes, she found herself confiding in him. She began telling him about her mother and the publicity job she'd had and how she hoped that one day she would be able to follow in her mother's footsteps.

Jimmy nodded. 'Publicity! That's more like it. You'd make a wonderful press officer in the fashion or travel industry. I'll keep an ear to the ground and let you know if I hear of anything going. It's surprising how in my job you get to know about these things in advance of them becoming general knowledge or the position being advertised,' he told her.

She felt overwhelmed by his interest in her future. Nervously she sipped her glass of white wine. It was deliciously cool and smooth and she felt her confidence returning as she took another sip and then another.

'You certainly don't want to spend the rest of your life cooped up in an office taking dictation from some pot-bellied, grey-haired old man,' he told her with a grin.

'It's not quite that bad.' Karen smiled, wondering what Mr Williams would think of such an unflattering description.

'You want to be out in the world seeing the action; travelling perhaps.' He studied her thoughtfully. 'If you worked for one of the big shipping companies as a press officer you would probably get the chance of worldwide travel,' he pointed out.

Karen's green eyes widened in appreciation. There was nothing she'd like more but she couldn't see her gran being very happy about her having a job like that.

Rather reluctantly she explained the situation to Jimmy and felt as if her high hopes were draining away as he pursed his mouth in a silent whistle and shook his head.

'That will never do,' he said solemnly. 'What you need to do is to get right away from granny and find a flat of your own.'

'One day perhaps,' she said dreamily. 'I couldn't afford to do that at the moment. In three years' time, when I'm twenty-one I will inherit the money my father left me, but until then I am dependent on my grandmother to put a roof over my head.'

Jimmy shook his head. 'That's not necessarily true. If you had the right job you would be able to afford to share right now. Think of the independence that would give you. I bet your grandmother wanted to know exactly where you were going tonight and that she will be waiting up for you to come home.'

'Yes, you're right about that. She wasn't at all happy,' Karen admitted, her colour rising.

'I bet she wasn't! Especially when you said you were going out with someone she has never met.'

Karen bit her lip and said nothing. It was too near the truth for her to want to comment. Instead she concentrated all her attention on the chocolate brownie served with cream and ice cream that he had ordered as their dessert.

'You really do need to get out from under your grandmother's thumb as soon as you can,' Jimmy commented as their coffee was served.

'Think about it, Karen,' he urged when she remained silent. 'As I said, you could always share with someone to start with and see how things went. You could even go back home to Granny if you weren't happy,' he added with a reassuring smile.

Karen nodded thoughtfully, then, suddenly aware that they had been talking for a very long time, she looked at her watch and was shocked to see the time.

'I must be going,' she gasped. 'I had no idea it was so late.'

'Granny will be cross?' Jimmy asked, raising his eyebrows.

'Well, she'll be concerned.'

'I understand.' Without another word he called for the bill, settled it, collected their coats and helped her into hers.

'How do I get hold of a taxi?' she asked. 'Will someone from here phone for one if I ask them?'

'Taxi. What on earth do you want a taxi for? It will be terribly expensive from here to Wallasey at this time of night.'

'I know, but I promised Gran I would get one and not travel home on the ferry if it was late.'

Jimmy smiled. 'You'll be quite safe. I'll be there with you.'

'You can't come all the way over to Wallasey and then back again,' Karen protested.

'I certainly have no intention of letting you go home on your own,' he said firmly. 'Granny would never forgive me,' he added in a mocking tone.

Karen bit her lip and said nothing. She knew he was teasing her but it made her feel childish and she didn't like it.

They talked of general matters as they walked to the Pier Head and on the rest of the journey home he told her something about himself and what his job at the *Liverpool Gazette* entailed.

Gradually, Karen regained her composure and once again she found herself enjoying Jimmy Martin's company.

When they reached Seacombe she told him there really was no need for him to come any further. She would take a bus to Wallasey Village and from there it was only a couple of minutes' walk to Warren Point.

Jimmy wouldn't hear of it. 'I certainly don't intend to abandon you half way home; I'll take you to your door,' he insisted.

Ten minutes later as they walked up the path to her home she wondered if perhaps she should invite him in and introduce him to her gran.

Jimmy forestalled her. When they reached the front door he said goodnight, gave her a fleeting kiss on her cheek, and turned and walked away before she even had time to thank him for a wonderful evening.

Four

Jenny Langton was worried. It was the end of the month and as she went through the pile of bills stacked up on the kitchen table her feeling of dread that she wasn't going to be able to pay them all mounted.

Karen had been at work for over six months now and had completed her trial period. She was now on a full wage. True, it wasn't a lot but even so she must ask her to hand over a little more towards the housekeeping if they were to keep their heads above water.

She had hoped that Karen would volunteer to give her more and that she wouldn't have to ask but Karen was spending every penny she earned on new clothes.

This month alone she'd bought a new trouser suit and two new dresses. She already had a very nice navy trouser suit so why did she need to go out and buy another one, Jenny mused. True, the new one had flared trousers and was in a pretty shade of green but she didn't really need it. She rather suspected that Karen was buying so many new clothes to impress Jimmy Martin.

Jenny wasn't at all sure that she approved of their friendship. Jimmy Martin was far too full of himself and, because he was several years older than her, Karen seemed to do everything he suggested. Furthermore he was bombarding her with all sorts of suggestions about changing her job for some sort of publicity work like her mother had done and that really worried Jenny.

She remembered all too well what had happened in the past; Fiona had become tired of Liverpool and wanted to move on to London. She didn't want Karen getting those sort of ideas in her head, at least not for many years to come.

No, Jenny decided, she'd speak to Karen that very night. She'd make something special for dinner and then explain to her that making ends meet was becoming more and more difficult. She'd ask her if she could contribute a little more of her wages.

Before she finally managed to broach the subject Karen put down her knife and fork and, looking most uncomfortable, blurted out, 'Gran, there's something I have to talk to you about.'

For a moment all thought of asking Karen for extra money went out of Jenny's mind as a rush of other worries took over. What on earth was wrong? Why was Karen looking so upset? Had she lost her job or, worse still, was she pregnant?

The thought of how that would ruin her young life, how it meant she had failed not only Karen but Eddy as well flooded Jenny's mind. Her heart was pounding as she waited for Karen to go on.

'I've changed my job,' Karen said hesitantly, pushing her thick blonde hair back behind her ears and tossing her head. Her green eyes were defiant as if she was expecting Jenny to make an adverse comment or even a scene.

A mixture of concern and annoyance flooded through Jenny. A feeling of tremendous relief that it was nothing more serious quickly followed this.

'I see,' she said quietly. 'So where are you going to work now?'

'That's not all,' Karen went on, ignoring Jenny's question.

'Go on. What else?'

'I'm moving out, Gran, I'm going to share a flat over in Liverpool,' Karen stated.

Once again a feeling of anger and concern battled in Jenny's mind.

'You can't afford to do that,' she expostulated. 'You will certainly have to hand over a great deal more of your wages than you do at the moment if you are going to pay your way sharing a flat. You certainly won't be able to afford to keep buying new clothes like you've been doing lately.'

The two women stared at each other in silence for several seconds, then Jenny went on, 'As a matter of fact, I was on the verge of asking you if you could contribute a little more each week to the housekeeping because I simply can't make ends meet. The cost of running this house is going up all the time and my income seems to be shrinking with the increased cost of living.'

'I'm sorry, Gran. I've already agreed to this new arrangement. Living and working in Liverpool will mean I have hardly any travelling expenses,' she added brightly, as if that explained everything.

'You haven't told me where you are going to work,' Jenny said. 'I thought you were happy at Premium Printing. Ever since you were a small girl you always said you wanted to follow in your dad's footsteps when you were old enough to do so,' she added with a sigh.

'I did, but this new job will be much more exciting. At Premium Printing I'm just the junior secretary, so I get all the duff jobs. I am even expected to make tea for all the directors and to do Mr Williams's filing.'

'You'll probably find it is much the same wherever you go,' Jenny pointed out. 'As the newest and youngest member of staff you have to expect that. Anyway, I would have thought filing was all part of a secretary's job.'

Karen shrugged her shoulders, giving her a pained look but no answer.

'So what is this new job?' Jenny persisted.

'Working for one of the shipping companies. As a press liaison officer,' Karen said abruptly.

'And where is this flat? Who are you going to share it with, then?' Jenny queried. 'Is it with one girl or several?'

Again Karen was silent and looked so uncomfortable that Jenny's heart began to pound again. Something wasn't right, she was sure of it. Karen wasn't telling her the complete story.

'I'm sharing with one other person, that's all,' Karen said at last, avoiding Jenny's eyes.

'I see. Can you afford to do that? Where does she work? Is she a lot older than you? Does she have a good job?'

Her barrage of questions fell on deaf ears. Karen pushed back her chair and stood up from the table and moved towards the door, eager to get away. Then she paused and turned to face Jenny.

'I suppose I may as well tell you, Gran, because you are bound to find out sooner or later.' She paused, colour flushing her cheeks. 'I'm going to share a flat with Jimmy Martin.'

Jenny stared at her granddaughter in stunned silence. This was something she had been afraid of hearing, and now Karen had voiced it aloud she didn't want to believe it.

'Are you sure you know what you are letting yourself in for, Karen?' she asked exasperatedly.

Karen straightened her shoulders and glared at her grandmother. 'Of course I do.'

'You won't find it as comfortable as living here, you know,' Jenny went on. 'You'll be expected to do your fair share of the housework, shopping, and the cooking. Have you actually seen this flat?'

'No.' Karen stared at her defiantly.

'Well, don't you think that perhaps you should take a look at it first?'

The silence hung between them like an invisible barrier. It was one that Jenny knew would never completely go away. She stared at Karen dispassionately as if seeing her as she must appear to other people. Karen was no longer the little girl she had nurtured and cared for since she was a baby; Karen was now a slim, elegant, eighteen year old and, with her dark blonde hair and lively green eyes, she was extremely attractive. Karen was no longer a teenager who was willing to accept guidance. She was a young career woman who was determined to fly the nest.

A vision of Jimmy Martin, handsome, self-assured, well-dressed and brash, filled Jenny's mind. She'd only met him once but she hated him. He had taken away Karen's innocence and now he was taking her into his clutches completely.

Ever since Karen had first told her about him she had hoped that he would find Karen too young and naive and rapidly tire of her company.

She knew Karen was deeply infatuated with him and that a break-up would result in bitter heartache for her; but better that than for him to ruin her young life completely. Now it seemed this was the very thing that was happening.

She suspected that it was Jimmy Martin who had not only persuaded Karen to change her job but also told her not to say a word about her intentions until the very last minute when it would be too late to do anything about it.

Jenny sighed. It meant that Jimmy Martin had complete influence over Karen and it also seemed that since she held him in such high regard there was not very much she could do about it.

Perhaps if she accepted what was happening she would at least remain friends with Karen. If anything went wrong, as she was quite sure it would, Karen would turn to her for help. Oppose Karen and she would lose out in every respect and perhaps never see or hear from her ever again.

Taking a deep breath, Jenny asked as calmly as she possibly could, 'So when are you moving out?'

Karen looked taken aback. 'Quite soon.'

'It's only a matter of a couple of weeks to Christmas, you're not moving before then are you?' Jenny asked.

'I'm not sure, I haven't fixed the exact date with Jimmy yet. There's no hurry is there?'

'No, not really, except that if you are leaving then I will have to make some plans myself for the future. If I want to go on living here then I will have to see if I can find a lodger or perhaps even two to help share the costs.'

'Lodgers!' Karen looked aghast. 'You wouldn't like to have strangers living here with you, would you, Gran?'

'No, I certainly wouldn't but as I have already tried to explain I simply can't make ends meet, so I will have to do something like that if I want to go on living here.'

'Perhaps you should get a job,' Karen suggested hesitantly.

'At my age! I'm sixty years old, remember, and I have no training or experience of working,' Jenny said sadly. She was suddenly conscious of the streaks of grey in her hair and her faded looks. She hadn't bought any new clothes for years, except for the black outfit she'd bought for Eddy's funeral.

Karen looked at her critically. 'You don't look all that old,' she said, frowning. 'They might be able to find a job for you at Premium Printing. I'm sure you could do proofreading or something of that sort.'

'I don't really think so,' Jenny said drily. 'You need training even to do that.'

'Then it will have to be lodgers, I suppose.' Karen shrugged. 'There are four bedrooms here and you will only be using one of them after I move out so there's plenty of room.'

She seemed to be so disinterested, that Jenny didn't pursue the matter, knowing that it was pointless to do so.

Karen's news had upset her far more than Karen realized. All she wanted to do was to sit down quietly on her own with a cup of tea and try and unravel her jumbled thoughts.

Five

As he braked to a stop in front of a terraced house in Dalrymple Street, the taxi driver looked over his shoulder at the well-dressed young lady in the back of his cab and asked, 'You quite sure this is the right place, Miss?'

Karen was already leaning forward and peering out at the grim three-storey building as if unable to believe her eyes. She consulted the slip of paper she was clutching in her hand to verify the address before nodding and murmuring, 'Yes, this must be the right place. It's the address I've been given.'

The taxi driver switched off the engine and leaned back to open the cab door for her. He jumped out, opened up the boot and heaved Karen's two heavy suitcases out on to the pavement.

As she climbed out of the back of the taxi and stood there on the pavement looking uncertainly at the row of houses, he held out his hand. 'Two quid.'

'How much!' she exclaimed in a startled voice. 'You've only brought me from the Pier Head!'

'Two quid, that's the fare for you and your luggage,' he demanded in a surly voice.

Karen searched in her handbag for her purse and then handed over the money. 'You are going to carry those cases as far as the front door for me?' she asked.

The man pocketed the money and then slid back behind the wheel of his cab. 'Not likely, you haven't even given me a tip.'

Before she could remonstrate with him he had switched on the engine and pulled away from the kerb.

Karen checked again that she was at the correct address. When Jimmy had told her that it was a penthouse flat she'd asked him what that was supposed to mean.

'That it is right at the very top of the building with splendid views out over the city, of course.'

His words rang in her ears as she studied the long terrace of identical houses. They all appeared to have stone steps leading down to the basement living area and then a shorter number leading up to the front door.

The ground floor flat had a large bay window; on the second and third floors there were medium-sized windows and then, right at the very top, there was a room running up into the eaves with a much smaller window. Was that the so-called penthouse flat, she wondered.

She picked up the heavy suitcases, one in each hand, and staggered towards number thirteen.

She paused at the bottom of the five stone steps leading up to the front door and decided that as the cases were so heavy she would have to take them up one at a time.

To her relief the scarred black painted door was unlocked, so she pushed the first case into the hallway and left it blocking the door open while she went back for the other one. Before she managed to reach it a stray dog was sniffing round it about to lift a leg. Angrily she shooed it away.

With both cases safely inside the building Karen stopped to get her breath back. In front of her was a steep flight of carpeted stairs leading up to a small, square landing. From there she could see another flight of stairs going up to the next floor.

She wished Jimmy had arranged to be there when she arrived, but since he wasn't she wondered if it would be safe to leave her cases in the hallway until he came home.

As she turned to close the front door she looked out into the squalid street outside and a shiver went through her. It would be foolhardy to leave her cases in the hallway she decided. Somehow she'd have to get her luggage up to the top flat even if it took her the rest of the day to do it.

Carrying one case at a time, she progressed from one landing to the next until she reached the very top.

She was so exhausted that her hand was trembling as she fitted the key Jimmy had given her into the lock and opened the door.

Once the two cases were inside she closed the door and collapsed into the first armchair she could find. She closed her eyes and waited for her heart to stop pumping like a wild thing and for her breathing to return to normal.

She was nineteen but she felt like ninety. In future, she resolved, whenever there was any heavy shopping, she'd make sure that Jimmy was with her to carry it up all those stairs.

Ten minutes later she felt back to normal and looked around with interest, eager to explore the flat.

Apart from the armchair she was sitting in, the only other furniture in the room was a sofa and a small drop-leaf wooden table with two straight back wooden chairs, a bookcase and an oak cupboard with solid doors.

What struck her most forcibly was that the living room was long and narrow with a sloping ceiling down one side. There was only one window and it was not very large. Remembering Jimmy's enthusiasm about the panoramic view she went over to look out. To her disappointment she found that the view was mainly of rooftops and chimneys with grey smoke drifting up from them into the sky. It was so high up that the people walking about in the street below looked like pygmies.

Turning away, she went to see what the bedrooms were like and was startled to discover that there was only one. It didn't even have a proper window, only a skylight, and one of the walls in there was also sloping.

She shuddered; the bed was pushed tight against the wall on one side and she was sure that if you sat up in bed on that side you would probably hit your head on the ceiling.

Apart from the bed, the only other piece of furniture in the bedroom was a small, dark oak chest of drawers with a mirror fixed to the wall behind it. There was no wardrobe, only a built-in cupboard. When she opened the door and looked inside she saw that it was so packed with all Jimmy's smart clothes that there would be no room in there for anything of hers.

The kitchen was also long and narrow with cupboards and worktop down one side – almost like a ship's galley. There was one small window that overlooked some sort of factory or warehouse building. At one end of the kitchen, partly concealed beneath the worktop, was the bath. The toilet was in a tiny room next door to the kitchen.

Lovely penthouse suite. The words drummed in her mind as she looked round at the shabby furnishings and she felt tears of disillusionment filling her eyes. After the spacious bedroom with its views out over the Mersey estuary and the misted Welsh mountains in the far distance, the warm scent-filled bathroom, the huge, beautifully furnished lounge and pristine dining room she had known in Warren Point, this place couldn't be more different.

She felt not only a sense of disenchantment but was overwhelmed with homesickness; not only for Wallasey and the lovely home in Warren Point where she had grown up, but also for her gran.

She was already missing Jenny. Although she had accepted that she was leaving, it had been obvious that her Gran had thought she was making a mistake.

If only she had listened to her reasoning and taken more time to consider what she was doing. It had certainly been a mistake not to insist that Jimmy showed her his flat before she had decided to move in – like Gran had suggested, she thought miserably.

It was too late to have regrets, she told herself. She went back into the kitchen to make herself a cup of tea but, although she found the electric kettle and switched it on, she couldn't find a teapot or even any clean cups.

The sink was full of dirty dishes, not only breakfast dishes but what looked to be those left from meals the previous day. Holding back a shudder of distaste, Karen used the hot water from the kettle to fill a small plastic bowl and washed them all up and stacked them up to dry. Then she refilled the kettle and searched again for the teapot so that she could make the cup of tea she longed for.

As she sat sipping her tea, she mulled over the drastic step she had taken. Had her gran been right after all? she asked herself. Had she been silly and rash to give up her safe job and lovely home to move in with Jimmy?

She still had no idea what her new job as a press officer would be like or even if she would be able to do it. What if they sacked her at the end of her agreed trial period?

Pride wouldn't let her return to Premium Printing, even if they would have her back. Still, as a trained secretary she could always find work somewhere else in Liverpool, she told herself.

She had almost finished drinking her tea when she heard a key turning in the lock and Jimmy came in. Her heart fluttered as she looked up at him. He was so tall and handsome, so smart in his sharp, dark grey suit, crisp white shirt and red and grey striped tie that instantly she felt all her niggling doubts vanishing.

'You've already made yourself at home I see.' He grinned as he came towards her. He bent down and kissed her on the brow. 'I hope there's still enough hot water in the kettle for me,' he said as he released her, shrugged off his jacket and loosened his tie.

'Yes, I'll make it for you,' she told him.

He drank it thirstily in one gulp when she brought it to him. 'Glad you are here?' He grinned again as he put his empty cup down.

Not waiting for her to answer he pulled her up out of the chair and drew her into his arms, kissing her passionately.

As she returned his kisses with equal fervour Karen forced all thoughts about the drawbacks she might encounter living in Dalrymple Street or when she started her new job from her mind.

She was in love with Jimmy and he was crazy about her and that was all that mattered, so of course it was going to be worth it, she told herself.

Six

Jenny Langton felt stressed. She had thought long and hard about having lodgers before eventually capitulating, and now that she had decided to take such a momentous step, she wasn't at all sure that she was doing the right thing.

There were several reasons why it was necessary to do so. One was that she simply couldn't manage to go on living in her beloved house on her meagre income without some form of additional help. She had practically used all the money Eddy had left her and if she had to fork out for any more essential repairs she'd have to start selling some of the furniture or some of her precious ornaments in order to meet the ever increasing bills.

Another reason was that she was desperately lonely. She was not used to living on her own with no one to talk to or look after.

Much as she loved her beautiful home, being on her own in a four-bedroom detached house could be quite frightening at times. It was bad enough in the summer months if there was a high wind blowing in off the Mersey but in winter when there were fierce gales or the occasional snow that had to be cleared away it was even worse.

She made a list of people who might be considered suitable as lodgers or as paying guests. After a great deal of deliberation she began striking out those who would not be acceptable.

She didn't want elderly ladies or schoolteachers who might be bossy or demanding; she didn't want very young women because she would feel too responsible for them.

She eventually decided that men would be the most suitable as lodgers; her list included bank managers, civil servants, retired army colonels, doctors and even lecturers at Liverpool University.

She hoped to find at least two, possibly three. She visualized them all sitting down with her to an evening meal that she had cooked and then relaxing over coffee in her comfortable lounge and conversing on their various topics in a friendly group like one big family.

With this in mind she wrote out a carefully worded card detailing the home comforts she was offering and added her address and telephone number. Then she set off to ask the newsagent in Wallasey Village to see if he would display it in his window.

'Yes of course I will, Mrs Langton. How many weeks? It's fifty pence a week payable in advance.'

'Oh, I think two weeks will be more than adequate,' Jenny said smiling confidently.

Feeling much more light-hearted about the matter now that she had taken some positive action, she returned home, prepared the rooms in readiness and waited expectantly.

At the end of the two weeks there had not been a single applicant. There was, however, a pile of bills on her desk that had to be paid immediately, which meant that once again she would have to make more inroads into her meagre savings.

The newsagent shrugged when she asked how it was she had not had any response to her advert. 'Not many people in Wallasey Village looking for accommodation,' he told her. 'Perhaps you should try placing your advert in the *Liverpool Echo*. I can arrange that for you if you like, Mrs Langton.'

Three days later she had two replies. One was from a Liverpool docker who arrived unshaven and in his dirty working clothes. To Jenny's relief he decided it was too far to travel from Wallasey to Liverpool each day. The other one was from a young man who said he was the manager at an office in the city. Jenny thought he looked far too young and brash for this to be strictly true and decided he was exaggerating. However, he was clean and friendly, well spoken and smartly dressed, so Jenny decided he was suitable and agreed to rent him a room.

Brian Coulson moved in the following weekend. Jenny gave him a bedroom that had a splendid view out over the Mersey and did everything she could to make him feel welcome. He said that he didn't want an evening meal but he would like her to provide him with breakfast.

After just one week Jenny knew she had made a ghastly mistake and that taking in lodgers wasn't working out, but she couldn't afford to tell him to go.

Brian Coulson was the most untidy person she had ever known. He left his room a shambles with his dirty clothes left lying on the floor and possessions strewn everywhere. Worst of all he left the bathroom in such a dreadful state with wet towels on the floor and shaving cream and toothpaste splattered all over the mirror that she dreaded going in there afterwards.

Something else that bothered her were the odd hours Brian kept. He was never home until after midnight and he always seemed to be in high spirits, banging the doors and making a lot of noise when he came in. Long after he went to his room she could hear his radio playing. This she decided was probably why he didn't get up in the morning until after nine o'clock and usually rushed out to catch a bus with his half-eaten piece of toast still in his hand.

The following week Jenny received a telephone call from a man called Austin Ford. He told her that he was a lecturer at the university in Liverpool and that he only wanted a Monday to Friday arrangement as he went home to his family in York every weekend. Jenny invited him to come and see the room she could offer him and discuss terms.

He was a lot older than Brian Coulson and was dressed in dark grey flannels, a dark red wool shirt and a tweed jacket with leather patches at the elbows. Jenny didn't like him very much but she agreed to rent him a room in the hope that once there was another man living in the house Brian Coulson might mend his ways.

Austin Ford was not only middle-aged and rather set in his ways but at times he could be extremely fussy and pompous. He brought with him a bookcase, which had a shelf that opened out to form a writing desk and he made a great to-do about exactly where it should be positioned in his room. He also gave Jenny strict instructions that she was never to touch it or rearrange any of the books and papers he left spread out on it.

It didn't take Jenny very long to realize that she simply didn't like having lodgers, but since she so desperately needed the money she forced herself to grit her teeth, smile politely and put up with their foibles.

She had told both men to 'make themselves at home' when they first moved in but she had no idea that they would take her quite so literally. Brian removing his tie and leaving it lying on the table or in the chair he'd been using, or draping his coat over the banister instead of hanging it up on the hallstand when he came in late at night was bad enough. When Austin Ford removed his shoes and placed his stocking feet up on the coffee table Jenny felt incensed. She sat tight-lipped wondering what she could do about it as he babbled on endlessly about the political tension that had arisen between Ted Heath and Margaret Thatcher.

A further problem was that the two men had to share the same bathroom and Jenny listened to the heated arguments between them each morning with growing concern. The tension between them whenever they met was palpable and Jenny knew she ought to do something about it.

The matter resolved itself at the end of the third week when Austin Ford announced that there had been a change in his plans and that he would not be there the following week.

At the time Jenny thought he was taking a week's holiday, but when she went upstairs to put clean sheets on his bed she found he had packed and taken all his belongings, even his books and book-case, with him and realized he had gone for good.

That same evening Brian Coulson said that it was too difficult for him to get back from Liverpool each night because the boats stopped sailing at midnight and he would be leaving for good in the morning. It appeared that when he said he was a manager he had failed to tell her that it was of a nightclub and that this was why he was so late getting home every night.

When the front door closed behind him Jenny walked round the house, opening windows, letting in gusts of fresh air in an attempt to cleanse the place of the presence of both of the men. It was wonderful, she thought, to have her home back.

As she stripped the beds and cleaned the rooms they'd been using she felt an overwhelming sense of freedom that they had both departed. It was such a relief not to have strangers there. If only she could turn the clock right back, she thought, and have Eddy back and Karen still a little girl and everything as it had been for so many years.

She knew that was impossible and knew she had to devise some other way of finding the money to maintain her beloved home. Perhaps Karen had been right and she should try and find herself a job of some kind.

Seven

Although she tried very hard Karen Langton found it difficult to settle in to her new surroundings and to adjust to living with Jimmy Martin.

It was not only that the tiny flat in Dalrymple Street was claustrophobic after her home in Warren Point but her relationship with Jimmy was so different from what she had anticipated it would be. His whole manner had changed in every way since she had moved in and Karen found it very disturbing.

He was moody; not only first thing in the morning but often for days at a time. The hugs, kisses and sweet talk with which he had charmed her and won her heart in the first place seemed to have vanished. He was curt, often disinterested in what she had to say and sometimes so downright rude and dismissive that she felt deeply hurt.

Furthermore he was lazy and slovenly at home. He seemed to expect her to wait on him as well as to be responsible for all the cleaning and cooking. She was willing to do her fair share but the way he treated her made her feel like a drudge.

All the romance and glamour seemed to have ebbed away and the old adage 'he only wants you for one thing' rang in her head when he made excessive sexual demands on her.

She quite liked her new job although she found it was much harder work than she had expected. Her immediate boss, Jason White, who was in his early thirties, was rather foppish. He dressed in a very arty manner and had overlong black hair that he kept sweeping back from his brow in an affected manner that irritated her.

He was the nephew of the owner of White Hart Publicity and he was both pedantic and demanding but Karen had to admire his artistic talents and his flair for dramatic presentations.

Jason was an ideas man who left all the leg work to someone else and that, Karen discovered, was usually her. She did all the mundane hard work and Jason basked in all the glory.

More and more Karen began to wonder if she had been rather hasty in her decision to change both her job and her home at the same time. Her job was nowhere near as glamorous as she had anticipated that it would be and her new home life was certainly disappointing.

She wondered how her gran was managing without her and sometimes felt a little guilty at having left her to cope alone.

For the first time in her life she realized what budgeting entailed. Jimmy didn't pay anything towards their food, saying that since he paid the rent for the flat and also all the lighting and heating bills then he expected her to pay for everything else they needed.

It had sounded ideal but she hadn't realized that food cost as much as it did or that there would be all the other things she was expected to supply like toiletries for both of them and cleaning items.

She had dreamed about all the new clothes she would buy and the trips to the hairdresser and perhaps even to a beauty parlour but found she couldn't afford to do any of these things.

True, Jimmy paid for the tickets if they went to the pictures or to a dance, but these outings didn't happen very often. He worked such odd hours that it was impossible to fit them in. Often he didn't come home until it was bedtime and usually there was the smell of wine or beer on his breath.

He always had a ready excuse that it was because he'd had to attend something to do with his work; reporting either a meeting or a business function of some kind. Even when she showed an interest and asked him to tell her about it he would never go into any details, which meant she could never check out in the next day's issue of the newspaper if his story was true or not.

Once or twice when she tried to press him to tell her more he accused her of nagging and not only refused to discuss the matter but sulked for days and completely ignored her when she tried to talk to him.

Karen bore it all as stoically as she could, partly because she didn't want to return to her gran and admit that she had made a terrible mistake. She desperately hoped that things between them would gradually get better. Jimmy was probably finding it was just as difficult having someone else in his flat as she did living there, she kept telling herself.

Yet surely he wouldn't behave in such a boorish manner if he really and truly loved me, she asked herself time and time again when they had one of their all too frequent spats.

When she blurted this out to him after a particularly bitter row in which they'd both said things to hurt each other, he told her that she was right – he didn't love her.

As she stared at him white-faced and aghast, he went on to tell her that he was in love with someone else and that was the reason he was so often late home in the evenings.

'You mean you've been taking someone else out?' Karen asked incredulously. 'How could you do such a thing when you know I'm here expecting you to come home and that I will have cooked a lovely meal and have it on the table waiting for you.'

His handsome face darkened. 'Because you bore me,' he said callously. 'You are so naive, so childish and such a goody-goody with your constant cooking and cleaning. I can't stand the way you pander to me and then expect me to do exactly as you want.'

'That's not true,' Karen said bristling, her green eyes swimming with tears. 'I try my best to please you. I cook you lovely meals and keep your flat spotless. When I arrived it was dirty and the sink was full of unwashed dishes. You never see it like that now.'

'That's the trouble, you're no longer any fun. You behave like an old married woman and you look like one. You even wear the same clothes day in, day out,' he told her contemptuously.

'That's because I have no money left over to buy any new ones,' she flared. 'I spend every penny I earn paying for food for you to eat. If I leave you'll probably starve to death.'

Jimmy shrugged but made no reply.

The tension between them became more and more strained. That night when they went to bed Jimmy made love to her, but he was so rough, almost as if he wanted to hurt her, that she yelled out in pain and pushed him away. Instead of taking her into his arms and comforting her he turned his back on her.

Karen lay awake afterwards feeling sore and miserable, listening to Jimmy snoring. When she woke the next morning she found that the bed beside her was empty and felt cold to her touch.

Three days later when they had still not spoken another word to each other and Jimmy had stayed out all night for two nights running, Karen packed her suitcases and left.

She wondered if she should have telephoned her gran to let her know that she was coming home but she was so confident that Jenny would receive her with open arms that she didn't think it would matter.

As Karen had anticipated, Jenny greeted her warmly with hugs and kisses, telling her how delighted she was that she was back home.

'Let's get these suitcases upstairs to your room and then we can have a cuppa before you start to unpack,' Jenny said in a matter of fact voice.

She helped to carry the cases up to Karen's room the same as she would have done if Karen had just returned from a holiday.

'Right, I'll go down and put the kettle on and give you a minute or two to freshen up,' she said, turning to leave the room.

She hesitated at the door and turned to give Karen a smile. She didn't pass any comments or ask any awkward questions but Karen knew that when she joined her downstairs Jenny would expect her to explain what had happened and why she had returned home.

Alone in her bedroom Karen breathed in deeply, relief flooding through her; she was so happy to be back in familiar surroundings once again. She crossed over to the window and stared out. The Welsh mountains to the left were shrouded in October mist. As she looked to her right at the Liverpool waterfront on the other side of the Mersey, it seemed so far away that it was like a different world.

Closing the window she looked around her bedroom with a sense of utter contentment. Everything seemed to be exactly as she had left it and her heart lifted. The events of the past eight months faded from her mind almost as if they were of no importance. All her books were still there, neatly arranged in the bookcase her father had bought for her tenth birthday.

She opened the wardrobe doors and found the clothes she had left behind were still all hanging there. She smiled; she really was back home. For the first time in months she felt free; her own person once again.

Nothing had changed, she thought happily. There didn't appear to be any sign of lodgers in the house so obviously her grandmother had found a way of managing without doing anything so drastic as taking strangers into her home.

Eight

Jenny had already made the tea, and as Karen entered the room she patted the sofa for her granddaughter to come and sit beside her, then she poured it out and handed Karen a cup.

For a few moments they sipped their tea in silence, enjoying each other's company. Then, as she replaced her cup and saucer on the tray, Karen began to tell Jenny all that had taken place between her and Jimmy Martin.

Jenny remained silent throughout apart from the occasional understanding nod or murmur of sympathy. By the end of Karen's story she was holding her hand in a mute attempt to comfort her.

'Aren't you going to say "I warned you", or "I told you so",' Karen asked heavily.

Jenny squeezed her hand. 'No, of course I'm not. I'm sorry it turned out so badly for you but you needed to find out for yourself. It's all part of growing up and being able to recognize what will work and what won't. So often when we come face to face with the real world it turns out to be quite different from our dreams.'

'You did warn me,' Karen gulped.

'True, but as I've already said, you have to find these things out for yourself. I've discovered that I am not cut out to take in lodgers,' she admitted with a sad little smile.

Jenny poured them each another cup of tea and then regaled Karen with the story of how she had fared with her two lodgers.

'So, we've both made mistakes and learned a lesson.' She smiled. 'We'll have to come up with a completely new plan about how we are going to manage in the future I'm afraid.'

'Well, I still have my job and since I have been promised promotion I shall be getting a pay rise so I'll help as much as possible,' Karen told her.

'I know you will, my dear, but I will still need to earn a living of some kind as well. The overheads here seem to be increasing all the time. I suppose we could move to a smaller place but I do love it here.'

'So do I,' Karen agreed, 'especially this room with its big picture window looking out across the Mersey estuary.'

She sat up straight, frowning as she looked around the room. 'There's something different about it today. You've taken the picture down from the opposite wall and the bureau has gone from the corner over there. Why have you moved them? Where are they now?'

'I sold them,' Jenny told her quietly.

'What on earth for? You loved them and you always said that they were very very old.'

'Yes, valuable antiques,' Jenny agreed with a sigh.

Karen stared at her, a puzzled look on her face. 'You mean that is why you sold them?'

'Yes,' Jenny nodded. 'I needed the money. I've sold several other pieces as well.'

'Oh, Gran! That is terrible. You were so fond of them; you were always telling me about their history.'

'I needed the money,' Jenny repeated quietly. 'I'll probably have to sell a good many more pieces to make ends meet. That is unless I manage to find a job and, as I have already discovered, my age and lack of business experience is making it difficult to do so.'

'Well, it's only a couple of months to Christmas so I am sure a lot of the stores in Liverpool will be taking on extra staff, so perhaps you might be lucky.'

'No.' Jenny shook her head. 'I wouldn't want to do all that travelling. Something local is what I would like. Didn't you find it tiring having to leave home so early to catch a bus and then the ferry and then another bus when you reach Liverpool?'

Karen shook her head. 'No, but then I enjoy travelling, and now I've got my new promotion I will certainly be doing plenty of that. Sometimes I am going to be away for days at a time, when there's a publicity event at one of the other ports in another country.'

Jenny sighed. 'You've certainly grown up and become very sure of yourself,' she remarked with a smile.

In that Jenny was right, and within a very short time she discovered that Karen was quite a different person from the girl who had left home to go and live with Jimmy Martin. In fact, in the weeks that followed there were times when she wondered if she knew Karen at all.

Karen also realized that things were different between them. She had learned to stand on her own two feet and to make decisions without referring to anyone else. Now she sensed the hurt and disappointment this caused her gran.

The frown that appeared on Jenny's face whenever she said, as she was leaving the house in the morning, 'I probably won't be back for at least three days' irritated her.

She knew she should have mentioned it to Jenny the night before, or even two or three days earlier, but she didn't want to have to explain her timetable or where she was going.

Karen found her new position so exciting and fulfilling that once she was on her way over to Liverpool all the problems relating to her home life vanished from her mind. It was like moving into a different time zone; a world that was exciting and glamorous.

She didn't know what she found the most fascinating; possibly entertaining travel agents, showing them hospitality at her company's expense and sometimes accompanying them on short trips on one or other of the liners the company owned.

Every trip was different but she always met people who intrigued her. Sometimes the brief friendships she formed with attractive men looked like developing into something more serious. They were usually from other parts of the country, however, so when their visit was over they went straight back home.

Sometimes a young, attractive man would hint that he would like to stay longer, but as she had no flat of her own it was impossible to agree to this unless they were prepared to book into a hotel and very few wanted to do that.

She assumed that it was because they didn't want their employers or their family to be able to trace their movements and find out what they had been up to.

More and more Karen began to wish she had her own place. She was earning good money and could well afford it if she didn't hand over so much to her gran, she reasoned.

The running costs of Warren Point were a constant source of concern. It seemed to Karen that no matter how much money she put into their home, although it was far more than Jenny did, it was never enough.

She brought the matter into the open over Christmas, the most solitary, frugal Christmas Day she had ever known. The two of them had sat down to a meagre meal of roast chicken, roast potatoes and Brussels sprouts. They'd forgone a drink and Christmas pudding. It might be advantageous for their figures but remembering all the pre-Christmas parties she'd attended in connection with her work it didn't seem a very good way to celebrate a festive occasion.

Jenny had managed to find three weeks' work before Christmas but that had ended when the shop she'd been serving in closed on Christmas Eve.

'Never mind, let's hope that a new year means things will be better,' Jenny commented as they washed up the dishes after their meal. 'I'm convinced that next year is going to be a fresh start,' she added optimistically.

'Well, it will be for me,' Karen said firmly. 'I'm moving out and into a flat of my own. Somehow life here hasn't been the same since I came home.'

'Whatever has brought this on?' Jenny asked in a shocked voice.

'I find living here is far too isolated, and much too restrictive and claustrophobic.'

'You've lived here all your life so how can it be all that much different? Are you blaming me?'

'No, Gran, it's nothing to do with you, it's me. I've changed. Living with Jimmy and having my own place has made me look at life in a different way. I want to have some fun and excitement in my social life as well as at work. I need to feel free to do what I want when I want to do it without having to mention my intentions to anyone else or ask their permission.'

'So it is living with me,' Jenny sighed. 'Well, can you afford to take on a flat on your own?'

'Oh yes. I've worked it all out. If I didn't have to hand over so much money to you each week I would be able to rent a flat and have money left over to enjoy myself.'

'I see!' Jenny stiffened and Karen tried not to notice the pained look on her grandmother's face. 'So that is what you intend to do?'

'Yes, Gran. It's wonderful being back with you but it's simply not working out because I've changed. Even living with Jimmy I had more independence than I have here; now I feel cramped. I promise I'll come and see you as often as possible.

'You mean I ask too many questions?' Jenny sighed.

'Partly that. I always have a feeling that you expect me to report to you about everything I do. I'm afraid to bring friends home in case you don't approve of them.'

'I'm sorry you feel like that, Karen. I am only trying to take an interest in your life,' Jenny said stiffly.

'Yes, and I get the feeling that these days you don't always like the same things as I do.'

'You know quite well that you can bring your friends here any time you wish and that I would always make them welcome,' Jenny persisted.

Karen shook her head. 'I don't think so, Gran. I'm not sure you would like them.'

Jenny didn't answer. She felt deeply hurt by what Karen said yet, at the same time, she understood. Karen was so like her father, Jenny reflected. Eddy had always demanded independence; always been quite sure that he knew what he was doing.

And look where that got him, she thought bitterly. He'd married the wrong girl and not only ended up heartbroken but with a young child to bring up.

She thought back to the countless sleepless nights she'd had when Karen was a small child and Fiona had been away from home for days at a time and she had been the one who had to try and soothe the little tot. She thought of all the traumas they'd known as Karen was growing up, the childhood illnesses she'd nursed her through, the dreaded exams. There had been joyous occasions too, like parties and holidays, she reminded herself.

Jenny sighed and stood up and went over to her desk. There was no point in dwelling on the past. She picked up the pile of bills lying there waiting to be paid; there were far more urgent things needing her attention than reliving the past, she thought grimly.

Nine

Jenny Langton sat at the dining room table trying to sort out the pile of bills she'd spread out there and place them in the right order. She scanned each one and then put it into the appropriate pile; those that had to be paid as soon as possible, the ones that could be put off until next month and those which she would forget about until the final demand notice reached her.

As the pile that had to be paid right away grew ever bigger she shook her head in despair. There really was no way she could cover them because she knew that there was nowhere near enough money in her bank account.

She had only just finished paying back the overdraft she'd had to ask for the previous month and she was pretty sure that the bank manager wouldn't grant her another overdraft so soon.

There was only one way out of the dilemma and that was to go and ask Karen if she would reconsider her decision about leaving home again; but would she?

Perhaps she'd do it if she told her that she proposed to divide up the house in some way into two separate flats. If she did that then Karen could live her life as she wanted without any interference from her, Jenny mused hopefully.

She looked at her watch; it was still only six o'clock. Since it was early May it would be light until at least nine o'clock so, perhaps if she went over to Liverpool right away, before her courage failed, and put this idea to Karen she might think about it.

Jenny wasn't sure where Bostock Street was, except that it was somewhere near Scotland Road. She had a tongue in her head, she told herself as she got ready to go, so she could always ask directions when she reached Liverpool.

She spent most of the time on the bus and on the ferryboat as it crossed over the Mersey going over in her head what she would say to Karen.

When she reached the Pier Head in Liverpool she set off up Water Street past Exchange Station and on into Scotland Road. It took her some time to find Bostock Street and when she did it looked so shabby that she couldn't believe that it was where Karen was living.

She once again checked the address on the slip of paper in her hand. As she hesitated at the bottom of the steps leading up to the front door a middle-aged woman in a black skirt and grubby blue blouse, a black shawl around her shoulders, came out and looked at her questioningly.

'You want summat, luv?'

'I'm looking for Karen Langton, this is the address she gave me.'

'Yes, well yer'll have to go down to the basement and knock on the door there,' the woman told her, pointing to some steps leading down to a battered green door.

Still unable to think she could possibly have the right address, Jenny went down the cracked stone steps to the small paved area littered with old paper bags and other rubbish that had blown in from the street and settled down there. Apprehensively she rapped on the door.

'I have got the right address then,' Jenny murmured as Karen opened the door.

'Gran! Whatever are you doing here?'

'I want to talk to you about something; can I come in?'

'Yes. Of course.' Rather reluctantly Karen opened the door back just far enough to allow Jenny to step inside.

'This way.' Karen took her through into a square room. Jenny needed a minute for her eyes to adjust. The long narrow window looked out on to the steps she had just come down, and as it was more or less below pavement level it didn't let in much light.

'Is something wrong?' Karen frowned.

'Not really; well yes, there is,' Jenny said rather breathlessly. 'It's about the house; I've had a splendid idea and I wanted to talk it over with you.'

'Sit down and let me make us a drink while you get your breath back.' Karen frowned as she waved Jenny into one of the shabby armchairs.

Left on her own Jenny looked round the room and shuddered. It had a low ceiling, the walls were covered in grey and pink wall-paper that was peeling away at the corners and the dark green curtains at the window were tied back with pink cord. The furniture was old and the two upholstered armchairs looked grubby.

There seemed to be nothing to mark that Karen lived there, and Jenny couldn't believe that Karen was happy in such surroundings. She will probably jump at the chance to come back to Warren Point she thought hopefully.

As Karen came back into the room with a tray on which there was a teapot, milk jug and two cups and saucers, Jenny took a deep breath ready to tell her what she was planning to do.

As they sipped their tea Karen listened to Jenny's tale of woe followed by her suggestion about turning the house into two separate dwelling areas.

'It sounds quite a good idea but where is the money coming from to carry out all the work?' she asked in a hard, tight voice. 'You've just been telling me about all the bills that are outstanding and how you can't afford to carry out the urgent repairs and decorating that needs to be done and your idea about making it into two parts will cost thousands. No, Gran, it wouldn't work.'

Jenny's mouth tightened. 'Please Karen, do think about it. We could take out a loan or even a mortgage to cover the cost,' she retorted and winced inwardly as she heard the pleading in her own voice.

'No, Gran. That's all pie in the sky. It wouldn't work and, anyway, I don't want us to live together again.'

'You're not telling me that you like living here in this . . . this . . . this squalor,' Jenny said tightly.

'No, I hate it here, but at present I cannot afford to pay out more. Fortunately I'm not here all that often. My work takes me all over the place and then I stay in top rate luxurious hotels.'

'So what am I going to do?' Jenny sighed. 'I was counting on you to be cooperative?'

'There is only one solution but you constantly close your eyes to it,' Karen said tersely.

Jenny looked puzzled. 'What's that?'

Karen's mouth tightened. 'Sell the house; sell Warren Point and move into a flat and let me have my share of the money and then I can afford to rent something better.'

Jenny stared at her in dismay. This was certainly not the answer she expected or wanted to hear. 'Surely you don't mean that,' she gasped. 'The house in Warren Point is our family home; your grandfather left it jointly to your father and me. Now it's our home, Karen, yours and mine. It's full of memories.'

'Yes, sad ones. Grandad and my dad both died there,' Karen said quickly.

'You spent such a happy childhood there,' Jenny said lamely.

'I know, but I'm grown up now and I want to break free and make a life of my own. It's time you did the same, Gran. Put the past behind you, and spend the rest of your life enjoying yourself, not worrying yourself into your grave because of the ever mounting bills.'

Jenny sighed. She knew there was a grain of truth in what Karen was saying but she was reluctant to take such a step.

'So you won't come back, not even if I try and convert the place into two separate entities?'

'No, Gran, because I know it won't work. There will always be bills piling up, ones which we can't afford to pay. Even as it stands the place needs updating and decorating. If we went ahead with your idea then that would take thousands and I'm not prepared to take on such a burden. Sell the house, split the money it fetches and let's both get on with our lives. Think of it as downsizing; lots of people are doing that these days.'

'I'd never get a mortgage on my own at my age,' Jenny stated, 'and I certainly don't want to move into a council place even if they would let me.'

'You won't need a mortgage and you certainly won't qualify for a council property,' Karen said impatiently. 'When we sell the house there will be plenty of money for both of us. We'll both be able to afford to buy a flat of our own.'

'There may not be as much left as you seem to expect, not after all the outstanding debts are paid off,' Jenny pointed out.

'Maybe not, but at least you will have cleared all the bills and not have to worry about them any more.'

Jenny nodded but she still didn't like the idea. She loved her house and the happy life she had known there until quite recently. If only she could turn the clock back and perhaps plan ahead for what had come to happen, she thought despondently.

'I don't think I could face living in a block of flats with children and dogs running around the place,' she prevaricated.

'Then buy one of those flats in a retirement block; ones that are specially built for the over fifty-fives.'

'I don't understand.'

'It's a new idea,' Karen explained patiently. 'People can only buy them if they are age fifty-five or over so there are no children and in many cases no pets allowed either. All the maintenance, including the cleaning of the windows, stairways and corridors as well as the care of the garden, is covered in an annual fee. All you have to worry about is looking after the interior of your own flat and doing your shopping and cooking your meals.'

'I'm not sure I want to share with other people,' Jenny said doubtfully.

'You own your flat and you have a front door the same as if you were living in a house. There's usually a communal sitting room where people can meet each other. It means you never need to be lonely but you don't have to go in there if you don't wish to do so. Some of these blocks also have a reception desk that is manned either full time or part time. In fact, it's very much like living in a hotel.'

'Where did you say they were building these sort of places?' Jenny asked dubiously.

'All over the country, but I'm sure you will be able to find some that have been built locally if you want to stay in the Wallasey or the New Brighton area,' Karen told her. 'Visit one or two estate agents; they will be able to give you all the details and tell you where they are being built.'

Karen collected their cups and put them on the tray then took it through to the kitchen that opened off the living room. Jenny hoped she was going to show her round the rest of the flat but Karen looked at her watch and frowned.

'Sorry, Gran, I hate to hurry you like this but I have to be at work in twenty minutes,' she said briskly. 'I'm catching an evening train to London and I'll be working there for at least the next four days,' she explained.

She bent and kissed Jenny on the cheek. 'I'll come and see you when I get back. But in the meantime why don't you go along to an estate agent and find out what sort of price he thinks you will be able to get for our house when you put it on the market. At the same time you can ask about these retirement flats I've been telling you about. They really are far more suitable than where you are living at the moment.'

Ten

Jenny returned home after seeing Karen, feeling tired and disillusioned. Awaiting her on the dining room table were the piles of overdue bills that had spurred her to visit Karen and make the suggestions she had.

Although it went against the grain she felt too tired to struggle any longer and resolved that on the following day she would do as Karen had suggested and visit an estate agent and seek advice.

The estate agent, Brian Hardy, was a thin man in his early forties, with a retreating hairline and a sympathetic manner, and seemed to be eager to help. He suggested putting Warren Point on the market to 'test the waters' as he put it. Once she knew how much her house would fetch then she would also know what sort of accommodation she could afford for herself.

In the meantime, he gave her sales literature to browse through which highlighted some retirement flats that were on the market. The price he proposed to advertise Warren Point at staggered her; it seemed much more than she had expected and she felt quite light-hearted. If it did reach that figure then her troubles were over. She would be able to pay off all her debts, give Karen her share and still have enough left over to buy herself a suitable apartment.

'Very well, will you take it in hand, advertise it or send out details or whatever it is you have to do?' Jenny told him.

'Right, I'll do that,' he agreed. 'You are happy for people to come and view? Do you want someone from here to accompany them or will you show them round yourself?'

Jenny hesitated. She hadn't thought of that aspect. The idea of taking people round and perhaps hearing them make disparaging remarks about her beloved home sent shudders through her.

'I would rather you sent someone with them,' she stated.

'Certainly, I can arrange to do that,' Brian Hardy agreed. 'Perhaps then you would like to leave a key with us,' he suggested. 'We will, of course, phone you in advance to make an appointment that suits you and our client but if you prefer not to be there then we can let ourselves into the house and handle everything on your behalf.'

When she returned home Jenny walked from room to room trying to see them through the eyes of a prospective buyer. She decided to make one or two changes in the way things were arranged in some of the rooms and also to put away some of her remaining precious ornaments just in case they were knocked over.

Leaving her home would break her heart but it seemed that it was the only solution, she thought, as she sat down and looked through the pamphlets about apartments that the estate agent had given her. There were none in Wallasey Village but there was a very attractive block of flats called Merseyside Mansions that had not long been built close to New Brighton. Her spirits lifted when she noticed that some of them had views and balconies overlooking the Mersey. As the building was only a mile or so further along the coast the view would not be so very different from where she was living now, she mused.

A week, ten days, two weeks passed without a single enquiry and Jenny began to panic. Then slowly a trickle of people came to view but no word came from the estate agent afterwards to say that any of them were interested in buying.

Jenny felt perplexed. How could people not want to live in such a lovely house, she wondered.

Karen sympathized but pointed out that the house required a great deal doing to it as the whole place needed decorating inside and out and it also needed the bathrooms updating as well as a completely new kitchen.

Slowly the offers came; and so did more bills. Jenny now felt desperate to sell and would have accepted the very first offer even though it was well below the asking price but the estate agent insisted she held out for more.

Two months later contracts were exchanged and Jenny suddenly realized that although she would now be able to settle all her bills she had nowhere to go.

'You could rent some furnished rooms on a short term lease and put all your furniture in store until you have decided where you were going to live,' Karen suggested.

'No.' Jenny shook her head emphatically. 'Having to move is bad enough, I don't want to prolong the agony. I'll have one of those retirement flats at Merseyside Mansions as long as it's one with a balcony and a view over the river.'

'I'm afraid all the ones overlooking the Mersey have been taken,' the estate agent told her.

'Then in that case I'll have to cancel the sale of my house,' she told him.

'You can't do that,' he exclaimed, 'not at this stage. Leave it with me and I'll see what I can do.'

Three nail-biting days later Brian Hardy phoned to say that he had good news. He had managed to secure a flat in Merseyside Mansions. It was one situated on the second floor and had a balcony as she had requested. There was just one snag, he explained, there was only one bedroom and she had stipulated that she must have two bedrooms. He offered to take her along there so that she could view it for herself.

'No, that is not necessary,' she stated after a moment's hesitation. 'I'll take it and leave all the details in your hands.'

'Very well, in that case I'll inform your solicitor and I'll let you know when to call into our office to sign all the necessary documents and to collect the keys.'

Jenny replaced the phone feeling as exhausted as if she had completed a five-mile walk or spent a whole day spring-cleaning. The deed was finally done. She had committed herself to a completely new kind of life.

She went into the kitchen and made herself a cup of tea, trying to clear her mind of doubts and make plans for the tremendous upheaval that lay ahead of her.

She had agreed to include all the carpets, curtains and light fittings in the sale, so now she had only to wait for the final completion date so that she could contact a removal firm.

She walked round the big house and realized it would be impossible to fit everything into a one-bedroom flat, so she would need to sort out what to take and what to send to the saleroom.

She telephoned Karen to tell her what was happening and to ask her if she wanted any of the furniture.

'No, Gran, nothing at all. I have no idea yet where I will be moving to or what size it will be until I know how much money you are giving me. Send whatever you don't need to the saleroom,' she advised.

'You mean you don't want anything at all?' Jenny persisted. 'I thought you would like some of the furniture or pictures or ornaments from your bedroom.'

'No, Gran, I don't want anything at all, and you will need to get rid of most of it. Remember there is only one living room and you'll have to fit dining room furniture in there as well as lounge furniture. I am quite sure that the big sofa and armchairs you have now will be much too large and so will the dining room suite. Perhaps you should think about sending everything to the saleroom and buy something more suitable for your new home.'

'That's a very drastic step,' Jenny protested.

'We're both setting out on a new life, so let's start afresh. Sell the lot, Gran, and buy new; choose something more suitable for modern surroundings.'

Jenny felt despondent when she put the phone down. She prized her furniture almost as much as she loved the house. Many of the pieces dated back to the early days of her marriage; furniture that she and William had worked hard and saved up for months to pay for and had chosen together. Could she bear to get rid of absolutely everything and start all over again? Surely it must be possible to take some of her favourite items with her.

There was only one way to find out she reasoned and that was to visit the apartment she was planning to move into and see for herself what size the rooms were. When she phoned and asked Brian Hardy for the keys he offered to accompany her but she said she would rather go on her own.

Her first impression was how small and boxy the apartment felt after her own home. Karen had been right, she thought, with a feeling of dismay as she looked around. None of her existing furniture would fit into such small rooms.

Then common sense prevailed. A double bed was a double bed so of course she could bring that; but hers was King size she reminded herself and so it would be far too big. She had no choice, it would have to be replaced by something smaller. The same fate awaited the heavy mahogany wardrobe with its matching tallboy and the triple-mirror dressing table.

There was a built-in wardrobe in the bedroom but it wasn't all that spacious. Unfortunately there wouldn't be room for another wardrobe so, it would mean that a great many of her clothes would have to go to a charity shop because there most certainly wouldn't be room for all of them when she moved.

Right, so that meant disposing of all her existing bedroom furniture, she decided. She still intended to have a double bed but she made a mental note to look for a divan that had storage drawers underneath it because that would be more practical. And instead of a dressing table she'd have a chest of drawers with a large mirror on the wall behind it.

Her existing lounge and dining room furniture would certainly take up far too much space in the living room. She needed more modern compact furniture and possibly a dining table that partially folded down when not in use.

The only things she could bring with her, she thought unhappily, would be her cooking utensils, china and glassware. Even some of those would have to go because there wouldn't be enough storage room for them all in the compact little kitchen.

Karen was absolutely right, she reflected. None of her existing furniture was going to fit into the apartment so she really was going to have to make a clean sweep of everything. It really was going to be a completely new start.

Eleven

Moving day came all too soon. Jenny had barely had time to contact the saleroom and agree which pieces they would take and then get in touch with a house-clearance firm to take the rest, as well as shop for all the new furniture she needed and arrange a date for them to be delivered to her new flat.

She had hoped that Karen would be on hand to help but she explained that she would be away on business for the next ten days. Tired and weary, Jenny wondered whether this was true or whether Karen simply didn't want to get involved.

Brian Hardy was outstandingly helpful; in fact Jenny didn't know how she would have coped without his helpful advice. He even came to the house on the day she was to move out to collect the keys so that she wouldn't have to travel all the way into Liscard Village to hand them over to him.

Karen kept well away and didn't even telephone to see if Jenny needed any assistance. She did, however, send a magnificent bouquet of flowers and a bottle of champagne to Merseyside Mansions as a welcome gift.

It was almost midnight by the time Jenny had finally arranged her new furniture, made up the bed and unpacked several large boxes of clothes and china and glasses. Exhausted, she took a shower and collapsed into bed.

She felt so disorientated in her new surroundings that she didn't expect to sleep, but she was so tired that the moment her eyes closed she knew no more until morning.

When she woke she wondered for a moment where she was. Then, very slowly, as she recalled the long strenuous move she'd made the day before, it all came back.

Pulling on her dressing gown she padded through to the kitchen and switched on the kettle. As she waited for it to boil she moved into the living room, pulled back the curtain and, opening the French doors, stepped out on to the small balcony.

It wasn't the view she was used to but if she strained her neck then to her left she could just see the misty blue outlines of the Welsh mountains. They seemed to be so far away that they almost disappeared into the distance and merged in with the skyline.

Immediately in front of her window was the promenade separating the block of flats from the shoreline. She could see New Brighton pier and wondered if she would hear the noise of the fairground in the nearby Tower grounds when it started operating later on in the day.

On the other side of the Mersey, slightly to her right, were the Liver buildings and the Liverpool waterfront where at that moment a huge liner was being pulled by tugs towards the Landing State at the dockside.

The whistling sound that indicated the kettle was boiling claimed her attention and she went back into the kitchen to make her tea. She carried a cup into the living room and stared round thinking how bare it looked, almost sterile; not a home at all.

The bedroom had the same feel; it lacked colour and atmosphere, those bits and pieces that transform a room and give it a personal touch.

As she went into the bathroom she was met by the overpowering smell of lilies. The welcoming bouquet that Karen had sent was still lying there in the washbasin. She had meant to arrange the flowers and take them into the living room after she'd had her shower the previous night but by then she'd felt so tired she'd simply left them where they were. She'd have to find a suitable vase and, although she'd unpacked her china, she wasn't quite sure where she'd put the big glass jug that she needed to hold such a large bunch.

Equally important, she mused as she dressed, was to find out all the rules and regulations governing the place before she put her foot in it and disgraced herself by doing something wrong. She'd asked the concierge if she had a leaflet listing the basic rules but she had said she would tell her anything she needed to know once she was settled in.

The concierge had said, however, that they held a regular midweek coffee morning and suggested that if she attended this it would give her the opportunity to meet most of the other residents.

Once she was dressed Jenny decided to take a walk round the inside of the building to get her bearings. It was four storeys high so that meant there must be two more floors above hers.

The lift was only a short way down the passage but when she pressed the button to summon it and stepped into it there was already a woman in there. She greeted Jenny with a tight smile that didn't reach her eyes and automatically assumed that Jenny was going down to the ground floor, the same as she was.

The woman was dressed in a dark brown skirt and a brown and white check jacket over a pale blue blouse. She had tightly curled dark grey hair, a sharp nose and high cheekbones, and looked so formidable that Jenny said nothing.

When they reached the ground floor the woman strode away, straight through the reception and out into the street.

Jenny looked anxiously at the reception desk hoping the concierge was there but the door into her office was closed. Indecisively, she turned and looked into the communal room. It was a very big room with a cream carpet and numerous brown and grey leather armchairs grouped round low tables. Bookcases lined one wall and people reading newspapers occupied several of the armchairs. There were wide windows at the far end and a double door leading out into a small landscaped garden.

Jenny was still hovering, wondering whether or not to pluck up the courage and push open the door and go into the room when a voice behind her boomed in her ear.

'You the newcomer?' a man's voice demanded. 'Heard you were moving in this weekend, what! Are you settled in or still unpacking confounded boxes?'

Jenny turned to find a tall, very upright man dressed in grey flannels, dark grey shirt and a green tweed sports jacket that had the elbows reinforced with leather holding out his hand in greeting. He was grey-haired with a ruddy complexion and sported a crisp grey moustache.

'I'm Major John Mitchell by the way. Retired of course. Been living here for the last six months, so if there is anything you need to know, then I'm your man.'

'Very pleased to meet you.' Jenny held out her hand. 'I'm Jenny Langton and yes I have only just moved in and I don't feel at all settled, not yet.'

'Quite, quite.' He ran a hand over his moustache. 'Make sure you come to coffee morning next Wednesday; meet all the troops at one go then, what!'

'Yes, I'll remember to do that,' Jenny murmured as abruptly he gave her a salute and continued along the passageway.

Jenny watched his retreating back for a couple of seconds and then with a tiny shrug made her way from the main reception area to the outside lobby where the postboxes were located to see if there were any letters waiting for her.

Two women were already there; both were grey-haired, one small and tubby and dressed in a green patterned blouse and plain green skirt, the other, tall and angular, was wearing a very smart mid-calf dark red dress.

The tubby woman was about to unlock her mailbox, the other one was taking the key out of hers and grumbling about the amount of junk mail she had found in it.

'Well, I suppose it's better than bills.' The tubby woman laughed as she extracted a sheaf of leaflets and quickly scanned through them before screwing them up.

They both looked at Jenny enquiringly as if not too sure who she was or what she was doing there.

'Hello, I'm Jenny Langton, I've just moved in,' she said, smiling first at one and then at the other.

'Second floor? I heard all the banging and noise and I knew the flat had been sold so I thought it must be someone moving in. My apartment is right under yours.'

'Oh dear, I'm so sorry if the removal men disturbed you,' Jenny said apologetically.

'That's all right; you can't help making a bit of noise at first. I'm Beryl Willis and this is Sandra Roberts,' she added, nodding in the other woman's direction.

'I live on the same floor as you,' Sandra told her in a quiet voice.

Beryl looked at her watch. 'If we are going to be over in Liverpool on time we'd better hurry,' she stated.

With a quick 'see you again sometime' they both scuttled off, and once more Jenny found herself alone and wondering what to do.

She went back to her flat and looked around. It was tidy but felt strange, almost as if she didn't really belong there. She looked out of the window at the neatly laid out communal garden and sighed. She was already missing her own garden and the pleasure of wandering out of the back door, strolling down the path, smelling the freshness of the soil as she pulled out the odd weed that had sprung up overnight and took note of what needed attention.

On impulse she reached for her outdoor coat, her hat and gloves and then picked up her keys. A brisk walk along the promenade was what she needed, she told herself.

It was no good moping or hankering for what had been. A good walk would blow away her feeling of depression. On the way back she would find out where the nearest shops were and buy some milk and bread and anything else that caught her fancy.

It would give her a chance to plan what she intended doing in future. She would have to find something to fill in her days. Perhaps she could help out at a charity shop, or even get a part time job, she told herself.

It was a bright day but the wind had a biting edge as it swept in off the Mersey. It was the sort of morning she loved; a morning to peg out the washing and watch it blowing as she rewarded herself with a cup of coffee.

Thinking of coffee reminded her about the coffee morning at Merseyside Mansions. Did she really want to go to it? Certainly it would be an opportunity to meet the other residents; but did she want to do that? Was it a good idea to make friends with the neighbours, or would it be better if she kept herself to herself, she wondered.

Up until now she had always led a very private life. After William died she had been too busy looking after Eddy and later on Karen to have much time for a life of her own. She had been perfectly happy with that arrangement and never craved outside interests.

Now, though, with both William and Eddy dead and Karen living independently, it was all so different, and there were times now when she had to admit that she felt lonely; very lonely.

The walk revived her spirits. Who could be downhearted on such a lovely morning she asked herself, as she watched boats plying up and down the Mersey, gulls swooping and screaming overhead and the first of the day-trippers already taking up their favourite spots on the beach.

As she left the promenade and made her way up Victoria Street she remembered her shopping needs. As she added bread, milk, meat from the butchers and some fresh vegetables from the greengrocers she found that her shopping bag was becoming rather heavy and it was quite a long walk back to Merseyside Mansions. She'd have to organize daily shopping trips or arrange for heavy items to be delivered, she decided.

Since she wasn't living all that far from Wallasey Village she wondered if it would be worth asking her previous suppliers if they would still be willing to deliver.

That would mean waiting in for them to come, she reminded herself. When she'd been living in Warren Point the delivery men had known that they could always leave whatever they had brought just inside the porch and that it would be perfectly safe there. Could they leave deliveries in reception if she was out, she wondered. That was another thing she would have to find out.

She wished Karen had been there to help her settle in. She would have found out the answers to all these questions for her.

She decided to phone Karen as soon as she got home to see if she was back from her trip yet and invite her over. She must be curious to see what the flat was like and she was quite keen to show her around it even though that wouldn't take very long.

Twelve

It was three weeks before Jenny heard from Karen and then it was to say that she hoped she'd settled in to her new home at Merseyside Mansions but she was too busy at the moment to visit.

Jenny felt disappointed but by then she felt quite settled and very much at home in her new surroundings. She had met a number of the residents at the Wednesday coffee mornings and could even remember most of their names and in some cases where they lived.

They were certainly a very mixed bunch of people, she thought wryly. As far as she knew only four of the residents were still working and went out at regular hours each day. The rest were retired and filled in their time in a variety of ways.

Some of them, like Clare and Peter Green, had a very regular routine. Clare was a very large lady and so severely incapacitated that she was unable to walk more than a few steps at a time. Even so she went out every morning at eleven thirty in a wheelchair with Peter pushing her.

He was the exact opposite of his wife; small and weedy. It took every ounce of his strength to manoeuvre the wheelchair and his face was usually a bright red with exertion by the time they came back from their walk.

Clare was extremely demanding. Jenny felt sorry for Peter. She saw the way he was constantly berated and belittled when he was obviously doing his utmost to please her.

Clare always seemed to be particularly aggressive towards him at Wednesday coffee mornings. Peter would leave her wheelchair in a convenient alcove and then help her out of it. She would lean heavily on him as she took the few steps necessary to reach the nearest chair.

On the second Wednesday she'd been there Jenny had rushed to help and offered her chair to Clare because it was the nearest one but Clare had waved her hand dismissively.

'He's quite capable and he'll be the one who decides which chair I am to sit in,' she stated imperiously.

Jenny felt her colour rising and quickly returned to her own chair as she saw several people trying to hide amused smiles.

'Take no notice, she's always like that. We put her rudeness down to her not feeling very well,' Sandra Roberts whispered.

Jenny nodded but made a mental note that in future she would avoid Clare Green as much as possible.

It was not difficult to do so; Jenny found that there were many other residents who were extremely friendly. Several times she was invited to go shopping in Liverpool or for a walk along the promenade with one or other of the ladies.

Some of the men were attentive but Jenny was guarded. She knew from various conversations that some of the other women hoped for an invitation to take a stroll or go out for a meal either from the Major or one or two other bachelors who resided there and she had no intention of causing any jealousy.

Jenny found her time fully occupied and although as the weeks slipped by she missed Karen, she never really felt lonely. There was always a great deal going on in Merseyside Mansions in addition to the Wednesday coffee mornings.

If she felt she needed outside stimulus she could always take a walk along the promenade to New Brighton. She also enjoyed going to Vale Park to listen to the band and did so most Sunday afternoons, whether on her own or with one of the other residents.

As the summer faded and the crisper days of October were followed by the fogs and rains of November, Jenny spent more and more of her afternoons in the communal lounge enjoying the company of other residents.

As she listened to the tales about their families and the get-togethers they'd enjoyed with them, it made her more and more aware that she hadn't seen Karen for months.

She knew that since she had sent Karen her share of the money that had resulted from the sale of the house in Warren Point, she had moved to a new flat on the outskirts of Liverpool and, one Sunday afternoon, feeling rather bored, Jenny decided on impulse to pay her a visit.

She might be out or entertaining some friends, she thought, as she caught a bus to Seacombe and from there the Royal Daffodil ferryboat over to Liverpool.

When she reached Liverpool Pier Head she checked on the address and then asked one of the bus drivers if he could tell her which bus she ought to take to get to Calderstones Park.

As the bus travelled through the city and out into the suburbs the houses grew bigger and looked more and more expensive. When she reached her destination the house seemed to be so grand that Jenny began to wonder if she had the right address.

Having come so far I may as well ring the doorbell and find out, she thought resignedly.

The young girl who answered the door looked surprised when Jenny asked for Karen. After Jenny explained who she was the girl invited her to step inside. She showed her into a beautifully furnished lounge and told her to take a seat, saying that she would let Miss Langton know that she was there.

Jenny looked round in amazement. Everything was top quality and beautifully coordinated; almost like a show house. The deep pile cream carpet on the floor, the dark red velvet drapes at the large bay window, the plush cream upholstered settee and matching armchairs and the numerous little tables with their elaborately carved legs were all top quality. It was far grander and more expensive than Karen could possibly afford and Jenny assumed she must be sharing with someone.

When Karen finally appeared, Jenny could hardly believe her eyes. Karen was looking extremely glamorous in a midnight blue velvet housecoat, her hair piled high on her head in a very sophisticated style. She looked astonished to see her grandmother and her greeting was cool rather than exuberant.

'Is something wrong?' she asked as she gave Jenny a brief peck on the cheek.

'No, not at all.' Jenny smiled. 'It is such a long time since we saw each other though that I thought I'd better come and see if you were all right.'

'Yes, of course I am,' Karen said with a frown, 'but I am very busy.' She looked at the expensive diamond studded gold watch on her wrist. 'I'm packing at the moment; I have to catch a plane in less than an hour on a business trip.'

'On a Sunday!'

'Yes, I have to be somewhere first thing tomorrow morning, which means leaving now. I'm sorry, Gran, but I really must go; my taxi will be here at any minute. You should have telephoned and let me know you were coming,' she added half apologetically.

'Mmm, I'll remember to make an appointment next time,' Jenny said quietly. She picked up her handbag from the small table beside the chair she had been sitting in. 'When will I see you?' she asked as Karen walked with her down the hall towards the front door.

'I have a very busy schedule for the next month or so but I'll try to be in touch before Christmas,' Karen murmured. She kissed Jenny on the cheek. 'I'm so sorry I can't stop and talk to you now, Gran. It's just unfortunate . . .' Her voice faded away.

'I understand,' Jenny said quietly. 'Make it as soon as you can because I really do want to know how you are getting on, Karen, and what your plans are for the future and so on, my dear. I also want you to come across to Wallasey and see my flat. I thought you would have done so long before this.'

'I know, I know,' Karen said contritely, 'but I have been very busy. Really I have Gran.'

By this time they were at the door and Jenny found herself once more in the street and the door closed behind her. She hesitated for a moment, feeling bewildered. Karen hadn't shown her round her new home or even offered her a drink, yet she knows how far I've come to see her, she thought, feeling slightly resentful. She didn't even ask me if I knew the way home, she thought, as she made her way back to the bus stop.

Jenny felt very curious about the house where Karen was living; it was not only in an expensive area but extremely tastefully furnished. She was also puzzled about the young girl who had answered the door. She wasn't old enough for her to be the person Karen was sharing with so who was she? Was she a maid? Surely such a luxury as having a servant was well out of Karen's pocket.

Jenny felt concerned and hoped that Karen hadn't let her inheritance go to her head and was living beyond her means. It wasn't only the grand house but Karen's appearance.

She realized that she probably had to look glamorous when she was at work but the watch she'd been wearing and the diamond stud earrings looked to be very expensive.

As the ferryboat ploughed its way across the Mersey, cutting through the heavy fog that had come down suddenly, Jenny felt both worried and despondent. Perhaps she should have tried harder to keep their house because it had been Karen's home as well as hers.

Selling it and not keeping more of an eye on Karen was letting Eddy down she thought guiltily.

She really must ensure that she kept in closer touch with Karen so that she knew more about what was happening in her life. She might be twenty and independent but she had led quite a sheltered life while she'd been growing up and she hoped she wasn't moving into the wrong sort of company.

Then she had a brilliant idea. They were having a Christmas party at Merseyside Mansions in December and they'd been told they could invite a friend or relative. If Karen hadn't paid her a visit before then she would send her an invite to the party.

Thirteen

The Christmas party at Merseyside Mansions was planned for Friday the seventeenth of December. So many people were eager to help with the preparations and to decorate the communal lounge that Jenny held back.

She knew she no longer felt confident about going up ladders or standing on steps to fix the decorations or put up the fairy lights and thought that the men were more capable of doing that sort of thing anyway.

She would have been quite willing to help to decorate the Christmas tree but so many of the other ladies were already intent on doing so that she felt it was better to keep out of their way.

Outside caterers had been hired to supply a spread of sandwiches, cakes, mince pies, biscuits and cheese and other seasonal titbits. They would also be there to pour out the mulled wine and soft drinks and hand them around. The concierge would be there to supervise them.

There was really nothing at all for her to do except send an invitation to Karen and hope that she would come. She'd already written a letter telling her the anticipated date and she had phoned her several times since and left messages on her answerphone to let her know that it was fixed for the seventeenth. So far there had been no reply, so she assumed that Karen must be away somewhere.

Jenny refused to let her disappointment spoil her anticipation of the evening festivities. She dressed with care in a floor-length dark red velvet skirt, a white lacy blouse and an elegant black patterned velvet stole which she draped loosely over her shoulders.

As she entered the communal lounge for the evening's event a waiter handed her a glass of mulled wine. She steeled herself to enter into the spirit of the occasion although she felt annoyed that Karen wasn't there to accompany her.

In addition to the fairy lights and glittering baubles on the Christmas tree, the lounge was so lavishly decorated that everywhere glittered. The room was crowded and everyone was suitably dressed up for the occasion.

The party was already in full swing, a cacophony of voices almost obliterating the music, when there was a loud rapping on the main door. The concierge went to open it and came back to tell Jenny that there was a young lady asking for her.

Jenny could hardly believe her eyes when she saw that it was Karen. Suddenly the whole evening took on a new appeal. She had been feeling lost and lonely as other residents introduced her to their sons and daughters and then went off with them happily chattering and laughing and enjoying their company while she had remained isolated and alone.

She hastened to greet Karen, offered to take her to her own apartment if she wanted to freshen up, but Karen declined. Heads turned as she shrugged off her grey fur jacket to reveal a short black figure-hugging dress with a very low-cut neckline, sheer black stockings and very high-heeled shoes. Against the whiteness of her skin an emerald necklace gleamed and she had earrings and a bracelet to match.

The concierge took Karen's fur jacket saying she would put it in her office. A waiter handed Karen a glass of mulled wine and Jenny, with a mixture of pride and happiness, began introducing her to some of the other residents.

Everybody seemed eager to meet the newcomer, especially the men. The Major took her hand and bowed low over it in a courtly manner, saying how charmed he was to make her acquaintance.

There was one surprising moment when Jane Phillips, a tall, imposing woman in her late sixties who had up until now more or less ignored Jenny, came over with a frosty smile and said in a rather condemning tone of voice to Karen, 'I'm very surprised to see you here.' She didn't stay to talk and, when Jenny looked at Karen enquiringly, she offered no explanation but immediately became involved in a conversation with Lionel Bostock and his son Edwin.

Jenny had only spoken to Lionel Bostock once before, but she knew that he was held in high esteem by most of the other residents. He was something of a character, very smart and upright with white hair and a white moustache. He had once been a well-known surgeon and his son, who was with him that evening, had also followed in the same profession.

They both seemed to be captivated by Karen while Jenny stood patiently waiting for them to acknowledge her presence. When the older man finally did it was merely to tell her that he hoped she would let him know when her delightful daughter was visiting again.

As midnight approached Karen looked at her jewel-studded wristwatch and said that she'd ordered a taxi and that she expected it to be there at any minute.

Although Jenny had enjoyed seeing Karen she was disappointed that she'd had no opportunity to talk to her privately and catch up with any news or even take her to see her new flat.

'Can't you stay over?' she asked hopefully.

'Impossible. I have to be away early tomorrow morning on a trip,' Karen told her. 'You know what my lifestyle's like. I'll come over again in the New Year and take you out for a meal,' she promised.

'I can come over to Liverpool if that is easier for you,' Jenny said eagerly.

'No. No, Gran, I'd rather you didn't do that. I don't like to think of you making such a long journey, not at this time of the year. I'll come again very soon, I promise you.'

Before Jenny could argue any further someone called out, 'Miss Langton, your taxi is here; it's waiting for you at the door.'

Once Karen had left, the enjoyment went out of the evening for Jenny. She accepted another glass of mulled wine but it tasted sickly sweet and she didn't really want to finish it. She was there yet she wasn't; her thoughts were focused on Karen and the Christmas celebrations they had known in the past.

She was so absorbed in her daydreams that when Jane Phillips suddenly appeared at her side she almost spilled the remains of her drink she was so startled.

'I take it that since you both have the same surname you are in some way related to Karen Langton,' she said frostily.

'Yes; she's my granddaughter.'

'Really!' Jane's thinly pencilled eyebrows rose. 'You must be very concerned about her reputation.'

'Her reputation? What do you mean?' Jenny asked in a puzzled voice.

'Surely you know where she is living?' Jane's eyebrows went even higher.

'Yes, of course I do. She's living in Liverpool, in the Calderstones area. A very nice house . . .'

'It should be seeing it's the home of someone in shipping who is reputed to be a millionaire,' Jane said with a sneering laugh.

Jenny stared at her, frowning in surprise. 'I don't think so. Karen is sharing with someone.'

'Sharing! Is that what it's called these days. Oh yes, she's sharing all right. Proper little love-nest they have there.'

Seeing that Jenny still looked bemused, Jane went on, 'She's living with Hadyn Trimm the shipping magnate. How else do you think a girl of her age could dress like she does and be able to afford a fur coat and emeralds?'

Her words were meant to shock but Jenny gave a disarming chuckle. 'Karen always has had good taste when it comes to clothes. You may have seen her at this Hadyn Trimm's house because he is the head of the shipping line where Karen works. She is their press officer and handles their publicity so she was probably there delivering some papers to him for his approval or something.'

'And staying there all night?' Jane sniffed.

'How do you know she did?' Jenny asked sharply.

'I know because my sister lives only two doors away and both my sister and her neighbours are absolutely disgusted by what is going on at that house. Your granddaughter appears to have moved in with him. She's in and out of there as if she owns the place.'

'You mean your sister and her friends are gossips who spend all their time watching other people from behind their net curtains?' Jenny murmured spiritedly. Her heart was thumping but she was determined not to let this obnoxious woman see how upset she was. Nor did she intend to let her spread scandalous lies about her beloved granddaughter.

'Hadyn Trimm's wife is desperately ill in a nursing home and what sort of effect do you think your granddaughter's behaviour is having on her,' Jane went on, ignoring Jenny's comment.

Jenny's heart sank. She had wondered how Karen could afford to live in such an area even if she was sharing with another woman. Now this revelation saddened her but she was determined not to let Jane Phillips know how she felt.

'I think you should get your facts right before you go around making accusations like that,' Jenny said quietly. She put her glass down on the table and stood up, preparing to leave.

'You believe what you like,' Jane retorted, 'but I know the truth. Anyway,' she added as a parting shot, 'you have only to look at the way she was chatting up old Mr Bostock and making eyes at his son to know the sort of person she is.'

Jenny found she was shaking when she reached her apartment; so much so that she could hardly fit the key into the lock.

Although she had refuted everything Jane Phillips had said she had the awful feeling that the woman spoke the truth. She wasn't shocked but she was certainly concerned. She also felt very sorry for Hadyn Trimm's wife and wondered if it was because of Karen's behaviour that she was so ill.

Although it was now well past midnight she no longer felt sleepy. Her mind was churning. Was it her fault that Karen had turned out like this, she wondered. If so, it meant that she really had failed Eddy. He had always been so proud of his daughter.

If he was still alive and they were all living in Warren Point then none of this would have happened, she thought sadly. She had failed his trust in her by not making sure that Karen had the right sort of guidance. She should have tried harder to find some way to keep their family home. She knew she must do something to put matters right and tried to think how Eddy would have handled the situation.

It had all started to go wrong when Jimmy Martin had persuaded Karen to leave Premium Printing to work for a shipping company and move in with him.

She should have stepped in at that point and insisted that because it was what her father had wanted, Karen should stay with her father's firm. Karen had been so determined to stand on her own feet though that she simply wouldn't listen, Jenny reminded herself.

Fourteen

At Merseyside Mansions, 1977 was heralded in with a party for the residents on New Year's Eve.

The lavish decorations were still up in the communal lounge and it was packed with people. Everyone seemed to be there, all of them dressed in their party clothes. As they waited for midnight they were all standing or sitting around in groups, holding a glass of wine in their hand, chatting away to one another about the wonderful Christmas they'd had with their families.

Jenny now knew most of the residents and was thoroughly enjoying herself until Jane Phillips made it her business to come over to where she was and pointedly ask her if her granddaughter was coming to the party.

'Not as far as I know,' Jenny murmured. 'I'm sure she is out enjoying herself with her own young friends, or she may even be away; she's out of the country quite a lot. She does a great deal of travelling in her job,' she added by way of explanation to others in the group who had stopped talking between themselves to listen to what Jane Phillips was saying.

'Travelling!' Jane gave a cynical little laugh. 'Oh yes, I know all about that.'

She immediately launched into a waspish account of Karen and her 'goings-on' followed by a detailed character assassination of Hadyn Trimm.

'I'm surprised you allow your granddaughter to associate with a man like him let alone live with him,' she commented. 'It's asking for trouble. Everyone knows he's flaunting the law. The police have been watching him for ages and sooner or later they'll catch him red-handed. Either that or they'll catch your granddaughter.'

'Catch them? What on earth are you talking about?'

Jane raised her eyebrows and stared back at Jenny with a look of cynical amusement on her face. 'The smuggling they're involved in, of course. All the illegal drugs and stuff they're bringing in and taking out of the country. Why else do you think your granddaughter is always going abroad?'

Jenny looked taken aback but kept her nerve. 'What a malicious story,' she said with a forced laugh. 'You've got it all wrong, of course. Karen's travelling is connected with her job but not in the way you are suggesting. I told you before, she works for Hadyn Trimm and handles public relations for the shipping line and her travelling is all to do with that.'

Jane's mouth momentarily gaped then she burst into laughter.

'That's what she's told you, is it?' she said scornfully. 'Believe me, it's not nearly as innocent as that. A good cover story, I'll give you that, but I've no idea who would believe it, except a complete simpleton.'

Jenny was sure that the barbed insult was directed at her and she felt herself bristle. She drew a deep breath to calm herself as an angry retaliation sprang to her lips.

She realized that there was no point in antagonizing this woman and was relieved when someone carrying a bottle of red wine came up to see if they would like a refill in readiness to greet the New Year, making it unnecessary for her to answer. Murmuring an excuse, she moved away while Jane Phillips was having her glass topped up.

Jane's words had made a deep impact and Jenny wondered if there was perhaps some element of truth in what she'd said. She certainly hoped not but she could see how such gossip might start and be spread amongst Hadyn Trimm's neighbours, especially if they were envious of his lavish lifestyle.

The moment midnight struck they all raised their glasses in a toast and handshakes, kisses and hugs followed. Jenny slipped away. The joy had gone out of the celebrations for her and she was anxious to seek solace in her own apartment.

She didn't want to meet up with Jane Phillips again until she'd had a chance to talk to Karen and see if she could discover how such awful rumours had come about. She was sure that it was all nonsense but nevertheless it worried her greatly that Karen's name was linked with such malicious gossip, especially if there was anything in Jane Phillips's comment about Hadyn Trimm and Karen being watched by the police.

After a disturbed night, Jenny was unable to get into her normal routine on New Year's Day. She kept to her own apartment because she didn't feel in the mood to be exchanging 'Happy New Year' greetings with anybody. She wished she could contact Karen so that she could talk to her and set her own mind at rest about the gossip. She was sure Karen would have an explanation as to how it had all started.

By midday Jenny felt so much on tenterhooks that she knew she could stand her own company no longer. She might not be able to contact Karen by phone but she knew where she lived and since she'd made the journey once before she'd have no problems in finding the house again.

It was a cold grey day so she put on a warm topcoat, a fur hat, and a thick scarf. Then, picking up her fur gloves and handbag, she set off. What she hadn't taken into consideration was that since it was a bank holiday boats and buses were restricted and it took her until almost mid-afternoon to reach the Calderstones area.

The street looked deserted and there was a hollow echo when she rang the doorbell. She followed it up by knocking loudly, and when that had no effect she was about to turn away, disappointed that they were obviously not there, when the curtains at the front window of the next door house twitched and a woman tapped on the glass.

For a moment Jenny was inclined to ignore her, then the thought that she might know when they would be coming home made her hesitate and she smiled at the woman.

The woman mouthed something that Jenny couldn't understand but within seconds her front door was opening. Jenny was surprised to see that she had on an apron and that she was pulling a coat around her shoulders as she came out into the driveway that separated the two houses.

'I'm afraid they are out so it's no good you ringing their bell or knocking because there's no one at all there,' the woman said. 'They sacked the young girl who worked for them at Christmas,' she went on lugubriously.

'Thank you for telling me,' Jenny said as she turned away.

'I come here next door to them to clean and one day they were there and the next morning they'd gone,' the woman went on. 'Moved right away. I work for a couple of other houses along the road and I did hear someone say that the pair of them had gone to live in Cardiff but I don't know for sure if that's right or not. They're a bit of a mystery though and there's always a lot of gossip going on about them.'

Jenny felt stunned. 'Are you sure they've moved and not just gone there on business?' she asked. 'I only saw Karen a short time ago and she never mentioned that she was thinking of moving.'

Her voice trailed away. The woman's green eyes were bright with interest, greedy for more information and Jenny knew that by thinking aloud not only was she giving away far too much information but in next to no time it would be passed around the street.

'Oh, it was a moonlight flit all right if ever I saw one though I'm not sure why . . . but one of the other ladies I clean for said . . .'

'Thank you for telling me they're away,' Jenny interrupted, pulling herself together, her voice sharp.

'Well, you might have stood there knocking all day or even have hung around thinking they'd be back soon. You could have been half frozen doing that on a day like this. There's sleet coming down and I wouldn't mind betting it will snow later on tonight.' She pulled her coat tighter around her. 'The best place to be is indoors sitting round the fire.'

'Yes, you are quite right,' Jenny agreed. She looked again at the house, this time noting how empty it looked and she felt quite disorientated. She couldn't believe that Karen had left there, left Liverpool, without telling her. She felt vaguely unnerved.

'Have you come from very far away? You look as though you're worn out. Either that or you're shocked by the news that they've skedaddled.'

'You're a relative are you?' the woman went on when Jenny didn't answer. 'You are very welcome to come in and have a cuppa and a warm by the kitchen fire, luv,' she invited when Jenny remained silent, ignoring her questions.

'No, no. That's very kind of you but I agree it does look as if it is going to snow and I'd like to get home before it does. If I leave now I should manage to do so,' she added as she began to walk down the driveway.

She was still puzzled by what could have happened and why Karen had left Liverpool without a word to her; that was, if what the woman said was true.

As she remembered the vicious accusations Jane Phillips had made and her character assassination of Hadyn Trimm she was worried in case Karen really was in some sort of trouble.

Fifteen

As they drove across the Severn Bridge into Wales, Karen glanced apprehensively at Hadyn's grim profile. They had been driving for hours; a devious route down through Birmingham and the Midlands to Bristol instead of taking the more direct route through Chester and the Welsh Border towns to Chepstow.

When they reached the other side of the Severn, Karen felt that it was almost like leaving England for a foreign country. British law still applied in Wales, of course, she reminded herself, and if Hadyn was apprehended and she was with him would the police decide that she was as guilty as him?

She had never been to Cardiff before but Loudon Square sounded quite imposing and she imagined it would be full of large Regency or Victorian houses and hotels.

She felt rather guilty about not letting her grandmother know that she was leaving Liverpool but Hadyn had been insistent that they told no one and that they should leave immediately. He was right, of course. If she had phoned Jenny then she would have wanted to know what was going on.

There were so many things she hadn't told her grandmother in the past few months, Karen reflected. She hadn't told her the truth about where she was living but had let her think she was sharing a flat with a girlfriend.

How could she tell her that because Hadyn was her boss she had not only let him make love to her after a rather wild party but had spent the rest of the night with him.

He was a wonderful lover and their love-making was so very different from the rough, boisterous coupling she'd known with Jimmy Martin. Although Hadyn was a gentle and sensitive lover he made her feel like a real woman. She had fallen crazily in love with him and had been more than willing to move in with him when he'd asked her to do so.

Her grandmother would have to be told eventually, Karen thought uneasily. Or would she ever need to know? If everything turned out all right then perhaps Jenny need never know the whole truth, especially about why they'd thrown their belongings into Hadyn's car and left Liverpool in such a hurry.

She studied Hadyn's jet-black hair and saturnine profile more intently. He might be almost thirty years older than her, old enough to be her father, but he really was devastatingly handsome; and charming. He exuded charisma; there was no doubt that she was completely under his spell. She must be or she would not have done all the things he'd asked of her, she reasoned.

It had all started innocently enough a few weeks after she'd moved in with him. He had asked her if on her next trip she would mind taking along a small package and handing it over to a friend of his who would contact her at her hotel.

Hadyn was her boss as well as her lover and she felt flattered, especially when he asked her not to mention it to anyone else as it was a personal matter.

After that it happened more and more frequently and became a regular chore. He seemed to have friends in every country she went to and when she handed over the package to them they usually asked if she would take one back for Hadyn.

She would probably never have known what was in the packages if she hadn't been caught in a torrential downpour as she was making her way from Liverpool Pier Head out to Calderstones and the wrapper had become so damaged that it split and the contents had been revealed.

At first she'd believed him when he told her that it was samples of vitamin pills. It was only later that she suspected that the pills might be drugs and that if that was so then she was acting as a courier.

When she voiced her suspicions, Hadyn had tried to laugh it off and tell her she was imagining things, but this had made her angry. 'They're simply different kinds of vitamin tablets that I've been asked to get for a friend,' he assured her.

'I'm not a fool,' she said, shaking her head. 'They're drugs of some kind, aren't they?'

'You're quite right, of course, they are,' Hadyn said, laughing. 'All pills are drugs of some kind or the other.'

'Yes, I suppose they are,' Karen agreed, 'but these are the kind of drugs that are termed illegal and I'm not prepared to carry them for you any more.'

'Why not? You've been doing it for months and what harm has it done?'

Karen felt taken aback. 'Surely you must know the effect they have on people; and what if they are getting into the hands of children . . .' Her voice trailed off. She had no idea what she was talking about except that she knew there were lots of dangerous drugs on the market and that they were reputed to ruin people's lives.

'I'm going to report what has been going on to the police,' she threatened.

'I see. And what proof are you going to offer them?'

'I'll tell them what I've been doing all these months and all about the men who collect the packages you ask me to take for you and the ones I am asked to bring back.'

'That would be very foolish,' Hadyn said quietly. 'If you do that you will be considered guilty because you have been carrying them backwards and forwards through customs.'

'I don't care!'

'You might not but I do. I thought you trusted me.'

'I did,' she admitted, 'but now I'm scared because I know what we're doing is so wrong.'

It was two nights after this that Hadyn had come rushing into the house and told her to pack and that they were leaving instantly.

'Where are we going and why?'

'Right away from here. I know someone who will let us stay with him and the police will never think of following us there.'

When she'd hesitated and said that she didn't want to do that, Hadyn had laughed harshly and told her she had no option.

'In the eyes of the law you're as guilty as I am,' he told her sharply. 'Pack your bag and stop arguing. The sooner we are on the road the better.'

It wasn't until they were approaching the Severn crossing that he had told her exactly where their destination was to be. When she questioned him about it and asked where they would be staying in Cardiff he'd merely shrugged. 'Loudon Square, but I haven't any idea what it's like there,' he told her crisply. 'This chap has a hotel but I've never been there before. We won't be staying long, only until the heat dies down.'

'Will we go back to Liverpool then?'

Hadyn shrugged again. 'Depends,' he snapped.

Karen looked at him in stunned silence. This was a new side of Hadyn, one she hadn't seen before. He seemed so hard and ruthless, so different from the kindly boss or the charismatic lover who had won her heart.

Although he claimed that he had never visited Cardiff before, Hadyn seemed to know precisely where he was going and was able to drive directly to Loudon Square without pausing to ask anybody for directions.

Karen felt her heart sinking as she looked around her. Loudon Square was a large 'square' of stunted grass with a couple of sad-looking trees surrounded by grim-looking grey terraced houses and a modern tower block of flats at one end.

'We're here,' Hadyn said as they drew up and he switched off the car engine. He waited for her to get out and, taking her arm, accompanied her to one of the terraced houses.

A dark-skinned man who was wearing a smock-type shirt over grey baggy trousers opened the door. Hadyn pushed her inside the door and said abruptly, 'Go with Jamil. I'll get the cases.'

'This way, please,' the man said with a little bow. He turned and led the way up a flight of stairs to the second floor leaving Karen to follow him.

He showed her into a drab room furnished with a double iron bedstead that was covered with a multicoloured candlewick bedspread, and then he stood by the door as if he was keeping guard.

Apart from the bed there was only an armchair, a small brown wood table pushed up against one wall with a mirror above it and a brown wood cupboard in the room.

Karen walked over to the window and was about to draw aside the heavy net curtain when Jamil let out a warning noise and grabbed at her arm, shaking his head in disapproval. 'No, no!' he scowled. 'Keep away from the windows, please.'

Before she could ask him why, Hadyn was in the room. He heaved their two suitcases on to the bed and then nodded at Jamil who had indicated with a movement of his hand that he wished to speak to him in private.

As the two men left the room, Karen returned to the window and, carefully moving an edge of the curtain away from the side, stared out into Loudon Square.

Within seconds she saw Hadyn leaving the house and get into the car. As he pulled away from the kerbside and drove off, Karen was panic-stricken for a moment in case he had deserted her. Then common sense came back; he was probably only going to garage the car somewhere out of sight, she told herself.

Sitting on the edge of the bed she drummed her fingers impatiently on one of the suitcases as she waited for Hadyn to come back. This place wasn't at all like she had expected it would be, she thought with a shiver as she looked round the drab room.

Loudon Square had sounded quite grand and she had expected to be staying in a luxury hotel or at least somewhere comfortable. This place was little more than a slum, she reflected in dismay and wondered how long they would have to stay there.

'How the hell do I know?' Hadyn said brusquely when he came back from garaging the car and she questioned him. 'We stay here as long as is necessary so shut up and make the best of it. I don't want to be here any more than you do,' he said irritably.

Karen stared at him in dismay. She felt hurt; he sounded so curt and unfeeling and completely oblivious to how she felt.

'It's so drab here and that man Jamil frightens me,' she whispered.

She expected Hadyn to put his arms around her and comfort her but he did nothing of the sort. Instead, he opened up both their suitcases. 'You may as well unpack, we'll probably be here for quite some time,' he told her curtly.

Sixteen

Karen detested living in Loudon Square from the moment she arrived in Cardiff. She particularly disliked Jamil; she was suspicious of his motives even though Hadyn seemed to trust him.

From the first days after their arrival, Hadyn insisted that they stayed in their room. Jamil brought them meals, most of which Karen found distasteful. She longed to go out and enjoy a good English meal but Hadyn insisted that it wasn't safe to do so.

'We don't need to stay around here, we could drive out into the countryside and find a restaurant there,' she argued.

'This is Cardiff not Liverpool, I don't know the area outside the city,' he told her.

'Then let's explore; it could be fun. Anything would be better than being cooped up in here,' she said tetchily.

'Not yet, it's far too dangerous. We might be recognized,' he cautioned. 'Have patience. Another few days and then perhaps we can do something like that.'

Each morning when Jamil brought in their breakfast, he always had some news of some kind that he confided to Hadyn in a conspiratorial whisper. All the time he kept glancing uneasily at Karen as if afraid she might hear what he was saying.

When Karen asked what Jamil had said Hadyn usually shrugged and said, 'Oh, nothing of any importance.'

His refusal to take her completely into his confidence irked Karen. She knew that if Hadyn was charged with drug smuggling then she would probably be regarded as an accessory or even considered to be as guilty as he was.

She certainly didn't want to end up in prison and she wondered if perhaps the best thing to do was separate from him before the police traced his whereabouts.

Apart from the fear of being caught there was no other reason why she should stay. Hadyn had changed so much that she was no longer in love with him and the hold he had once had over her was gone.

They were no longer lovers. He hadn't made love to her once since they'd arrived in Cardiff.

That first night in Loudon Square when she had longed for the comforting feel of his arms around her, of his lips on hers; when she had needed to know he cared and that he still loved her, he had turned his back towards her in bed and there had not been any reconciliation since then.

The problem of how to make her escape filled every minute of Karen's waking hours. To start with she was in a strange city and she had very little money, so how was she going to be able to afford to buy a train ticket back to Liverpool?

Then there was the problem of escaping from the house without either Jamil or Hadyn seeing her leave. Even if she could avoid them she wasn't sure that there weren't other people living in the house and if there were then they might tell Jamil.

She had almost abandoned the idea when Jamil came rushing into their room to tell Hadyn that he must come with him at once and move his car.

'Someone has spotted it and asked who it belongs to,' he said in a nervous voice. 'They are talking about reporting it to the police. I know of a warehouse on the dockside where you can hide it away out of sight and it will be safe there from prying eyes.'

'I'll do it after dark tonight,' Hadyn told him. 'It's too risky to do it now.'

'No, you must do it now. You must take the risk. You don't seem to understand that here in Tiger Bay the police are very suspicious. Once they are informed about the car they will start asking questions. Come. I will accompany you.'

Hadyn's mouth tightened. 'Very well, if you think it is that important. You wait here, lock the door behind me, and don't open it to anyone,' he told Karen.

'Will you be gone long?'

'As long as it takes,' he told her curtly. 'Remember now, lock the door and don't open it to anyone and keep well away from the window.'

Although she promised to do so and nodded as though in agreement, the moment Hadyn and Jamil left the room she went straight to the window and pulled one corner of the curtain aside so that she could see when they left the building.

The minute she saw them walk down the road and then turn a corner, she put on her hat and coat, picked up her handbag and headed for the front door.

She hoped she wouldn't meet anyone but if she did and they questioned where she was going she decided she would tell them that she was hurrying to catch up with Hadyn and Jamil because they had left something behind.

Once she was out in Loudon Square breathing fresh air Karen felt elated. She had no idea which way to go but that no longer seemed to matter. She was free; not only from being imprisoned in the house but from Hadyn as well. All she had to do now was get well away from Loudon Square and for that matter from Tiger Bay.

As a trolley bus lumbered past her with the destination 'CITY CENTRE' emblazoned on it she decided to walk to the nearest stop and catch the next one that came along.

She'd find a cafe or restaurant once she reached the main part of the city and have a cup of tea while she planned what to do next. If she decided that she wanted to go straight back to Liverpool she would ask someone to direct her to the railway station. Or perhaps, since she had never been to Cardiff before, she would have a quick look round before she left, she told herself.

As she explored the shops in the city centre, Karen lost all count of time. There were so many large department stores, some of them even better than the ones she knew in Liverpool.

Eventually she stopped for a cup of tea and a sandwich, but instead of making for the railway station she went on exploring. She loved the maze of brightly lit arcades all packed with individual shops. They seemed to lead from one to the other all over the city centre.

Emerging from Castle Arcade she found herself facing the crenellated walls and towers of Cardiff Castle. She was so intrigued by the site of the original Norman castle high on the hillside beside it that she followed the road round to see where it took her.

Suddenly she found she was in the civic centre and its breathtaking panorama of Portland stone buildings; the impressive city hall, its clock tower and dragon emblem outlined dramatically against the sky, and close by it the National Museum. She went into Cathays Park with its marble memorial and stared across the road at the imposing edifice of the Law Courts.

The sight of the stream of policemen going in and out of that building brought her back to reality. Quickly she turned on her heel and made her way back towards the shopping centre. She knew it was possible that one of them might recognize her, that was if her description and that of Hadyn had been circulated, and there was no sense in taking unnecessary risks.

It would be better not to delay her departure from Cardiff any longer, she told herself. By now both Hadyn and Jamil would have returned to Loudon Square and when they discovered she was missing they might set out to look for her.

'You'd be better going to St Mary Street,' a woman told her when she asked someone in Queen Street where she could get a bus to the railway station, 'There's buses to everywhere from there. Mind you, it's a bit pointless getting one there because you are only a hundred yards or so from Wood Street where the station is.'

'So how do I get to St Mary's Street?' Karen asked.

'Cut through the David Morgan arcade, *cariad*, and then when you come to the other end ask somebody to direct you and you'll be there in next to no time.'

Karen took her at her word and followed her instructions. Fifteen minutes later she was sitting on the station platform waiting for the next train to Liverpool.

She spent the journey home trying to sort out in her mind what she was going to do next. She couldn't go back to Hadyn's house in Calderstones in case the police were watching the place.

When she reached Lime Street she went into the ladies' room and checked on how much money she had left in her purse. As she feared, there was very little left after paying for her train ticket. And she certainly didn't have enough money left to book into anywhere, not even for one night.

She had enough to buy a ticket across to Wallasey on the ferry. So the only option she had, she reasoned, was to go to Merseyside Mansions and see if her grandmother would give her a bed and let her stay there with her for a few days until she could make other plans. It was far too late to do that tonight so she would have to stay where she was.

She made herself as comfortable as she could in the waiting room and settled down to sleep. If a porter came along then she would say she was waiting for an early morning train or something, she decided.

She felt cold and hungry and was so uncomfortable that she only slept in short spells. Her mind was churning with the trauma that lay ahead. The biggest problem was, she thought worriedly, what am I going to tell my grandmother? She certainly didn't want her to know that she had been carrying drugs as she went backwards and forwards on her various trips. Or tell her that Hadyn was a drug smuggler and that the police were on his trail and that she could very well be considered as guilty as him.

So what am I to tell her? she pondered. Could she make up a story about ill health, or would that give rise to complications because Jenny would want to know the details. Should she tell her she was tired of her job and wanted a change. It sounded feasible but if she said that then her grandmother would want to know why she was giving up her life with Hadyn.

Perhaps, if she told her that she had quarrelled with Hadyn, that would give her a plausible reason for giving up her job as well. Would her grandmother believe her if she said she'd been forced to leave because she couldn't bear to work in the same company as him any longer? Or should she say that Hadyn had sacked her? If she said that then Jenny would want to know why, and try as she might she couldn't think of a valid reason.

It was all so complicated that she decided to leave a decision about what she would tell Jenny until she reached Wallasey. Perhaps she'd be lucky and Gran wouldn't ask too many questions or, if she did, by then she'd have had some sort of inspiration and know what to tell her.

Seventeen

Most of the residents at Merseyside Mansions were gathered in the large communal lounge, their eyes glued to a television set that someone had brought down and set up on a low table in the middle of the room. They were all clutching slips of paper carrying the name of a horse and, with their glasses primed, they were so intent on waiting for the start of the 1977 Grand National that very few of them noticed Karen's arrival.

Jenny was startled to see her. She had not heard from her for weeks.

Momentarily she was shocked by Karen's appearance. Her dark blonde hair was straggly and looked as though it was in need of a wash; her clothes were crumpled almost as if she had slept in them. Jenny immediately wondered if she'd been ill.

Karen put a restraining hand on her grandmother's shoulder as she stood up to greet her and shook her head when Jenny offered to take her along to her apartment.

'There's no rush. Stay and see what the result of the race is first,' she said in a low voice as she perched herself on the arm of Jenny's chair.

It was the Major who first caught sight of Karen and all his attention was immediately focused on her. Ramming his monocle into one eye, he regarded her with interest. 'Good to see you again, m'dear,' he greeted her enthusiastically. 'Staying long?'

Karen smiled warmly as she returned his greeting but didn't commit herself in any way, so Jenny constrained herself and said nothing although she, too, was curious to know.

Someone shushed them to silence and pointed towards the television screen where the big race of the day was in progress.

Red Rum was the favourite and no one knew who held the ticket bearing that horse's name. Dan Grey had organized the draw and he'd given them all sealed slips and asked them not to open them until the race was over.

Tension grew as the race drew to a close and when Red Rum

was pronounced the winner, there were cheers and clapping. Everybody tore open their slip, each one of them hoping that they would be the one to find that name on it.

When Lionel Bostock discovered that he was the one holding the winning ticket there were further cheers all round.

Lionel raised his glass as everyone toasted his success and Dan Grey duly handed over the winnings. Lionel insisted on fetching a bottle of champagne from his apartment and so the glasses were refilled and the jollity continued for over an hour.

Then, one by one, they took their leave and went back to their own apartments. As soon as Jenny could prise Karen away from the Major's long rambling stories about race meetings he had attended in the past she shepherded her up to her own rooms, eager to know why she had come and how long she would be staying.

Karen knew that the moment she had been dreading, the moment when she would have to explain things to her grandmother, had arrived. She couldn't put off telling her that she was no longer working for Hadyn Trimm.

'Really!' Jenny raised her eyebrows in surprise. 'Why is that?'

Karen hesitated and then took a deep breath, deciding that she might as well tell her the truth and get everything over at once rather than prolong things.

'Moving in with Hadyn Trimm was a terrible mistake, but I had no idea what he was really like,' she admitted in a contrite voice.

'You mean you fell for his looks and charm and found they'd worn thin,' Jenny commented drily. 'What did you expect, he's twice your age, in fact he's old enough to be your father. You might have known he wanted you for one thing only,' she added bitterly.

'It was nothing like that,' Karen said in a small voice. 'I didn't know that he was into buying and selling drugs,' she explained, her voice trembling.

'He was doing what!' Jenny looked at her in horror, realizing that the rumours Jane Phillips had hinted at were probably true.

With an exaggerated shiver Karen recounted an edited version of what had happened over the last few days and how Hadyn had forced her to go with him to seek refuge in Loudon Place in Cardiff and how she had managed to escape and get back to Liverpool again.

'Surely you must have thought it odd that he always wanted you to carry and collect packages for him whenever you went abroad,' Jenny said with a frown.

'Not really,' Karen told her. 'He was my boss, remember. I was only doing what I was told.'

'Yes, I suppose that's true enough.' Jenny sighed. 'So what happens now?'

'I don't know, Gran, except that he is hiding because the police are looking for him and want to question him. I do hope the police don't think I had anything to do with it,' she added.

'You did though,' Jenny pointed out worriedly. 'You may have acted in all innocence but you were the carrier, the go-between, so if they have been watching him then they are bound to know that you were involved as well.'

Karen shuddered. 'I don't really want to talk about it, Gran.' She sniffled.

Jenny felt nonplussed. She didn't know much about the law but she was pretty sure that if they were looking for Hadyn Trimm they must know all about his activities and would be looking for Karen as well because they would consider her to be an accomplice.

'So what are you planning to do?' she asked anxiously. 'It might be best if you went to the police and told them exactly what you have been telling me. That way they might be lenient and you might get let off with a caution.'

'No.' Karen shook her head. 'I can't do that; it would be too risky. I was hoping I could stay here for a while until all the fuss died down. After that I'll try and find a new job.'

Jenny felt alarmed. Could she be in trouble if she was found to be harbouring a criminal, she wondered. Still, that was a chance she would have to take. After all, Karen was her granddaughter and, although she was now in her twenties, she still felt responsible for her.

'Of course you are welcome to do that but you will have to sleep on the settee, so you won't be very comfortable.'

'That will be fine, Gran. At the moment I'm so tired I could sleep anywhere. I spent last night in the ladies' waiting room at Lime Street Station because I didn't have enough money to go anywhere else and I didn't think that you would want me arriving on your doorstep in the early hours of the morning.'

'What are you going to do about your own flat and your clothes and so on,' Jenny questioned her.

Karen looked puzzled. 'I haven't got a flat, and I can hardly go back to Hadyn's house for my clothes and stuff without running into the police. They'll be watching his place, probably searching every inch of it, and they'll probably turn his office over as well,' she said dramatically.

'So what are you going to wear in the meantime?' Jenny frowned.

'You'll have to loan me some of your clothes. We are about the same size, though I'll probably look a freak in them.' She giggled.

Jenny ignored the jibe. She was too busy planning ahead.

'So if you haven't bought a flat then you still have all the money I gave you after I sold Warren Point,' she said thoughtfully. 'That means that we could both make a fresh start. If I sold this flat then we could buy a bigger place and live together again.'

'What on earth would you want to do that for, Gran?' Karen asked rather irritably. 'You like it here, don't you?'

'It's all right, but it does have its drawbacks,' Jenny said with pursed lips. 'Too many older people for my liking. Most of them have nothing else to do but watch what goes on and either criticize or grumble.'

'Surely you enjoy the company though, Gran. Each time I come I've found you are in the community lounge mixing with them all.'

'What else can I do except sit here on my own and watch television or read a book. I walk or go shopping during the day but I don't like going out at night, not on my own.'

Karen shook her head but remained silent, her green eyes looked troubled.

'Think about it Karen,' Jenny persisted in a cajoling voice, 'If we were sharing then I would be there to look after the place and do your washing and cook your meals. If we bought the place as a joint venture then when I died it would be yours.'

'Forget it, Gran. We can't afford to do it.'

'Rubbish, of course we can. If I sell this place and you put your money with mine . . .'

'Stop right there, Gran,' Karen ordered in a tight voice. 'I can't go halves with you because I haven't the money to do so.'

'What on earth are you on about? After the sale of the house I gave you half of the money like your father wanted me to do.'

'I let Hadyn invest it for me and . . . and . . . well that's it; there's no way I can get it back unless I admit that I was an associate of his and then I'll be accused of smuggling drugs and . . .' Tears overtook her as she broke down into a sobbing heap.

Jenny stared at her for several minutes in silence. The colour had drained from her face and she was shaking like a leaf. She couldn't believe that every penny of Karen's inheritance had been fleeced off her by that scoundrel Hadyn Trimm. How foolish could Karen be, she thought, aghast; how had he talked her into parting with a small fortune when he was supposed to be such a wealthy man? Surely there must be some way they could reclaim it without divulging the sort of things Karen had done for him.

Or, as she had suggested earlier, would it be better if Karen went to the police straight away and gave herself up. If she pleaded innocence and told them that he had fooled her into thinking it was all part of her job to act as a courier they might even let her off with a caution.

The enormity of the problem went round and round in Jenny's head, hammering at her skull until she found it impossible to think clearly.

Karen was still curled up in a heap in the armchair, her shoulders heaving, still sobbing as if her heart would break. Surely there must be some sane solution to all this, Jenny thought wearily.

Eighteen

Jenny felt worried. Karen had been sleeping on the sofa for three weeks now and she seemed to have done nothing at all about making any plans for her future.

She'd not even applied for any jobs. Most evenings Jenny had tried to encourage her by reading out two or three from the Liverpool paper that she thought might interest Karen, but she didn't even comment on them.

During the day she would wander off into the community lounge and, whenever Jenny went in to see if she wanted to go for a walk or go shopping, she always found her sitting with Lionel Bostock. They were usually deep in conversation and Jenny wondered what they found to discuss.

Lionel Bostock might be very fit and alert for his eighty-three years but surely he had nothing in common with a young woman in her early twenties.

Jenny knew that their closeness had been noticed by several of the other residents. She'd overheard a number of sly comments; waspish words that she hadn't liked and had tried to ignore but nevertheless that had worried her.

Jane Phillips had been very outspoken in her comments. She had made it quite obvious from the very first time she had encountered Karen that she didn't approve of her lifestyle and her association with Hadyn Trimm. Now she was making it equally clear that she shouldn't be living at Merseyside Mansions. 'This place is for people of fifty-five and over, and your granddaughter, Mrs Langton, is certainly not in that category,' she stated in a censorious voice at the Wednesday coffee morning.

'I own my apartment and I can offer hospitality to whomever I wish,' Jenny defended.

'You have only one bedroom so where is your granddaughter sleeping?'

'That is entirely our business,' Jenny told her in a quiet but firm voice.

'We do have a management committee you know,' Jane retaliated, 'and I shall be bringing the matter up at our next meeting. An overnight stay is one thing but she has been here for several weeks now and there doesn't seem to be any sign of her leaving.'

'Leaving? Who's leaving?' Major Mitchell asked. He inserted his monocle into one eye and stared round the room, letting his gaze come to rest on Karen. 'Not you, young lady, I hope? Ray of sunshine in this drab place, what!' he commented jovially, looking round at the sea of faces for agreement.

'We don't approve of permanent lodgers,' Jane Phillips told him.

'Lodger? Who is a lodger? The young lady in question is Mrs Langton's guest and I can't see anything wrong in that,' Tom Fieldman intervened.

'We tolerate guests but we don't expect them to stay for weeks at a time,' Jane Phillips stated testily. 'Especially since it is only a one-bedroom flat. Exactly where is this so-called guest sleeping; that is what I want to know?'

'I don't really see that it is any concern of ours,' Mavis Grey said mildly.

'It most certainly is,' Jane said heatedly and in such a commanding voice that everyone in the room stopped talking to listen to what was being said.

'We have standards to maintain and if you let one person get away with this sort of thing then the next thing you know is that some people will be taking in paying guests during the holiday season.'

'If it's a bed you're short of then I can offer one,' Lionel Bostock blustered.

'Yes, and it would be yours I imagine,' Dan Grey said with a boisterous laugh.

Several similar quips from other residents quickly followed Dan's rather ribald remark.

'Perhaps the ladies should be buying new hats in readiness for the next wedding,' old Mr Packard chuckled.

'No, no, you've all got the wrong end of the stick,' Lionel Bostock blustered. 'I have a second bedroom and that is only used when my son Edwin stays the night and that is a very rare occasion indeed. No, the room is there and if Mrs Langton's granddaughter would like to avail herself of it then she is most welcome to do so.'

'That is most kind of you,' Jenny said, smiling. 'There is really no need for anyone to be concerned. Our sleeping arrangements are fine and Karen most certainly isn't a lodger. She's merely staying with me for a few weeks' holiday, isn't that right, dear?' she said, turning to Karen, who had remained silent, sipping her coffee and listening with a half-smile on her face.

Later, when the coffee break was over and most of the residents had dispersed, Karen went over to Lionel, who was still sitting in one of the armchairs, and touched him on the arm.

'That was very sweet of you to offer me the use of your spare room,' she said with a smile.

'Not at all, and the room is there if you wish to use it.' He fumbled in an inside pocket of his tweed jacket, brought out a Yale key and pressed it into her hand. 'Here, this is the spare key to my flat. I want you to feel free to use the room whenever you like,' he urged as he folded her fingers around the key and patted her hand.

Jenny felt a mixture of annoyance and unease as she tried to catch Karen's eye to warn her not to take the key. When she failed to do so she looked quickly round the room to see who else had noticed what had happened and was dismayed to find that Lorna Hill was taking it all in and that she had a knowing smile on her face.

Jenny knew very little about Lorna but had heard that she was a gossip of the worst sort. She was one who listened and said nothing but then repeated what she had heard with added embellishments that often led to trouble.

As soon as Lorna left the room, Jenny told Karen that she shouldn't have accepted Lionel's offer. 'You should have refused to take the key,' she admonished, 'especially when you knew that Lorna Hill was listening to everything that was being said.'

'Give the old bat something to think about,' Karen said with a smile. 'Don't worry, Gran, they're going to talk anyway, even if I had refused, and after all it could come in useful if you suddenly decide you've had enough of my company and want me out.'

'That's hardly likely to happen, my dear, as you very well know. Mind you,' Jenny added cautiously, 'I suppose you will want to get a place of your own soon.'

'All in good time,' Karen told her. 'I'm still planning what to do next.'

'First thing is to try to find a job.'

'No, I think for the moment it is better to lie low until I hear what happened to Hadyn Trimm. The police still suspect him of handling drugs and if they take him to court he may spill the beans completely and involve me in his illicit dealings.'

'Gracious, I hope not,' Jenny said, concern etched on her face.

Karen shrugged. 'Knowing him as well as I do I wouldn't count on him not doing so if he thinks that by admitting who his accomplices were he might get a lighter sentence.'

Jenny was extremely worried although Karen didn't appear to be overly concerned by what the prospects might be. Every time the phone or the doorbell rang, Jenny jumped guiltily and then hesitated before answering either of them.

When a couple of weeks later they read in the newspaper that Hadyn Trimm had been arrested they followed the details avidly. Over the next few weeks, since no one had come to question Karen, and her name had not been mentioned, Jenny finally relaxed.

She felt drained. Having Karen living with her under such circumstances and in such cramped conditions was making her edgy. Now, with Hadyn Trimm safely locked away awaiting trial, she felt it was time for Karen to find herself a job.

As the days passed and Karen seemed to be making no attempt to do so, Jenny had the uneasy feeling that she was prepared to sleep on the sofa in her living room for the rest of time.

She'd thought that by now Karen would have grown tired of geriatric company, yet she seemed quite content to mix in the communal lounge every day and chat to Lionel Bostock and any other elderly people who happened to be in there.

They all seemed to think she was delightful because she listened to their catalogue of illnesses, treatments and litany of pills so sincerely. She even offered helpful advice whenever she could or willingly popped to the shops or the post office for them to 'save their tired old legs'.

'You are so lucky having your granddaughter living with you,' they told Jenny. 'She's such a sweet girl and must be such a great help to you.'

Jenny smiled and kept her thoughts to herself.

Having Karen there as a permanent lodger was proving very expensive. Karen seemed to be oblivious of the fact that she wasn't making any contribution at all towards paying for all their food or any of the other bills.

Tentatively Jenny broached the subject about her plans for the future and to her surprise Karen agreed with her.

'Yes, I think it is time for me to get back out into the real world. It's been wonderful staying here with you, Gran, but it is very cramped and I certainly do need to earn some money.'

'I shall miss having you, of course, Karen, but you know you can always come back if things don't work out.'

They smiled at each other as if in full agreement; each of them waiting for the other to say more.

'You've finally made some plans for the future then?' Jenny pressed.

'Yes! Give me a few more days and then you can have your flat to yourself again,' Karen said with a dismissive smile.

Jenny waited for her to go into details but when she didn't she gave a mental shrug and decided not to pry. She was sure Karen would tell her when she was ready to do so.

Nineteen

It came as something of a shock to Jenny the following morning when she found that the duvet and the pillow that Karen used each night for her bed on the sofa were neatly stacked and there was no sign of her at all.

As she made a pot of tea and poured milk over her cereal she wondered why Karen had gone out so early. She hadn't said the night before that she was going out somewhere special. Then, come to think of it she hadn't mentioned very much at all lately, Jenny thought resignedly.

For some reason Karen had become very secretive, Jenny mused as she washed up and put away her breakfast dishes. She'd said that she was making plans for the future but she certainly hadn't confided what they were.

As she tidied the living room, picking up the evening newspaper to put it in the waste bin, she found a note lying on top of it.

> I'm off to start a new life, Gran. Don't worry about me. I'll be in touch.
> Karen xx

Jenny read it though over and over again. What on earth did it mean? What sort of new life. Why hadn't she given her any details? She couldn't have gone back to Hadyn Trimm because he was in prison, so where had she gone?

A myriad of questions went round and round in Jenny's head. She made herself a cup of tea and tried to reason out what had happened to Karen. It was no good, she couldn't think of an answer. She put on her hat and coat and went for a long walk along the promenade hoping that the fresh air would clear her mind.

There were two liners lying at anchor on the other side of the Mersey, and Jenny wondered if Karen had gone back to her old job and was on one of them.

When she returned to the flat she tried to fathom out exactly what Karen had taken with her, hoping that might help to shed some light on her absence. She spent the rest of the day in a haze, going back over their conversations of the past few days, searching for any clues in what they had discussed, but it was useless.

Finally, she accepted that her granddaughter had gone and that she could do nothing until Karen got in touch with her.

She still felt piqued by the fact that Karen hadn't said what she was planning to do. She had obviously fixed up something because the past week or so she had gone around with a secret little smile on her face. Jenny felt she was being childish.

Over the next few days Jenny delighted in having her flat to herself. She opened all the windows wide to let in fresh air and whatever sunshine there was. She turned out the living room from top to bottom, getting rid of all traces of Karen living there. Any items that Karen had left behind she stored away carefully in a card-board box. She would give them to her the next time she saw her, although when that would be she had no idea.

Anyway, Jenny told herself, she wasn't going to let that worry her, she was far too happy. Now, on her own, she could live life to her own timetable; get up when she wished, eat when she wanted to and indulge in the foods she enjoyed rather than have to pander to Karen's tastes. It was sheer bliss.

Jenny was so content with her own company that she didn't even attend coffee morning that Wednesday. She was far too busy enjoying her feeling of freedom. Instead she went for a long walk along the promenade, watching the busy life on the Mersey. She walked as far as Warren Point and regarded her old home with nostalgia. On the return walk she even stopped and bought an ice cream from a roadside kiosk and sauntered along eating it.

She felt so cocooned in her own happiness that she didn't even stop to talk to the other residents when she met them in passing. She thought they gave her a funny look but she was too immersed in herself to let it bother her. They probably thought she was being snooty; or else if they had heard that Karen had gone thought that she was upset about it and wanted to be on her own.

The following Wednesday morning when she went along for coffee there was a momentary pause in the general chatter when she walked into the room. All eyes turned to look at her, followed by curious stares and whispered talk.

Jenny walked over to a vacant chair in one of the large circular groups. As she sat down she was aware of the tension all around her; it felt like the electrically charged air before a thunderstorm.

There was an uncanny silence as she accepted her cup of coffee from the concierge and chose a shortbread biscuit from the plate on the table in front of her.

When she looked up Jenny found that Richard and Lorna Hill were sitting directly opposite her and that Lorna had an expectant look on her lined face as if hoping to hear some interesting news.

Jenny groaned inwardly, remembering what an avid gossip Lorna was, but knew it was too late to do anything about it and hoped the woman wasn't going to start asking awkward questions about Karen.

Before Lorna could speak, Jane Phillips walked across the room from another group and stood beside Lorna. She was wearing a dark grey pinstripe skirt and a black sweater that made her look like a Gestapo interrogator as she stood there with arms akimbo.

'So are you going to tell us all exactly what has happened?' she demanded in a domineering voice.

'What has happened?' Jenny looked at her blankly. 'I don't understand what you mean. About what?'

'About your granddaughter, of course,' Jane said pointedly.

There was a sharp intake of breath from those nearby, uneasy coughs from one or two of the men and a trembling high-pitched laugh from Lorna.

'Well?' Jane looked smug. 'Go on then.'

'Perhaps Mrs Langton doesn't wish to talk about it,' the concierge intervened.

'I bet she doesn't,' Jane Phillips murmured. 'She's certainly kept herself hidden away ever since it happened. She's probably hoping that by now we will have lost interest.'

'My granddaughter is no longer living with me because she has a new job. Not that it is any business of yours,' Jenny said stiffly.

As Jenny stopped speaking a titter broke out and rippled round the room. She felt uneasy; unable to understand what she had said that gave rise to mirth.

'Is that what you call it,' Jane said in a ribald voice that brought even more titters.

Jenny looked at her questioningly, shaking her head in bewilderment.

'By Jove! You really don't know what they're talking about,' Major Mitchell guffawed. 'Either that or you're a damn good actress, what!'

Jenny picked up her cup of coffee and took a sip, then put it down again on the table because her hand was shaking so much that she was afraid she was going to spill it.

'No, I don't know what you are talking about,' she agreed. 'My granddaughter left here the weekend before last and I have been busy ever since so I have obviously missed something that has been going on.'

'It's your granddaughter we are talking about,' Jane told her. 'Your granddaughter and Lionel Bostock.'

'What about them?'

There was an uneasy silence, then several people spoke at once all eager to tell her the news.

'She's gone off on a cruise with him. Not sure if it's down to the Mediterranean or across to the West Indies.'

'They left the Saturday morning before last in a taxi. I saw them with my own eyes,' Beryl Willis confirmed with relish.

'He always books a double cabin when he goes on his annual cruise in the hopes that he might get lucky.'

'Seems that this time he got lucky before he even left Liverpool,' someone guffawed.

'His son Edwin told me that they're off for a month in the sun,' Mavis Grey piped up, her small dark eyes almost popping out of her round podgy face with excitement. 'When I told my Dan he could hardly believe it.'

Jenny felt stunned. 'Neither can I. Are you sure you have your facts right?' she protested.

She spoke in a quiet, controlled voice but inside she was churning as she listened to the babble of talk going on all around her. Lionel Bostock was an old man of eighty-three and her granddaughter was only in her twenties. She felt sick. She couldn't believe Karen had done anything so foolish as to go off on holiday with Lionel Bostock.

Jenny looked round the room at the elderly ladies in their twinsets and pearls, the men in tweed jackets and flannels or dark trousers, all of them so prim and proper, all of them delighting in this scrap of juicy scandal.

Surely it was idle gossip. Karen had happened to leave Merseyside Mansions at the same time as Lionel Bostock had, she told herself.

He had probably offered her a lift in his taxi, nothing more irregular than that.

Jenny felt indignant that they should think Karen had gone on a cruise with him. If only Karen had been more open with her and told her what her new job was, and where it was, or even where she would be living then she would have been able to scotch these foolish rumours right away.

She wanted to get up and run from the community room and seek solace in her own flat but her legs felt so shaky that she wasn't sure she could do it.

She needed to have time to calm down and get her thoughts in order. Time on her own to go back over every conversation she'd had with Karen before she'd left to see if there had been anything that confirmed what these people were saying.

Twenty

Jenny found it difficult to accept that Karen had gone away on a cruise with Lionel Bostock. Nevertheless, she absented herself from any further coffee mornings. For the moment she didn't want to face the barrage of questions and innuendo about Karen and Lionel. She knew she would have to do so sometime but she decided to wait until they returned and see what happened then.

She still couldn't believe that Karen would do something so utterly foolish. She waited impatiently for a postcard or letter from Karen telling her where she was and what she was doing. Once that arrived she could quash all the ridiculous rumours that were going around.

But the postcard when it did arrive brought confirmation that all the rumours were correct and that Karen had gone on a cruise with Lionel Bostock.

Jenny was aghast. Surely it must be a joke; a very silly one at that. She went for a long walk to put the matter out of her head. She'd give Karen a good talking to when next she saw her and explain how much gossip this might have caused if anyone else at Merseyside Mansions had accidentally seen it and read what she'd written.

When she returned from her walk Jenny found small knots of people in the reception area clustered around the notice board and all excitedly chattering about a new notice that was on display.

She went to walk past, deciding she would read it later when there wasn't quite such a crowd there, but found her way barred. Everyone wanted to talk to her about the cruise.

To her dismay she learned that was what the notice was all about. Lionel had sent a letter to the concierge telling her all about his cruise with Karen and asked her to display it on the notice board so that everyone at Merseyside Mansions would know all about it.

As she tried to fend off the many questions Jenny felt like a stag at bay.

She kept telling them that she'd had no idea that anything of this sort was happening until she had received a postcard that morning.

She still insisted that she hadn't even known that Karen had intended to go on a cruise with Lionel Bostock.

No one seemed to believe her, and she was on the verge of tears when Tom Fieldman took her by the arm and led her towards the front door, explaining over his shoulder that they had arranged to meet some friends for lunch.

'I thought it best for you to get well clear of that mob until after all the excitement dies down,' he said grimly as he steered her towards his car. 'They're almost like a lynch party.'

'Thank you,' Jenny said gratefully in a voice that was little more than a whisper, reflecting how upset she felt.

'We'll drive out into the Wirral and have lunch at a very quiet little pub I know in Heswall. If you want to talk about Lionel and Karen you can, otherwise we'll forget all about them until they return from their cruise.'

Lionel had talked so much about his forthcoming holiday that Jenny knew not only which ship he was on but also its destination. On impulse, the very next day, she went over to the company's offices in Liverpool and was delighted to find that she could check their progress. After that she went in every day and followed the progress of the liner they were on.

Afterwards, knowing she couldn't settle to anything at home, and wanting to avoid meeting any of the residents at Merseyside Mansions, even Tom Fieldman, she stayed on in Liverpool. She would go into Lyons Corner House or the Kardomah for a coffee and then wander around the Bon Marche, C&A's, T.J. Hughes or one of the other big department stores, idly eyeing up all the latest fashions.

After a time the assistants recognized her and seemed to know that she had no intention of buying anything, so apart from the occasional hopeful smile they ignored her completely.

The four weeks that Lionel and Karen were away were the longest Jenny had ever known. Yet, much as she longed for them to be back she was also rather apprehensive about the sort of reception they would receive from the other residents.

Why, oh why, had Karen acted so foolishly as to take up with a man who was so much older Jenny kept asking herself over and over again. Had Karen done so because he was reputed to be very wealthy, as so many of the residents seemed to think she had, or was she genuinely fond of the old man. He certainly dressed smartly and he was well spoken; witty even. He was wonderful for his age but there was no denying that he was often quite slow in his movements and in collecting his thoughts together.

They were due to return on a Monday and when Jenny made enquiries she was informed by a clerk at the shipping office that it would probably be late evening before passengers disembarked. She waited for Karen to call her but when midnight approached she gave up and went to bed.

She tossed and turned for most of the night, wondering whether their ship had been delayed for some reason or if Karen was putting off making contact until the next day.

Tuesday passed without any word from Karen. Jenny stayed in her apartment waiting for the phone to ring or for there to be a knock on her door. None came; she neither heard nor saw anyone the entire day.

Wednesday was coffee morning and Jenny was still unsure what to do. She didn't have a telephone number for Lionel's flat, so she couldn't ring him to find out if he and Karen were back; she had no idea if they intended to brazen their return out in public or not.

Partly from curiosity, partly from a sense of duty, Jenny felt she ought to be there to support her wayward granddaughter. She dressed with care. A dark brown tailored skirt, a beige top and a pink and white floral neck scarf. She kept her make-up simple apart from a bright lipstick so that she didn't look pale and washed out.

Head held high she walked into the community lounge and her heart pounded as she saw that Karen and Lionel were already in the room. She was aware that all eyes were on her, watching to see her reaction as she walked towards them and then hesitated as the concierge served them their coffee.

As Karen accepted a biscuit from the plate the sapphire and diamond ring on her left hand sparkled and so too did the matching earrings and sapphire and diamond pendant at her neckline.

Jenny smiled brightly as she stopped by their chairs. They certainly looked as though they'd had wonderful weather. Lionel's face was tanned and Karen's skin was a warm golden shade and was well displayed by the low neckline of the sleeveless navy dress she was wearing.

'You both look as though you had good weather,' Jenny murmured as she bent down and kissed Karen on the cheek.

Karen smiled sweetly. 'We had an absolutely terrific time, Gran,' she agreed enthusiastically, ignoring the titters that broke out from those sitting nearby.

Although the chair beside her was vacant, Karen didn't invite Jenny to join them, so Jenny went over to the other side of the group where Tom Fieldman greeted her with a warm smile and indicated that the chair next to him was vacant.

'Where have you been for the past couple of weeks?' he asked quietly. 'I haven't seen you since we had lunch in Heswall and I've missed you,' he added in a low voice as she sat down.

The concierge bringing her coffee saved Jenny from having to answer; it also distracted her sufficiently for Karen's remark to take several minutes to register.

For a moment she wondered if she had misheard, but the babble of excited chatter and flood of questions directed at Karen and Lionel left her in no doubt. Karen really did say that she and Lionel had been married on board ship and that the captain had performed the ceremony.

Did that make it legal, Jenny wondered, or was it merely a perfunctory ceremony like the one that was enacted when someone was crossing the equator for the first time.

Lionel and Karen were very much the centre of attention, so it was impossible to ask her. Although Lionel said very little, Karen was in full sway about how spectacular the trip had been and how much they had enjoyed it and how wonderful the other passengers had all been. She also went into great details about all the different places they'd visited and the wonderful sights they'd seen.

'Yes, she's quite right, we had a wonderful time and I feel like a new man; in fact twenty years younger,' Lionel boasted.

'Surprising what a new woman can do for an old man,' Dan Grey commented shrewdly.

His remarks brought renewed titters and made Jenny feel uneasy. They were all being relatively polite but she sensed that there was tension in the air. As she saw the exchange of raised eyebrows between Sandra Roberts and Jane Phillips she knew that there was trouble brewing.

She was not left in doubt for very long; before the end of the coffee morning Jane turned to Karen and asked sweetly, 'Are you over fifty-five, Karen?'

Jenny heard the suppressed fury in Karen's voice as she replied tartly, 'You know damn well that I'm not.'

'Then really you have no right to be living here, have you? These retirement flats are strictly for the over fifty-fives. We know Lionel comes into that category but . . .' Her voice trailed off and everybody waited expectantly for Karen's reply.

'Don't let it worry you, Jane. I'm well aware of the rules and restrictions,' Lionel told her. 'I'm planning on buying a house as soon as I have recovered from our cruise.'

'That's going to take a while at your age,' Sandra said waspishly. 'In fact, I would have thought you were far too old to move, especially into a house. All those stairs and a garden to look after! Surely, Lionel, that was one of the reasons why you came here; because you couldn't cope with such things.'

'Well, maybe I'll settle for a bungalow this time,' Lionel murmured. 'Give me time; with my new wife's help I'll soon have something sorted out, so there's no need for you to be concerned about us.'

'Surely, in the case of a married couple, as long as one of them is in the right age bracket that is all that matters,' Tom Fieldman protested mildly.

Nobody seemed to know what the ruling was about this and a variety of theories and arguments followed. Tom held up a hand in an attempt to halt the discussion. 'I think Lionel is trying to say something,' he said.

'In the meantime, until I have managed to make other arrangements I hope that you will do all you can to make my new wife very welcome here,' Lionel stated, patting Karen's knee.

Before anyone could reply he pulled himself up out of his chair and, reaching for his walking stick, gave a brief nod to everyone as he made his way towards the door. Karen immediately jumped up and rushed to open it for him.

There was complete silence for a couple of minutes after they left and then a general babble of conversation broke out. Jenny was bombarded by comments and questions. Tom endeavoured to answer some of them on her behalf but without much success.

Jenny made her exit, as soon as it was possible to do so, with an apologetic smile at Tom. She didn't want to listen to the gossip, the criticism or snide remarks about Lionel and her granddaughter and she certainly wasn't prepared to answer any of their questions.

She went back to her own flat and wondered how long she was going to have to wait before Karen contacted her. The news that Lionel was thinking of moving away made good sense to her but she wondered where they intended going. She hoped it wouldn't be too far away.

She felt sure that even though Karen was keeping her distance at the moment there would come a time in the not too distant future when she was going to need all the help and support she could give her.

Lionel was in his eighties and although he was claiming to be fit and well it was obvious from the way he'd got up from his chair and paused to get his breath back before walking towards the door that this was far from true. Not only were his movements very slow but he was walking as though he was in great discomfort. It seemed that either his knees or his hips were giving him some sort of trouble.

A major operation at his age could be serious, Jenny reflected. It would certainly mean that he would need a lot of nursing afterwards and she didn't think Karen would be able to cope with such a situation on her own.

Twenty-One

Jenny was very aware over the next couple of weeks that Karen was avoiding her as much as possible. In fact, the only time she saw her was when they met at the Wednesday coffee morning, and Karen always made sure that she and Lionel sat with other people.

Jenny felt rather piqued. Karen had not been to her flat once since she got back from her cruise. Nor had she invited her up to her flat since she had moved in with Lionel, but she suspected that it was because Karen felt a little uncomfortable about doing so.

She had, however, expected Karen to come and tell her about the cruise and the wedding. In the past as she was growing up she had always confided in her about everything. Her affair with Hadyn Trimm had stopped all that because Karen had realized the need for utter secrecy about their activities.

Now she was wondering whether or not the wedding had been a spur of the moment decision and that Karen was either regretting it or afraid of being criticized because she had taken such a drastic step as marriage to such an old man.

If this was the case then surely Karen needed the opportunity to confide in someone who understood her, and Jenny felt saddened that she was being excluded from her company.

Jenny was grateful that Tom Fieldman always made a point of arriving early on Wednesday coffee mornings and saving a chair for her even though she knew this caused raised eyebrows.

Tom acknowledged her concern about Karen and nodded understandingly when she confided in him that she was worried. Apart from agreeing with her that the age difference between Karen and Lionel was far too great for the marriage to work, he made no comment.

Rumours about Lionel buying a bungalow were rife. He gave very little away when he was questioned on Wednesday mornings except to confirm that they had found one they both liked and that they were going to buy it and were now awaiting the contract. Until that was signed they had no firm date for when they would be moving out of Merseyside Mansions.

Karen looked smug when it was being discussed but like Lionel she refused to go into any details about it. She wouldn't even say if it was in Wallasey or further out in the Wirral.

When Jenny talked to Tom about it he agreed with her that it was sheer folly for Lionel to take on the responsibility of a bungalow at his time of life. 'After all,' Tom said, 'Lionel moved into Merseyside Mansions because he had found that coping with a house had become too much for him.'

'I think that is why most of us are here,' Jenny agreed.

'I hope Karen realizes that she is the one who is going to have to run the place,' he added in a serious voice.

'I don't think she will find doing that and looking after Lionel very easy at all,' Jenny murmured. 'What's more, I think Lionel is rapidly going downhill. He is walking very much slower these days and he is beginning to look quite frail; a strong gust of wind off the Mersey would blow him over.'

She had said it in jest and was shocked when a few days later she heard that was exactly what had happened. Lionel and Karen had gone for a stroll along the nearby promenade and a sudden high gust of wind had caused him to sway and fall.

People had rushed to help but he was unable to get up and in so much pain that in the end someone had called an ambulance. He had been taken to the Liverpool Royal Infirmary where it was found that his fall had resulted in a broken hip.

Karen immediately turned to Jenny for help and support. 'You must come over to the hospital with me, Gran, I can't face it on my own,' she pleaded.

Jenny hesitated. After Karen's selfish attitude over the past weeks she knew she should refuse, yet the sight of Karen's tear-stained face touched Jenny's heart. She looked like a little girl who had dropped her favourite doll and broken it.

'Yes, very well,' she conceded. 'You should have gone in the ambulance with him, you know.'

'I couldn't go on my own.' Karen shuddered. 'When they picked him up from the pavement he . . . he was unconscious and I was afraid that he was dead.'

She looked so young, so visibly shaken by what had happened that Jenny's heart softened. All the slights of the past weeks were forgotten.

'Very well, I'll come with you,' she repeated. 'They probably won't let us see him though because if he has broken his hip they will be getting him prepared for an operation I imagine.'

Jenny was more or less right in her assumption that they wouldn't be allowed to see Lionel.

'Please, can we see him just for one minute, Sister,' she pleaded.

The Sister hesitated, looked at her watch and then gave an imperceptible shrug. 'Very well, but you can only stay two minutes. He probably won't even know you are there, as he is already under sedation prior to going into theatre for his operation,' she warned.

As they followed her to the small side ward where Lionel had been placed, she paused at the door. 'Only one of you. You can go in Mrs Bostock but not your daughter.'

'Karen is my granddaughter and I am not Mrs Bostock; Karen is,' Jenny corrected her.

The Sister looked very taken aback. Frowning, she turned back to Karen, shaking her head in disbelief. 'You are Mr Lionel Bostock's wife?'

'Yes, I am,' Karen affirmed, tossing back her hair and staring at the Sister defiantly.

The Sister said no more but took her into the room. As she had warned, Lionel was too sedated to be aware that she was there. Karen took one look at the frail, inert figure and turned away, biting her lip, saying nothing, her whole body shaking.

As she rejoined her grandmother Jenny saw how distressed she was and her heart ached. She put her arms around the trembling girl and held her close, murmuring words of comfort and stroking her hair as if she were a small child.

What problems had Karen brought on herself, Jenny wondered as she tried to calm her. She thanked the Sister for her help and asked when the operation would take place.

'As soon as we can get Mr Bostock into theatre,' she said briskly. 'There is no point in you waiting though as it will take several hours and he will probably spend some considerable time in the recovery room afterwards. I suggest you go home and ring in later this evening for a report. You certainly won't be able to see him today.'

On the boat as they crossed over to Wallasey, Karen stared unseeingly at the water, tears running unchecked down her cheeks, lost in a world of her own.

'Have you informed Edwin Bostock about what's happened?' Jenny asked.

'Edwin Bostock?' Karen stared at her blankly as if she didn't understand what she said.

'Yes, Lionel's son,' Jenny said rather impatiently.

'No.' Karen said, shaking her head. 'Do you think I ought to?'

'Of course you must.'

'I thought that the hospital would do that,' Karen muttered as she sniffed back her tears.

'They might have done at one time when Edwin was down as "next of kin" but now, as Lionel's wife, you are "next of kin".'

Karen looked uneasy. 'What do I tell him?'

'Tell him exactly what's happened of course. That you were out for a walk, Lionel fell, and that now he is in hospital with a broken hip and they're about to operate.'

Karen shuddered. 'I'd rather not be the one to tell him; could you do it for me please, Gran.'

'No, certainly not! I think you should do it,' Jenny said firmly. 'He'll think it extremely odd coming from me.'

'I've fallen out with Edwin and I don't want to have to talk to him,' Karen protested. 'He said some very nasty things to me when he came to meet us off the boat when we got back from our cruise and Lionel told him it had been our honeymoon.'

Jenny didn't ask for details, she had a pretty good idea what Edwin Bostock had probably said. She could hardly imagine that he would be pleased to discover that his aged father had married a girl young enough to be his father's granddaughter.

More than ever, though, she felt that Edwin must be told about what had happened to his father and that Karen should be the one to tell him.

When they got back to Merseyside Mansions, however, despite all Jenny's efforts, Karen refused to phone Edwin, so reluctantly she undertook the onerous task.

'Thank you for letting me know, Mrs Langton. Keep me informed if there is any further news and I will arrange to come to see him tomorrow. The hospital will probably not tell me very much if I contact them, so may I telephone you first for details of his progress?'

'Of course,' Jenny agreed. 'If we hear any news in the meantime I will let you know immediately.'

'There you are, that wasn't so very difficult now was it,' Jenny commented as she put down the receiver.

'He couldn't very well be rude to you but he would probably have ranted at me and said it was my fault that his father had broken his hip.'

Jenny dismissed the matter with a shrug. 'Well, what are you going to do now? Do you want to stay here and have something to eat with me or do you want to go back to your own flat?' she asked as she filled the kettle and switched it on.

'I'll stay here with you,' Karen said quickly. 'I don't want to be up there on my own. That flat gives me the creeps. I'll go up later and collect some clothes and my night things and I'll sleep on your sofa like I did before, Gran.'

'What about if the hospital try to contact you? The telephone number you've given them is Lionel's number, isn't it?'

'Yes, but it's hardly likely that they will be ringing me, not tonight at any rate. I'll give them yours the next time I go in there,' Karen answered airily.

Jenny bit down on her lower lip to stop herself from saying anything. Surely Karen must realize that it was extremely hazardous for a man of Lionel's age to have a general anaesthetic and a major operation. He could have a relapse and deteriorate at any time and if that happened then Karen would be the one they would ring so that she could be there with him.

Twenty-Two

It was two days before Karen was allowed in to see Lionel. Jenny went to the hospital with her but she was not allowed to accompany Karen into the side ward where Lionel was receiving intensive care.

When Karen emerged ten minutes later she was white and shaking, her green eyes were misted with tears and when she tried to speak her voice was so husky that Jenny couldn't understand what she was saying.

Jenny held her close, stroking her thick hair until she calmed down a little. Then she insisted that they went to the hospital canteen for a hot drink before they set off on their return journey back to Wallasey.

As they sat sipping their cups of tea she asked Karen if she had remembered to give the Sister her home telephone number in case Lionel deteriorated and she needed to contact her urgently.

'I gave her the one at his flat and I also gave them yours,' Karen replied. 'I explained that I was living with you most of the time.'

'Good. I think you ought to ring Edwin Bostock and let him know how very ill his father is,' Jenny said in the long silence that followed.

Karen shook her head. 'There's nothing to tell him. It would be a waste of time coming here to see him; Lionel only opened his eyes once and I'm not sure then that he knew who I was,' she said in a pitiful little voice as she sniffed back her tears. 'You ring Edwin if you want to, I'm not going to do so, because he'll only say hateful things if I do.'

They had been back home barely an hour when the phone went; the call was from the hospital to say that Mr Bostock was sinking fast and they should come at once.

Before they left the house Jenny insisted on ringing Edwin to let him know the situation.

'Thank you Mrs Langton, I'll be there as soon as I can,' he told her.

* * *

Edwin, dressed in a smart pinstripe grey suit and crisp white shirt, was already at his father's bedside when Jenny and Karen reached the hospital.

He was visibly shocked at the state his father was in. 'Why on earth didn't you notify me about his condition earlier?' he asked tersely as he gently released his hold on his father's hand and turned to face Karen.

Karen shrugged her shoulders but didn't answer. Once again tears were spilling down her cheeks and in her short pale blue dress and white jacket she looked very young and vulnerable.

'We did ring you to let you know that your father was in hospital and the moment we received their call to say he was sinking fast I immediately telephoned you to let you know,' Jenny protested.

'Yes, Mrs Langton, I'm sorry. You have done all you could. It's just extremely distressing to find that he is so very ill.'

All three of them stayed by Lionel's bedside for the next half hour, until a nurse came in and asked them to leave so that she could make him comfortable and change his drip.

Outside in the corridor Jenny suggested perhaps they should all go for a coffee. Edwin abruptly declined.

'You two go and I'll stay here with my father. When you get back then possibly I'll take a break,' he said curtly.

When they returned about twenty minutes later, the Sister was bending over Lionel's inert body and Edwin greeted them with a terse, 'He's gone.'

Karen looked at Edwin blankly and for one awful moment Jenny was afraid she was going to ask 'where?' Then, as Karen stared wide-eyed towards the bed and saw that Lionel was no longer breathing, the floodgates opened and she began to sob hysterically.

Jenny put her arms round Karen and tried her best to console her. It was all so dramatic that she wasn't sure if it was the shock of seeing a dead person for the first time or genuine grief because Lionel had died.

The Sister looked from one to the other with a slightly puzzled look on her face. 'Mrs Bostock, if you will come to my office there are some papers I need you to sign.'

'Do you want to do it? He was your father,' Karen said in a muffled voice as she looked appealingly at Edwin.

Again there was an uncomfortable silence. 'Very well,' Edwin agreed. 'Do you also want me to make the funeral arrangements?'

Karen sniffed and nodded.

'I'll telephone you with the details Mrs Langton,' Edwin said, giving Karen a contemptuous look. 'I'll try and arrange the funeral for the beginning of next week and . . .'

'No! No! It mustn't be until the end of the week,' Karen interrupted quickly.

Edwin raised his eyebrows and looked questioningly at Jenny. She was as puzzled as he was and gave an imperceptible shrug and shook her head to indicate she didn't understand why this was important.

Karen avoided their eyes and didn't offer any reason.

'Would you prefer it to be the Wednesday or the Thursday?' Edwin asked.

'Thursday; yes, I'd rather you made it Thursday. Thursday would be more suitable,' Karen gabbled, giving a watery smile.

'Very well, that's if the undertakers and the crematorium have a slot available that day. I'll telephone and let you know.'

'Thank you, Edwin. You are being extremely helpful and I am most grateful,' Jenny told him.

'Since I have no immediate family, perhaps we should hold the Wake at Merseyside Mansions,' Edwin suggested. 'If you agree with that then I'll contact the concierge to see if that is acceptable.'

'That sounds perfect, doesn't it Karen,' Jenny said with a grateful smile. 'Do let us know if there is anything we can do to help. We will have to provide drinks and food of some kind, I suppose.'

'If we are having it at Merseyside Mansions then I'll arrange with a catering firm to provide food and wine. I will also ask them to send along a couple of waitresses,' Edwin stated.

'That sounds perfect,' Jenny agreed. She felt relieved to know that it wouldn't be her responsibility to do so.

Once they said goodbye to Edwin and went their separate ways, Karen seemed to put her grief to one side. Before they left the hospital she went into the ladies' toilet and bathed her eyes with cold water and combed her dark blonde hair, flicking it back behind her ears and renewing her lipstick. There even seemed to be a jauntiness in her step as they made their way to the Pier Head to catch the ferry.

On the way home Jenny asked why she was so adamant about Lionel's funeral not taking place until the following Thursday.

'It's not Quarter Day until then,' Karen told her.

'Quarter Day? What has that to do with anything,' Jenny asked in a puzzled voice.

'It's settlement day for legal affairs. Lionel was old-fashioned about such things and he asked the solicitor to arrange for completion on Quarter Day and that's next Thursday twenty-fifth September.'

Jenny frowned. 'Completion? On what?'

'On the bungalow he's bought for us.'

'You mean he actually bought a bungalow before putting his flat at Merseyside Mansions on the market?' Jenny gasped.

'That's right. He said he could afford it and by doing it that way then we could take our time over moving from one place to the other. There are quite a few alterations I want to make and he agreed we should have all new furniture and furnishing and so on.'

'Well, surely none of that matters now does it? You won't want to move in there now will you?' Jenny cut in sharply.

'No, I don't suppose I will ever move in there, not on my own.'

There was a long silence and Jenny wondered if Karen was going to ask her to move there with her and suggest that they should live together again. When Karen next spoke her hopes were dashed.

'I don't suppose I'll be able to stay on at Merseyside Mansions for very long because they'll all say I'm too young to be there even if I do own the flat. I don't really fancy the bungalow, I never did. Still, now I'll be able to sell both of them and choose a place I really like.'

'Hold on Karen,' Jenny warned. 'You don't know that. It depends how Lionel's estate is divided up.'

'Lionel made a new will after we were married; he's left everything he possesses to me,' Karen told her smugly.

'You mean he's cut Edwin, his own son, out of his will completely!' Jenny exclaimed in a shocked voice.

'That's right. He said that now Edwin was a fully qualified surgeon, and would soon be a consultant, he was earning a good salary and didn't really need anything from him.'

'I'm not at all sure that Edwin will agree to that. He may very well contest his father's will,' Jenny warned.

Karen shrugged. 'He can try, but after the twenty-fifth of

September everything, even the bungalow, will be legally mine. That's how Lionel wanted things to be so I hope Edwin will accept that and not make a fuss.'

Privately Jenny felt taken aback that not only had Karen inveigled Lionel into changing his will so completely in her favour but that she had no qualms at all about how Edwin might feel about the matter.

She was well aware that this would cause a lot of malicious gossip among the residents at Merseyside Mansions. The majority of them had disapproved of Lionel marrying Karen and this would set tongues wagging even more.

Jenny sighed. They would certainly regard Karen as a scheming little minx once the news leaked out that she had inherited all of Lionel's estate.

Jenny wasn't at all sure, however, that because of the brief space between Lionel changing his will and his death, there was a sufficient time span for it to be considered legal.

She remembered Tom Fieldman telling her that he had been a solicitor before he retired so she wondered if he would know the legal situation.

She decided she would definitely have a word with Tom and ask his opinion as soon as she reached home. She needed to do it before the news became general knowledge and recriminations and gossip began to circulate.

Whatever happened or whatever was said, she would have to defend Karen even though in her heart of hearts she deplored the situation.

Eddy would have been horrified had he lived but then, he would have been heartbroken by so many of the things that Karen had done since he had died, she thought sadly.

Not for the first time she wondered if it was her fault; if she was in some way to blame. She had tried so hard to guide Karen but she was wilful and headstrong and determined to do whatever it was she wanted to do.

She seemed to have inherited the worst attributes from both her parents, Jenny thought sadly. She was headstrong and independent like Eddy had been and she yearned for the bright lights and glamorous lifestyle her mother, Fiona, had craved.

Twenty-Three

Jenny tried to reason with Karen about her appearance as the sleek black limousine that Edwin Bostock had hired to take them to the crematorium at Moreton carried them down Leasowe Road.

'You really can't go to your husband's funeral dressed like that Karen. What on earth do you think people will say?

'I'm wearing a dress Lionel bought for me and he loved to see me in it,' Karen pouted.

'I agree it's a lovely dress, my dear, but it is not suitable for a funeral, least of all your husband's,' Jenny said firmly.

Karen's fingers lingered over the low neckline of the crimson bodice and tugged the red and black patterned skirt over her knees.

'Well, I like it.'

'I understand your reasons for wearing it, my dear, but while we are at the crematorium please cover it up,' Jenny persisted in a more gentle voice.

'Gran, don't talk nonsense, how can I do that?' Her green eyes blazed angrily and she tossed back her dark blonde hair defiantly.

'I've brought my black raincoat. Will you put it on please,' Jenny said quietly.

Karen looked out of the car window at the dull, overcast September sky. 'You may need it yourself, it looks as though it's going to rain.'

'I won't need it. I brought it especially for you to wear, Karen. You simply can't go in to the chapel looking like that,' Jenny asserted firmly.

Karen was still protesting about wearing Jenny's black raincoat when the car drew up at the crematorium. As the liveried chauffeur opened the door on Jenny's side she handed him the raincoat. 'Please help Mrs Bostock into this when you open the car door for her,' she said firmly.

The chauffeur made a slight bow in acknowledgement of her instructions before walking round to the other side of the car.

Jenny held her breath, expecting Karen to refuse to put it on, but to her relief Karen gave the chauffeur a sweet smile and allowed him to help her into it. As Jenny reached her side, Karen gave her an amused look.

'Fasten it up; for goodness' sake don't leave it open,' Jenny said in a low voice. 'The idea is to hide your red dress. Stand still and I'll do it for you.' She sighed when Karen made no attempt to obey.

The organ was playing and they were not the first to arrive. Several of the residents from Merseyside Mansions were already there. Jenny smiled and nodded at them as she and Karen made their way to the front pew. Karen walked as though in a dream.

Edwin was already there, sitting in the front row, but he moved out in to the aisle to allow them to pass.

'I'd better sit on the outside because I will be saying a few words about Dad during the service,' he said in a low voice.

The service was extremely brief. Edwin spoke about his father's career as a surgeon and how proud both his parents had been when he had followed in his father's footsteps.

He made no reference to the fact that his mother had died a few years earlier nor that his father had recently remarried. He did say how happy his father had been at Merseyside Mansions.

Edwin rode with Jenny and Karen in the leading limousine as the long line of cars snaked back up Leasowe Road on the way back to Merseyside Mansions. As soon as they were in the car, Karen removed the raincoat and Jenny was aware of Edwin's sharp intake of breath when he saw what she was wearing.

Karen seemed to be oblivious to his frown of disapproval. Throughout the journey she stared out of the window, humming softly to herself, and left Jenny to talk to Edwin.

When they arrived back at Merseyside Mansions they found that the caterers were already there ahead of them and that they had set out an excellent spread of sandwiches, a variety of cheeses, several bowls of black and green grapes and bite-size savouries as well as a wide selection of small cakes.

Edwin immediately took over. He gave instructions to one of the waitresses to fill a dozen or more glasses with white or red wine and stand by the door and hand a glass to each person as they came into the room.

Within half an hour the large communal lounge was packed. As well as those who had attended at the crematorium there were many other people who had known and liked Lionel. Most of the men wore dark suits, white shirts and either black or dark ties. The women were discreetly dressed; some in black dresses or black skirts and white blouses, others in brown, beige or navy blue outfits. Karen, in her vivid red and black, stood out and was the focus of all eyes. Jenny felt humiliated but there was nothing she could do, and Karen seemed to be unaware that people were exchanging glances with each other and raising their eyebrows.

Most of the residents made a point of conveying to Edwin their deep regrets that Lionel had died and extolled what a wonderful man he had been. Most of them ignored Karen as if by doing so they expressed their disapproval of her.

Karen ignored their attitude but Jenny felt most uncomfortable and very much aware that so many of the people present were ignoring them.

Karen appeared to be thoroughly enjoying herself. She had refilled her plate with food and twice had her glass refilled with red wine. Jenny was grateful to Tom Fieldman, who remained by their side throughout the afternoon. He was very attentive and insisted that Jenny should have a second glass of wine even if she couldn't bring herself to eat anything from the sumptuous spread.

As the event drew to a close, the residents left one by one, most of them again expressing their sympathy to Edwin but ignoring Karen.

As the room emptied, Edwin came over to where Karen, Jenny and Tom Fieldman were standing near the window, looking out into the garden. Jenny was silently counting the minutes until they could go. She felt humiliated and longed for the seclusion of her own apartment.

'Karen, we can't deal with the matter of my father's will now so can you meet me at the solicitors' tomorrow morning at eleven o'clock?'

Karen gave him an amused look. 'There's no need. I know what is in it. I was with Lionel at his solicitors when he made out his new will and I can tell you now that he has left everything to me.'

Edwin looked very taken aback and for one moment there was a stunned silence. Jenny looked from one to the other of them in bewilderment.

'I think you should do as Edwin asks, Karen,' she murmured. 'It is the normal procedure.'

'I've already told you, I know what is in the will. Lionel changed it when we got married and he has left me everything, including the bungalow he recently bought. There is really no need for you to see the solicitor at all, Edwin, because it is all mine; you're not even mentioned in it. It all became legal on Quarter Day, which was on Tuesday,' she told him in a lofty tone of voice.

'You mean that was why you asked me to put the funeral off until today?' Edwin asked in an angry tone.

'That's right. I wanted to make sure that you wouldn't argue about the will and now you can't because it would be pointless to do so. Everything Lionel owned in his bank account as well as the flat and the bungalow are all mine,' Karen said triumphantly.

'If you want the furniture from the flat then you are very welcome to it,' she added. 'I certainly don't want it. I think it must have come out of the ark! Lionel insisted on keeping it but that was probably because he'd had it when he set up home for the first time.'

Edwin's face darkened with fury but his voice when he spoke was controlled. 'You are quite a little gold-digger aren't you,' he said, his voice full of contempt. 'Even so, I still think you should attend the solicitor's office for the reading of my father's will tomorrow morning. You may find that everything is not quite as cut and dried as you seem to think it is.' With that, he turned on his heel and strode away.

'Karen, how could you behave so rudely and so childishly,' Jenny remonstrated. 'Edwin is very upset by his father's death even if you don't appear to be. He must have deplored your attitude over Lionel's will.'

'Rubbish!' Colour stained Karen's cheeks but she tossed her hair back defiantly. 'He's annoyed at being cut out of the will, that's all, but there's absolutely nothing that he can do about it.'

'I'm not at all sure about that. I have a feeling that he can contest a will,' Jenny warned, 'What do you think Tom, you were a solicitor before you retired?'

'No, he can't. I made sure that it was all drawn up properly, and it was witnessed and signed,' Karen stated angrily before Tom Fieldman could speak. 'It was what Lionel wanted and there's absolutely nothing Edwin can do about it.'

'I'm not sure you are right about that,' Tom Fieldman warned. 'Edwin might claim that his father was very old and not fully aware of what he was doing. If the doctors say that he was suffering from dementia then . . .'

'Are you saying that Lionel had gone mad?' Karen protested hotly.

'I'm not saying that at all but Edwin may claim that it was so because his father was in his dotage. He might claim that Lionel didn't know what he was doing and was coerced by you into changing his will. Lionel was in his mid-eighties and if the case goes to court then there is every possibility that the judge may agree with Edwin.'

'I don't care what anyone says, everything is mine,' Karen muttered, her green eyes bright with tears.

'Incidentally,' Jenny warned, 'if it does go to court and you insist on staking your claim you will have to pay for a lawyer and so on so it might end up costing you most of what Lionel has left. It might make more sense to humour Edwin and go along to the meeting tomorrow morning. If, as Lionel said, Edwin doesn't need the money and you explain in a reasonable manner why it means so much to you then Edwin might capitulate without a fight.'

Twenty-Four

The next morning Karen refused to go to the solicitor. She was still in bed when Jenny received a phone call from Edwin to say that it was imperative that Karen should attend immediately and that they were sending a taxi to collect her and that it would be there within twenty minutes.

Under duress from Jenny, Karen eventually complied, although she staunchly maintained that it was unnecessary and that Edwin was simply being awkward.

'You are legally Lionel's next of kin,' Jenny pointed out. 'I don't know for sure but it might be necessary for you to be present in order to sign the relevant papers or something.'

Karen waved a hand dismissively. 'Load of poppycock. It's simply Edwin being difficult. All right I'll go,' she capitulated. 'It will be a laugh to see the look of disappointment on Edwin's face when the solicitor confirms that Lionel hasn't left him anything, not a single memento even.'

She insisted that Jenny went with her and she was still protesting loudly about what a waste of time it was when the taxi reached Liscard and drew up in front of the solicitor's office in Wallasey Road.

Edwin, in his dark grey pinstripe suit and sombre dark tie contrasted strongly with Karen, who was wearing tight fitting black slacks, a gaudy white and red top and a bright red woollen jacket.

'Well?' she demanded haughtily as they were shown into the solicitor's office. 'Why do you need me here? If it's simply to sign something then surely you could have sent me all the documents.'

'Not really, Mrs Bostock.' The solicitor took off his gold-rimmed spectacles and regarded her with shrewd blue eyes. Then he polished his glasses and replaced them before explaining.

'I understand that you are under the impression that the late Lionel Bostock has left everything he owned to you.' He looked at her sternly from over the rim of his gold-framed glasses. 'I am afraid this is not so,' he said curtly.

'What are you talking about, what's he been telling you?' Karen asked, colour rising in her cheeks. 'I knew you would try and make things as difficult as possible,' she said, glaring in Edwin's direction.

'The only thing which comes directly to you is the bungalow Mr Lionel Bostock was in the process of purchasing and which has your name on the deeds,' the solicitor went on, ignoring her outburst. 'I'm afraid, however, that he had not completed negotiations and had only paid a minimum deposit and made an arrangement with his bank for a bridging loan to cover the rest of the payment.'

'You're wrong.' Karen almost spat the words at him. 'You and Edwin Bostock are trying to cheat me out of my inheritance. You know very well that I am telling the truth. I was here with Lionel the day he changed his will and bought the bungalow.'

'You were here, yes,' the solicitor continued drily, 'and he did change his will in your favour. It was drawn up and read over to you both but it was only the draft so of course he never signed it; he would not be required to do so at that stage. He had arranged to come back in two weeks' time to do that after we had drawn up a new document.'

'I was right here at his side. I saw him sign both documents,' Karen protested. 'One was his new will and the other was for the bungalow,' she insisted stubbornly. Her voice was no longer strong but almost whining and the colour had drained from her face.

'I think the documents you saw my father sign were in respect of the bungalow only,' Edwin explained. 'One was to sign that he was proposing to buy it and the other was for his bank agreeing to a bridging loan which would cover the rest of the purchase price that was not covered by the deposit.'

'That is quite correct,' the solicitor affirmed. 'Those were the two documents he signed. Neither of them had anything to do with his will.'

Although he was obviously the victor, Edwin retained his dignity. 'I'm sorry, Karen, that you misunderstood what was going on. All you inherit is the deposit Dad paid on the bungalow.'

'So I don't even own that?' Karen said in a shocked voice.

'I'm afraid not. Well, not unless you can afford to pay the outstanding ten thousand pounds to complete the deal.'

Edwin looked expectantly from Karen to Jenny and back again.

'You know I can't,' Karen muttered angrily. 'I want the money that Lionel put down as a deposit on the bungalow and I want it now.'

'That's not possible,' the solicitor told her quietly. 'You will have to wait for that until the bungalow is sold and then you will receive any money that is left after the estate agent has taken his fee. You will also have to pay interest to the bank on the borrowed money and any other banking costs that may have accrued. What is left will then be legally yours.' He shook his head. 'I'm afraid there will not be very much left as Mr Bostock only paid the minimum deposit.'

'This is your fault,' Karen said, rounding on Edwin. 'You were jealous because I was getting your father's money and not you. He said you didn't need it because you already had plenty of money and you earn a good salary.'

'Very true,' Edwin agreed, 'but until he met you I was his only family and sole beneficiary and that is how it remains.'

'It means that I have nothing at all now.' Karen's green eyes were brimming with tears and her lower lip jutted in a sulky pout.

'I'm afraid that is so,' Edwin agreed sombrely. 'You don't even have anywhere to live because I now own the flat in Merseyside Mansions.'

'You can't turn me out, I have nowhere to go,' Karen protested in a hostile tone.

'I most certainly can but I wouldn't be so uncharitable,' he assured her. 'You are welcome to stay there until the flat is sold or you decide to move, whichever comes first.'

'Very generous,' Karen said in a scathing voice. 'You take everything else do you?'

'I do and it is all legal and above board.'

'Don't you even care that Lionel said he was leaving everything to me? I don't suppose you've even seen his new will.'

'As far as I am concerned it doesn't exist because he never signed it,' Edwin told her indifferently.

'You are going against his wishes,' Karen argued.

Edwin shrugged. 'As a measure of goodwill I will waive the matter of you paying me any rent while you are in his flat.'

'You might as well because I have no intention of doing so. What's more, I'll leave when I'm ready not because you want me to,' she retorted, tossing her head defiantly.

As soon as the news about Lionel's will reached Merseyside

Mansions gossip was rife. Jenny knew that it would be the topic of conversation at the next coffee morning and she would have preferred not to go, but Tom Fieldman pointed out that she had to face the music sometime and the sooner she did so the better.

'I'll be there, at your side,' he promised and he was as good as his word, waiting to accompany her when she arrived at the communal lounge on Wednesday morning.

They were left in no doubt that everyone had heard the news and they all held strong opinions. Some openly approved when they heard that Karen had not been left anything.

'Serve her right, marrying a man old enough to be her grandfather.'

'We all said it wouldn't last.'

'Not as much of an old man's darling as she thought she was.'

'Nothing but a little gold-digger.'

'The sooner she's out of his flat the better.'

'Silly old fool; we all said that getting married again at his age would kill him.'

'Hope this will be a lesson to some of the other old boys here.'

'I think her grandmother has set her cap at someone so look out for developments there. We might all be buying new hats again.'

The last comment brought gales of laughter.

Unable to stand their sour recriminations and insinuations, Jenny excused herself and stood up to leave despite Tom Fieldman's whispered advice to 'stick it out' as he placed a restraining hand on her arm.

'Going to try and sort out the mess your granddaughter's in are you?' Jane Phillips said waspishly as Jenny reached the door.

Jenny didn't answer. She wished she'd done the same as Karen and steered clear of the community lounge. She had suspected that there would be tittle-tattle but she hadn't expected there to be so many unkind remarks.

If Tom Fieldman hadn't been at her side, talking to her as if nothing was amiss, she was sure she would have made a fool of herself and broken down in front of them all.

Once outside the room she thanked Tom for his support but declined his suggestion that they should go out for a drink.

'It's very kind of you but I would rather not. I simply want to get back to my own flat,' she told him as she struggled to hold back her tears.

She felt so miserable that she wondered if she should move away from Merseyside Mansions. She loved her flat and until now she had quite enjoyed the mixed company there, but this incident over Karen had brought it all crashing down around her ears. Inside her head she could still hear some of the waspish remarks that had been made about Karen and they stung.

What she needed was a strong cup of tea and then she'd take a brisk walk along the promenade. That would clear her mind, she told herself as she let herself into her flat.

To her dismay she found Karen was there, curled up in an armchair, her eyes red from weeping.

'You're back early,' Karen said, sniffling.

She gave a watery smile and Jenny's heart went out to her, she looked so pathetically young.

'Yes, I felt like a brisk walk,' Jenny said. 'Want to come? I know it's blowing a gale out there but if we wrap up warm it will do us both good.'

Karen shook her head. 'No . . . No, I won't come with you, Gran.'

'Look, Karen, it's no good crying about all that's happened, certainly not over the money. You're young and healthy, so put the past behind you and start a new life.'

Karen stared at her wide-eyed. 'I can't do that.' She burst into gulping sobs. 'Gran, I don't know what to do, I'm pregnant . . . I . . . I am going to have a baby.'

Twenty-Five

'Edwin really must be told about this, Karen,' Jenny insisted.

'For one thing your child will be his half-brother. Also, it may change his mind about his father's estate. You said he agreed that he didn't need the money so perhaps under the circumstances he will see his way clear to let you have some, if not all of it.'

'No, Gran, I don't want him told. He will only say unkind things and I can't stand it . . . not at the moment anyway.'

'Rubbish! The matter has to be dealt with right away. It changes everything,' Jenny said brusquely. 'Are you going to telephone him and tell him the news or shall I do it?'

Jenny's heart went out to Karen as she shook her head and curled into an even tighter ball, her shoulders quivering as though with fear. She felt she was being very harsh but it was for Karen's own good, she told herself.

'Come here, let me give you a cuddle,' she said in a softer voice, holding out her arms.

Slowly, Karen stood up and came over to the settee where Jenny was sitting. As Jenny gathered her into her arms and stroked her hair Karen once more burst into tears, sobbing as if her heart would break.

'Come on, come on, worse things happen at sea.' Jenny crooned the mantra she had used so often when Karen had been small and come running to her in tears. 'We'll get through this together; we'll manage somehow. If you don't want me to tell Edwin then I quite understand.'

Slowly, Karen's tears subsided. 'You're right, Gran, he ought to know,' she said at last. Pulling herself upright and away from Jenny, she asked, 'Will you tell him for me?'

Jenny was silent for a moment. 'I think we should talk it through with Tom Fieldman first and see what he thinks is the best thing to do.'

'Must we. It will be all round Merseyside Mansions in next to no time if we start asking other people's opinions.'

'Nonsense. Are you forgetting that before he retired Tom was a solicitor. I'm sure he will be most discreet.'

'You like him, don't you.' Karen smiled.

'Yes, I do. He has been a staunch friend to me and without his help I don't think I could have got through the last few months,' Jenny agreed.

'I should never have come here, it's caused you nothing but trouble. I'm sorry, Gran.'

'That will do, we can't turn the clock back so let's deal with this situation in the best possible way. I'll invite Tom to come and have a cup of tea with us this afternoon and then we can ask his advice.'

'I think it might be best if you asked Edwin to meet you at the solicitors' who are handling Lionel's affairs,' Tom Fieldman told them. 'That way Edwin will appreciate the seriousness of the matter and, if he does decide to make you some sort of allowance out of his father's estate, then you not only have a legal witness but you won't have to tell your story to the solicitor all over again.'

'You will come with me, Gran, if I do that; I can't face them on my own?' Karen asked anxiously.

'Of course I will. I'll telephone Lionel's solicitor right away and make an appointment. The sooner we do it the better. I'll ask him to contact Edwin and then to let us know when they can see us.'

To Jenny's great relief a meeting was organized for the following morning at eleven o'clock.

'Mr Edwin Bostock is due to come in to sign some documents so I'm sure he will be agreeable to seeing you at the same time. Would you like to tell me what this is about?'

'No, I think it might be better if we tell you in Edwin Bostock's presence,' Jenny said cautiously.

She spent a restless night thinking over what Karen had told her and all its many implications. Once again she felt it was her fault; that she had failed Karen, and Eddy. She tried not to think of what he would have made of the situation.

Next morning, to her surprise, Karen appeared dressed in a simple black skirt and pale blue jumper. Her thick tawny gold hair was drawn back into the nape of her neck and she was wearing no make-up or lipstick. She looked pale and washed out, very different from the rather brash figure she had appeared to be at the cremation.

Jenny made no comment but a feeling of relief swept over her. Thank goodness Karen was taking this matter seriously. She hoped Edwin would also understand how grave it all was and that he would show compassion when it came to settling Lionel's affairs.

Karen hardly spoke a word over breakfast or while they cleared up and got ready to go to the solicitors'. Jenny kept thinking of things she wanted to tell her or ask her but decided it was better not to say anything. Karen looked quite composed as if she had sorted out everything in her own mind, so perhaps she ought to let her deal with the forthcoming meeting in her own way.

Edwin was already there when they arrived at the solicitors' office and, judging by the pile of documents on the desk, they had already dealt with the matter he had come about.

He looked impatiently from Karen to Jenny. 'I understand you wished to discuss something with me?'

'Yes, Karen has something to tell you,' Jenny said quietly. 'Go on, tell them,' she prompted, touching Karen's arm.

Karen hesitated for a moment and then she said in a low voice, 'Gran thought you ought to know that I am expecting a baby and . . .'

Edwin's outburst of laughter halted her.

'That's one of the oldest tricks in the book,' he said caustically. 'I suppose you are hoping that I will make you a handsome allowance so that you can bring the child up and educate it.'

'You can laugh. It will be your half-brother or half-sister,' Karen shouted at him, her cheeks flaming with indignation.

'Indeed it won't. You may be pregnant but it is nothing to do with me,' he retorted in an amused voice.

'One moment please.' The solicitor held up his hand for silence and concentrated his attention on Karen. 'You are telling us that you are pregnant and that the late Lionel Bostock is the father of the child you are expecting?'

'That's right.' Karen sniffed, her voice low.

'Impossible!' Edwin's voice rang out in denial. 'My father had the snip over thirty years ago.'

'Are you quite sure about this?' the solicitor frowned.

'Quite sure; I was eleven years old at the time and I can remember the discussion over breakfast the morning he was due to have it done as clearly now as then.'

'Discussion over breakfast?' Jenny frowned. 'You a mere child! I hardly think your parents would discuss such a topic in front of you.'

'You seem to forget, Mrs Langton, mine was a medical family. My mother was a hospital matron when she married my father and he was a surgeon and such matters were discussed openly,' Edwin said curtly.

'Is there any way you can confirm this?' the solicitor asked.

'Of course he can't. Lionel's been cremated so he's just bluffing,' Karen said triumphantly, wiping away her tears with the back of her hand.

'You can look at my father's medical records,' Edwin said quietly. 'You'll find all the details there.'

Jenny looked from one to the other of the two men in bewilderment. 'If what you say is true then how is it that my granddaughter is pregnant?' she asked.

'Possibly a one-night stand while she was on the cruise,' Edwin stated, his eyes hard and accusing.

'How dare you say such a thing,' Jenny defended hotly.

'I feel sick.' Karen clamped a hand over her mouth, stood up, and headed for the door. The solicitor hurried after her, summoning his secretary from the outer office and instructing her to take Karen to the ladies' room as quickly as she could.

Edwin looked at his watch. 'I'm afraid I have to go. I'm due in theatre in an hour. If you need me or wish to discuss this matter any further you have my telephone number, Mrs Langton, so please feel free to call me.'

'This is a very unsatisfactory state of affairs, Mrs Langton,' the solicitor said sympathetically as Karen came back into the room. 'I am afraid there is nothing more I can say or do at the moment but I will pursue the matter diligently and I'll be in touch with you as soon as possible.'

A sleeting rain was falling and there was a distinct chill in the air when Karen and Jenny came out of the solicitors' office into Wallasey Road.

'Shall we go to the milk bar up by the Liscard roundabout for a hot drink or to the nearest pub for a bar meal and a drink?' Karen suggested. 'The Boot is the nearest public house or we can go to The Wellington on the corner by Liscard Road.'

'I thought you were feeling unwell, so perhaps we should catch a bus back to New Brighton and go straight home?'

Karen shook her head. 'I'm all right again now, except that I'm cold.'

'Well, I could certainly do with something stronger than a coffee,' Jenny agreed. 'I feel absolutely drained, but what about you? You shouldn't be drinking if you're pregnant.'

'It's the pub then,' Karen said decisively. 'I like The Boot best because they have roaring log fires, so let's go there.'

It was only just turned midday so they were able to find a secluded table. Jenny ordered shepherd's pie; Karen asked for sausage and mash with onion gravy and they both decided to have a sherry while they waited for their meal to be served.

'You really shouldn't be drinking that if you're pregnant, Karen. Still, I don't suppose one glass will matter too much, but you must be careful in future,' Jenny murmured as they warmed themselves in front of the open fire before sitting down.

'Stop fussing, Gran. I'm not pregnant. I thought if I said I was then Edwin would feel he had to stand by his father's new will even though Lionel hadn't signed it. I didn't know the old boy had had the snip.'

'You mean you've been telling lies about being pregnant!' Jenny exclaimed, her eyes widening in disbelief.

'I'm afraid so, and the way things have turned out it looks as though I will have to forget all about it because Edwin holds the trump card and he knows it. There's certainly no chance of him changing his mind about his father's estate now that he knows I'm making it all up!'

She shrugged and took a sip of sherry, then she raised her glass in the air. 'Here's to a new start.' She laughed and drained her glass.

Twenty-Six

Jenny couldn't sleep. She tossed and turned, sat up and took a drink of water from the glass on her bedside table, thumped her pillow into different shapes, but still sleep would not come.

She lay there staring into the darkness, trying to fathom out where she had gone wrong in bringing up Karen.

She'd been such a lovely baby and an enchanting toddler. She'd enjoyed school and done well in all her exams. She'd had such a promising future when she left school and started work at Premium Printers, so where had it all gone wrong?

The question drummed in Jenny's head like a hammer. Why had Karen become such a scheming little money-grabber? She still couldn't believe that Karen had dreamed up such an evil plot as to tell them she was pregnant in the hope of getting Lionel's fortune.

Was it her fault, Jenny wondered? Had she harped on so much about money and making ends meet and saving for the future that she had made Karen so money conscious that she needed to amass money to give her a feeling of security.

No, it couldn't be that, because when she had given her a handsome nest egg after selling Warren Point, Karen had squandered it all. How she had managed to spend every penny of such a large sum in such a short time Jenny simply couldn't understand. Karen had said that Hadyn Trimm had invested it on her behalf and so she assumed that meant it had all been lost when he was arrested, but now she wasn't so sure because Karen was so devious.

In some ways she felt relieved that Eddy wasn't still alive to see what his daughter had become. He would have been devastated by her marriage to an eighty-three-year-old man; he would have been even more shocked if he had heard her saying she was pregnant and then found out that it was a lie.

Perhaps though, if Eddy had still been alive Karen would have behaved differently. She had adored her father and she would never have done anything to upset him. Perhaps it was because she missed her father so much that Karen was behaving in this way. Had she been looking for a surrogate father when she married Lionel?

Jenny was still dwelling on this aspect of Karen's behaviour when she drifted off to sleep. It was not a restful sleep but one that was more like a nightmare. Karen was in it and although Jenny called out to her time and time again to stop what she was doing and behave herself, she continued to cavort wildly with a medley of leering and jeering faceless characters.

Jenny was in a cold sweat when she wakened at first light. Shaking and stumbling, she went to the kitchen to make herself a hot drink to try and calm down.

Her hand was shaking so much as she lifted up the kettle to pour the hot water into her cup that the kettle slipped. Desperately she tried to control it and in doing so the scalding water went over both her hands.

Jenny's agonized screams woke Karen who, still half asleep, came to see what was happening.

She stood in the kitchen doorway staring as Jenny, screaming with pain, begged her to do something.

'What do you want me to do? Shall I make you a cup of tea?'

'Do something for my hands,' Jenny sobbed. 'Turn the tap on for me. I need cold water over them to cool them down.'

As Karen took a bottle of water from the fridge, Jenny shouted at her to stop. 'Not from the fridge, it will be icy cold. Turn on the tap so that I can hold my hands under the running water.'

'Very well, if that's what you prefer,' Karen said in a sulky voice. 'Cold water is cold water and that's what you asked me to get for you.'

She turned on the cold tap and then stood back. Shaking with shock, Jenny stumbled towards it. Leaning against the edge of the sink for support, she edged her hands forward.

'Can you turn it down a bit? It's coming so fast that it hurts.'

In silence Karen turned the tap until there was only a trickle.

'More than that,' Jenny begged, tears of pain flowing down her cheeks.

'Oh, make your mind up,' Karen said crossly and turned the tap full on. The water came with such force that Jenny screamed again as it hit her hands and arms, which were already swollen and blistering.

Realizing that Karen had no idea what to do she asked her to get help.

'The concierge won't be on duty yet so I'll pull the emergency cord,' Karen muttered.

It was answered immediately, but when a remote voice asked if she needed help, Karen looked helplessly at her grandmother. Choking with pain, Jenny tried to explain what had happened and how she'd scalded herself.

'I'll send an ambulance, Mrs Langton. Meantime, cool the scalds with tepid water and then cover them with a piece of clean linen. Don't apply any creams. Take a painkiller if you have some. The ambulance will be there in a few minutes.'

While Jenny had been talking on the intercom Karen had refilled the kettle and made herself an instant coffee. 'There's still hot water in the kettle, do you want a coffee?' she asked as she picked up her cup from the worktop.

Jenny shook her head. 'The ambulance will be here any minute. Will you help me out of this wet nightdress and fetch me a dry one to go out in and my dressing-gown and slippers,' she requested, wincing with pain and ignoring Karen's question.

'Yes, when I've finished my coffee. I want to get dressed myself first,' she murmured as she wandered away.

Before she returned Jenny heard the wail of the siren as the ambulance drew up outside, and seconds later there was a loud banging on her door and someone calling, 'Mrs Langton, are you there? Ambulance.'

Karen opened the door and let in the two paramedics. They took one look at Jenny's scalded hands and arms and were immediately concerned, agreeing that she must be taken to hospital right away.

'Have you a coat or dressing gown you can put on?' one of them asked.

'If not don't worry, I'll bring in some blankets when I go to get a chair to take you out,' the other one assured her.

For the second time Jenny asked Karen to fetch her dressing gown and slippers. This time Karen did so, but she made no attempt to help Jenny into them. Instead she handed them to the paramedic and then moved away so that he had no option but to take them and help Jenny into them.

By this time the other paramedic had returned with blankets and special sterile wraps in which he gently encased Jenny's scalds. Then between them they wrapped the dressing gown around her shoulders and helped her into her slippers. Although by then she was flinching with pain, they wrapped her in a blanket before carefully strapping her into a chair to convey her to the ambulance.

'Are you coming with us, Miss?' one of them asked Karen.

'No point, there's absolutely nothing I can do is there?' she said quickly.

'You will come to the hospital later, Karen?' Jenny asked anxiously.

Karen shrugged. 'Perhaps. I'll phone the hospital after I've had my breakfast and find out if they are going to keep you in.'

'She'll be in for a few days, possibly a week,' the ambulance man stated. 'Nasty scalds, and with them being on both hands she won't be able to do very much for herself for a while.'

It was Tom Fieldman, not Karen, who was sitting at Jenny's bedside when she came round from the mild anaesthetic she'd been administered. Both her hands and arms were encased in dressings up to her elbows and they were throbbing painfully.

'Where's Karen?'

Tom didn't answer right away. 'I heard about what happened,' he said quietly. He looked at her arms. 'Pretty painful I imagine.'

Jenny made a face. 'It is very painful and such an awkward time to happen just days before Christmas. You still haven't told me how you knew I was in here?' she persisted.

'Someone put a note under my door. I assume it was Karen.'

'I see. You haven't spoken to her though?'

'I haven't seen her.'

There was a silence while Jenny digested this piece of news and wondered why that was. Was Karen keeping away from everybody in Merseyside Mansions because she didn't want to face the gossip or had she gone off somewhere on her own for the day.

'Is there anything I can get you?' Tom asked.

Jenny shook her head. 'Not really, but you could ask Karen to bring me in some nightwear and my clothes ready for when I can come home.'

'Very well, I'll do that.'

'Thank you.' Jenny closed her eyes so that he wouldn't see her tears of gratitude. He was so kind and considerate, such a good friend.

A few minutes later, assuming that she was feeling tired, Tom took his leave but not before insisting that he would come back next day. He made her promise that if they did decide to let her out and she couldn't contact Karen then she would let him know and he'd come and collect her.

When he did return the next day it was to report that he still hadn't seen Karen and to ask if she had been in touch.

'No.' Jenny shook her head. 'I feel quite worried about her. I wonder where she is?'

'Have you heard when you are likely to come home?' Tom asked.

'Not for another few days; the Sister said I may have to stay here until after Christmas. It depends on how well my hands and arms have healed when the doctor looks at them tomorrow. At the moment they are very tender and I can't use my hands. I must look an utter mess because I can't even comb my hair,' she added with a self-conscious laugh.

'You look fine to me,' Tom told her gallantly. 'But even so, let's hope it is good news and they let you come home,' he said smiling.

'Yes, that would be wonderful; apart from the fact that I have nothing to wear to come home in,' she said ruefully. 'I'm not sure if they will let me go home in a hospital gown and apart from that I have only my dressing gown which I was wearing when I came in,' she added worriedly. 'I would be very grateful if you would try and get hold of Karen and ask her to bring in my clothes.'

'I will certainly do my best,' Tom promised, 'but if I can't get hold of her I can always collect them for you if you give me your keys and tell me exactly what you want and where to find them.'

The blood rushed to Jenny's face at the thought of Tom rooting through her wardrobe and underwear drawer but she knew there was really no alternative. Reluctantly she agreed to his suggestion.

Twenty-Seven

Jenny was in hospital until the third of January. Tom Fieldman came to visit her every day. No one else came from Merseyside Mansions although several sent good wishes and hoped she would soon be back with them, There was no word at all from Karen, and Tom said that no one had seen her.

'What a way to start 1980,' Jenny sighed when Tom came to collect her late in the afternoon.

Her hands and arms were now uncovered but the skin was very red and tender. She felt the bite of the cold wind as he helped her into the taxi, carefully avoiding holding her arms. After the warm cocoon of the hospital ward the real world felt cold, unreal and rather frightening, and she shivered uncontrollably.

Tom had put the heating on in her flat before he had come to collect her and after he had taken her case through to the bedroom he came back into her lounge and insisted on making her a cup of tea before he left.

'I imagine you will want an early night to give yourself a chance to get used to being home. Are you going to be able to manage to make yourself a meal? I have stocked up your fridge for you; it was completely bare,' he added.

'It was fully stocked when I left.' Jenny frowned. 'Karen must have been here after all. Are you sure she isn't still here? She could be in Lionel's old flat. Would you mind checking for me, Tom?'

He returned a couple of minutes later to say that he had knocked several times but there was no reply.

'I'll phone Edwin, he may know where she is.'

'Would you like me to do it for you?' Tom offered, his hand reaching out for the receiver.

'No, it's all right. I can manage to do that. You've done quite enough for me. One way and another I have taken up most of your day.'

'That's of no importance,' Tom assured her. 'I'll leave you now because I expect you want to get an early night. You are probably feeling quite tired.'

Jenny smiled gratefully. 'That's true and thank you once again for all your help.'

'I'll look in tomorrow morning to make sure you are all right,' Tom told her. 'If you want a lie-in then, if you have a set of spare keys, I can come and make you breakfast and you can have it in bed.'

'Thank you but I am sure I will be able to manage. Karen has my spare keys, I'm afraid.'

Before she went to bed Jenny telephoned Edwin, but all he could tell her was that he'd asked Karen to vacate the flat the week before because he had managed to sell and the new owner wanted to move in over the Christmas holidays.

'I don't think they have done so; Tom Fieldman went to see if Karen was there and there was no answer when he knocked on the door.'

'They've moved their belongings in but they said they would be spending Christmas and New Year with their son,' Edwin told her. 'They're a very nice couple, I'm sure you'll like them,' he added airily.

'So you have no idea where Karen is; she didn't say where she was going?' Jenny pursued.

'Sorry, I've no idea at all. I shouldn't worry, I'm sure she is well able to look after herself.'

She didn't expect to sleep at all, but as soon as she put the phone down she undressed and went to bed. The next thing she knew was that the cold January sun was sneaking in around the edges of the curtains.

It took Jenny a few minutes to gather her wits together and remember where she was. Almost at once her thoughts went to Karen. Where was she, what had happened to her, why had she not made contact or even enquired about her all the time she'd been in hospital?

She felt too worried to stay in bed any longer. Carefully, she washed and dressed and made her breakfast. It took much longer than usual. She found her movements stilted and painful. When she lifted up the kettle she felt sharp needle-like jabs of pain run up her arms, and fresh spasms when she tried to cut her slice of toast in half.

Tom called at ten o'clock and found her in tears. She tried to brush them aside but the feeling of helplessness that assailed her refused to go.

'Come on, put your coat on, we're going out for a coffee. You need to get back into the real world and you'll never do that moping around in here,' he said firmly.

As they made their way through the reception area several people came up to them to ask how she was. To her surprise they seemed to be genuinely pleased that she was home again and most sympathetic about her accident. None of them mentioned Karen.

Over the next couple of weeks Jenny made splendid progress thanks to Tom's constant attention and care. He shopped for her and made her meals but he also left her to get on with her life in her own way.

He was always there though when she needed him and he made sure that weather permitting they went out for a walk each day. Sometimes it was along the promenade; at other times, if the weather was particularly rough, they went up Victoria Road, looking in the shop windows and stopping at one of the cafes for a coffee on their way home. Or they took a bus to Liscard Village where there was a better selection of shops and a cinema which they went to occasionally.

When he took her back to the hospital for a check-up she was delighted to be told that they were discharging her. Her hands and arms had recovered completely and they didn't want to see her again.

Tom was extremely pleased at the news. 'What about seeing if we can get into a matinee?' he suggested. 'We're not often in Liverpool so it would be a lovely way to celebrate.'

Jenny pulled a face. 'I'm not very keen on pantomime and that's what's on at all the theatres at the moment.'

'No.' Tom said, shaking his head. 'I've checked it out; there's a new play on at the Royal Court Theatre, so why don't we see if we can get tickets for that?'

It turned out to be a romantic comedy and Jenny found it was like a tonic after the pain and stress of the last few weeks.

She took a sideways glance at Tom and thought how lucky she was to have found such a stalwart friend. He might be in his late sixties and his hair might be beginning to go grey but he was still strong-featured, gentle and kind.

When the show was over and they emerged into the busy city

streets again, Tom suggested that they finish off such a memorable day by having dinner at the Adelphi.

'It sounds wonderful, but I am really not dressed for such a glamorous venue,' Jenny told him with an apologetic smile.

Tom frowned. Then his face lightened. 'We can soon put that right,' he told her.

Taking her arm he steered her through the crowds towards George Henry Lees and into their fur department.

Excusing himself for a moment, he walked away and spoke quietly to an assistant who looked over to where Jenny was waiting and nodded her head understandingly.

The next minute Tom was back at her side and within seconds the assistant appeared with a pale cream wrap which she held out to Tom for approval.

'Do you want to try it on or wait until we get to the Adelphi?' he asked.

Jenny looked nonplussed. 'You mean it's for me?' she said, wide-eyed.

'Of course.' He smiled at her.

'I can't accept a present of that sort,' she protested.

'Think of it as a late Christmas present,' he told her with a broad smile. 'Now, do you want to put it on or have it wrapped and take it with us.'

When she looked bemused and didn't answer he told the assistant to 'pop it in a bag' and they would take it with them.

When they reached the Adelphi, Tom handed over the bag to her and directed her to the ladies' room.

For a moment Jenny was on the point of refusing but it seemed so ungrateful and he seemed to be deriving such pleasure from giving it to her that she accepted graciously.

When she took the wrap out of the bag she drew in her breath sharply. It was palest cream fur, exotically soft to the touch. She slipped off her winter coat and when she draped the wrap round her shoulders it transformed her rather plain dark red dress and made her look extremely elegant.

She stared at her reflection in the mirror and marvelled at her appearance. She looked so happy; her hazel eyes looked larger, her mouth lifted at the corners in a smile and there was a look of contentment on her face.

Tom's obvious pride as he escorted her into the dining room filled her with happiness. She caught sight of herself in the mirrored walls and felt delighted by their reflection. They looked the perfect couple. Tom was a few inches taller than her and looked quite distinguished in his dark suit, white shirt and discreet tie. The gorgeous cream fur stole transformed her own plain red dress, making it look chic and expensive.

It was a wonderful meal; the perfect ending to a day Jenny would never forget. She had left home feeling nervous and apprehensive about what she might be told and returned radiant.

In the taxi on the way home Tom told her how much he had enjoyed the evening and the past few weeks.

'You mean playing nursemaid?' she'd asked teasingly.

'I've enjoyed being needed and having someone to care about. We seem to get on so well that it has been a pleasure rather than a chore or a duty,' he said gravely, his blue eyes shining warmly.

'Yes, I agree. It has been rather comforting to know that someone cared so much about me. I really am grateful to you,' Jenny admitted.

'I don't want gratitude. As I've said, I've enjoyed it. In fact,' he paused, reaching for her hand and almost stumbling over his next words, 'since we are both on our own and such good friends then perhaps we should think about moving in together.'

'I don't mean right away,' he said hastily as he saw the look of surprise and consternation on Jenny's face. 'I'd like you to give it some thought though,' he said, earnestly squeezing her hand.

Twenty-Eight

Tom's suggestion was still ringing in Jenny's head when she went to bed that night. It had been such a momentous day, so packed with surprises that she wondered if she had misheard or misunderstood what he had said.

She stroked the beautiful cream fur wrap then buried her face in its softness. It felt so luxurious and was such a personal gift that she wondered if she should have accepted it. By doing so had it given Tom the wrong impression, she wondered?

It was thirty-five years since William had died. Her marriage had been such a happy one that she had never wanted to marry again. She had lived on her own for so long now that she wasn't sure she'd welcome the restrictions that could result if she was living with another person. That was selfish, she reflected, when Tom had been so good to her while she had been ill.

Living with Eddy and Karen had been different because she had been the one in charge, even though Eddy had always considered himself to be the man of the house.

They had been a good team. He had been someone to talk things over with and he had helped her to crystallize her thoughts whenever there were important decisions to be made. He had also taken care of any of the heavier jobs around the house and garden.

Bringing up Karen had been a shared duty and Karen knew from a very young age that her father and her grandmother agreed on all major decisions so it was no good trying to play one off against the other. It was an amicable arrangement; one which suited them all.

Eddy had been dead now for seven years and although she still missed him she had come to terms with life and no longer grieved or felt lonely.

Moving in with Tom Fieldman, however, would be a major decision, not one to be taken lightly.

She cared a great deal for him but there was no question of being in love like she had been with William. Rather, he would be a replacement for Eddy's companionship. Would he accept that she still felt responsible for her granddaughter?

She was still worried about Karen's present disappearance and went over and over in her mind what had happened to Karen since Eddy had died. If only she had kept her job at Premium Printing, she thought sadly.

Things had started to go awry, Jenny reflected, from the moment Karen had met Jimmy Martin. He had made her discontent with her ordered life; he had agreed with her that there were more glamorous ways of earning a living and had encouraged her to try her luck.

That had been Karen's undoing. It had led to her disastrous relationship with Hadyn Trimm and the possibility of being arrested as a drugs courier.

Marrying Lionel Bostock had been an even greater calamity. Jenny still believed that Karen had only done that because she felt the need of a father figure in her life; not as a scheming little money-grabber like so many of the people in Merseyside Mansions seemed to believe.

Jenny sighed. She certainly couldn't contemplate making any changes in her own life until she knew where Karen was and that she was safe. She would also need to know what her plans were for the future.

On Wednesday morning she decided to put a brave face on things and to go along to the coffee morning. She hoped Tom would be there to boost her confidence if people started questioning her about Karen.

It was a bitterly cold day even for the middle of January, so she put on a high-necked red woollen sweater and black trousers. She arrived before Tom and was immediately greeted with a babble of news about Karen.

'What a windfall for your granddaughter! You must both be over the moon!' Beryl Willis chuckled, her plump round face creased in a smile.

'Lucky girl! She really was "an old man's darling" and it has paid off,' Lorna Hill commented acidly.

'Where is she now?' Dan Grey questioned.

'Off making the most of it if I know anything about her,' someone said with a laugh.

'Probably taken herself off on a luxury holiday?' Lorna Hill mused.

'I know that's what I would do if I was lucky enough to have an unexpected windfall like that.'

'Surely, it wasn't that much of a surprise. I imagine she'd thought she would do a lot better than that. Old Lionel was very well heeled, remember.'

'She could have waited for you to come home and taken you with her. You might have found her another rich old man to marry,' Sandra Roberts commented rather sarcastically.

There were jests and jibes from so many that Jenny's head felt in a whirl; especially since she didn't really know what they were talking about.

She had no idea what the 'windfall' was, but it was not long before Jane Phillips's comment, 'so generous of Edwin Bostock,' gave her a clue what it was all about.

She took a seat next to Mavis Grey and after she'd been served with her coffee asked her tentatively if she knew what the windfall was that they were all talking about.

Mavis looked rather startled, then smiled nervously. 'I thought you looked rather bewildered. They're referring to the very generous settlement Edwin Bostock has made on your granddaughter of course,' she said quietly.

'Settlement?' Jenny looked even more puzzled.

'You really don't know, do you?' Mavis murmured.

'I don't. Do you know the details? If so then please tell me.'

'I can tell you what I've heard. It does come from Jane Phillips,' she said in an apologetic tone, 'but I gather it was Edwin Bostock who told her.'

'Edwin Bostock?' Jenny's eyebrows lifted in surprise. 'I didn't know Jane was that friendly with him!'

'Apparently he told her ages ago when she asked him what was happening about Lionel's flat. If Edwin sold the flat then it meant that Karen would have to find somewhere else to live.'

'Yes, I knew that was his intention,' Jenny murmured.

'Edwin then went on to explain to Jane that although his father had changed his will in Karen's favour when they had got married he hadn't signed it before he died so Lionel's previous will, in which he left his entire estate to Edwin, was still valid.'

'I see.'

'However,' Mavis went on, 'Edwin said that as a goodwill settlement he was giving her ten thousand pounds. He hoped that by doing this it would save them going to court about his father's estate. He said that if they did that then probably they'd both lose a great deal of money in the process.'

'Ten thousand! Good heavens!' Jenny put her half empty coffee cup down on the table, her hand shaking as she stared at Mavis astounded. 'So do you think all this is true?'

Mavis picked up her own coffee and took a sip. 'I imagine so. You mean Karen hasn't mentioned any of this to you?'

'No; she hasn't said a word. Mind you, I haven't seen her since the night I scalded myself and had to go into hospital. I couldn't understand why I hadn't heard from her and I have been very worried but now you've told me this it begins to make sense.'

Jenny picked up her coffee cup again and pondered over this unexpected news as she drank what remained. She wondered why Tom had never mentioned it.

When he arrived a few minutes later and came and sat in the chair next to hers it was the first thing she asked him.

'I heard rumours but I didn't attach any importance to them; I didn't for one minute think they were true and it seemed pointless repeating them to you.'

'It could account for why she is missing and why I've not had any news of her,' Jenny said rather sharply.

'True. If she was going away on a holiday, though, I would have thought she would have told you or at least left you a message,' he mused.

'Perhaps she thought I wouldn't approve. I might have told her she shouldn't waste the money but do something useful with it. In fact,' Jenny added more brightly, 'probably that's what she has done, put it to some good purpose.'

'Like what?' Tom asked dubiously.

'Now Edwin has sold Lionel's flat then Karen must have found somewhere else to live.'

'You mean you weren't willing to let her move back in with you?' Tom said in a surprised voice.

'As everybody keeps reminding me, it's breaking all the rules if I let her stay with me,' Jenny pointed out. 'According to Jane Phillips, even as a guest you have to be over fifty-five to stay here more than a couple of days.'

'I think Jane may have been exaggerating,' someone murmured. 'Perhaps you should have a word with the concierge and get a proper ruling.'

'Well, Karen's not here now so it doesn't really matter,' Jenny stated rather sharply. 'Anyway,' she added, 'it's not convenient.'

'Not for you perhaps, but she didn't seem to mind,' Tom reminded her cryptically.

'She had to sleep on the sofa and you can only do that for so long; it's not comfortable and you don't get a proper night's sleep,' Jenny pointed out.

'Yes, I suppose that's true,' Tom agreed.

'I think she's found herself somewhere else to live and is waiting until she has found a job and is back on her feet before letting me know anything because she doesn't want me to be worried,' Jenny stated loyally.

Tom nodded but made no comment. He hoped she was right even though from what he knew of Karen it seemed to him to be highly improbable.

He didn't pursue the subject. The conversation all around them was now focused on the impact Margaret Thatcher was having on the country. She had been elected the previous May and because she was the very first woman prime minister the men in particular were dubious of her ability to carry off such a role.

Jenny listened to the heated arguments and comments going on all around her for a few more minutes and then made an excuse to leave. She wanted to get away and be on her own. She needed the seclusion of her own flat, where she could digest the information she'd learned about Karen.

She needed to be alone to try and work out what Karen might have done or where she might be without listening to other people's theories. She also wanted to telephone Edwin Bostock and hear the details direct from him. She was still wondering why he had changed his mind and why he was now being so generous.

Twenty-Nine

It was August before Jenny heard from Karen. Eight long months during which she had grown thin and nervy with worry; eight long months without giving Tom an answer to his proposal.

Gossip about Karen was no longer a topic at the Wednesday coffee mornings apart from one or two genuine enquiries from some of the more kindly and friendly residents. So many other things had taken their interest. Since Christmas there had been two deaths, three people had moved away, several new people had moved in. Life went on. Jenny and Tom were the only ones who were really concerned about Karen's welfare and anxious about her whereabouts.

Jenny kept telling herself that 'no news was good news' but it did nothing to set her mind at rest. Lurid details about the fate suffered by victims of the Yorkshire Ripper filled her mind. Karen was young, pretty and vulnerable, so had she fallen prey to this evil man? she kept asking herself.

When she answered the telephone early one Tuesday morning and a woman's voice said, 'Hello, Gran, I'm back in England,' Jenny thought she was hallucinating. 'I'm on my way to see you but I was just checking that you were still living at Merseyside Mansions,' the voice went on.

Jenny pulled herself together. It sounded like Karen's and yet it didn't. It had an odd twang. Jenny wasn't sure if it was because she was speaking on the phone and it was a bad line or if it was someone impersonating Karen.

'Where are you?' she asked.

'London; Heathrow Airport. Can't you hear the planes?'

'What are you doing there?'

'Just flown in from Australia. We're going to take a train to Liverpool, so we will see you later in the day if that is all right. I wanted to make sure that you would be at home.'

'We?' Jenny asked.

'That's right, Bill and me.'

'Bill?' Jenny knew she must sound simple but things were moving too fast for her. After all these months of worrying, just hearing Karen's voice was sending her blood pressure spiralling.

'His name is Bill Walsh. I met him while I was in Australia. You'll like him, Gran. Look, I've got to go now or we'll miss our train. I'll see you later in the day. All the news then.'

Karen had rung off before Jenny could ask any more questions. She stood holding the receiver for several seconds before she replaced it in its cradle. Had that really been Karen? She said she'd been in Australia. And who was Bill Walsh?

She picked up the phone again and dialled Tom's number. He was as taken aback by the news as she was. Like her he was curious to know more about Bill Walsh.

'We had better wait until later today and see what she has to say for herself when she gets here,' he said thoughtfully.

'You're right, I suppose,' Jenny agreed, 'but I am worried about what this means; I've never heard her mention Bill Walsh before.'

'Well, she wouldn't have done if she met him out in Australia,' Tom reasoned. 'You haven't heard from her since she went there.'

'No, I suppose you are right, but I can't help feeling concerned; Karen seems to make such bad choices in men.'

'True,' Tom agreed. 'Look, why don't you let me take you out to lunch somewhere; it will help pass the time and might even stop you worrying about Karen,' he added with a light laugh.

Karen arrived just before five o'clock. The man with her was in his early thirties, tall, broad-shouldered, clean-shaven and with well-spaced dark brown eyes and thick dark brown hair. His handshake was firm and his voice decisive but well modulated. He was wearing dark brown trousers, a brown tweed jacket and an open-necked brown and cream checked shirt.

Jenny's initial fears were dispersed. She liked him on sight. What was equally important was that she thought Karen had lost weight and seemed happier than Jenny had seen her in years.

Jenny introduced Bill Walsh to Tom and, as the two men shook hands she saw that as they weighed each other up Tom appeared to be perfectly happy with what he saw.

'Have you two eaten?' Tom asked, looking from Bill to Karen and back again.

'Not since we landed, but we want to find somewhere to stay first,' Karen stated.

'That's no problem,' Tom told her. 'You can stay here tonight, I have a spare bedroom.'

'Thank you,' Karen said gratefully, 'but won't that set all the old tabbies squawking?'

'Karen!' Jenny said in a reproving tone, but nevertheless she laughed with the others.

'I'm sure we can avoid you meeting any of them if you are worried about what they will say,' she said quickly.

'No, not in the least worried,' Karen told her airily. 'I've told Bill all about my murky past. Oh, and I've turned over a new leaf, Gran, in case you were wondering,' she added, smiling at Bill.

Jenny noticed the warm smile he gave Karen in return and her heart lifted. These two really were made for each other, she thought happily. In that one glance she had seen so much honesty, trust and love between them that she was reassured.

'Right then,' Tom said briskly, 'that's settled. Come on Bill, let's take your cases along to my flat and get you settled in and then we'll go out for a meal.'

'You two carry on while I stay here and have a quiet word with Gran,' Karen told them. 'I know where your flat is Tom and I'll join you in a minute or two.'

'I'm sorry not to have been in touch, Gran,' Karen said contritely when the door had closed behind the two men. She crossed over to sit beside Jenny and took one of her hands and held it between both of her own. 'I have missed you and I knew you would be worried but I needed time to come to terms with myself. If you remember I always wanted to travel and see something of the world, but when I left school you were so anxious for me to start work right away at Premium Printing that I couldn't do so. I promised myself I would do it one day and when Edwin gave me that ten thousand pounds I thought it was an ideal opportunity.'

'Why didn't you tell me that was what you were planning to do?' Jenny sighed.

'Because I knew you would try and stop me and tell me I ought to invest the money as a nest egg for the future or something sensible like that.'

When Jenny said nothing Karen went on, 'I was in Australia and met Bill quite by chance and was astounded to know that he came from Heswall and was a geography teacher at a private school in

Wiltshire. He was visiting Australia during the school summer holidays because that was one of the things he had always wanted to do. Odd wasn't it that we should both turn up there at the same moment and bump into each other.'

'Some people might say it was fate,' Jenny said, smiling.

Karen grinned. 'Or sheer luck. Tell me that you really like him, Gran.'

'I've only just this moment met him but I certainly do like what I've seen of him so far,' Jenny agreed cautiously. 'Tom certainly seemed to approve of him; he must do or he wouldn't have offered to let you stay in his flat.'

'True, but then Tom is a very understanding person and he's also very nice and I do approve, Gran, so go on and enjoy a little happiness the same as I am doing. I think you two were made for each other,' she added with a broad smile.

'Karen! What a thing to say.' Jenny felt the colour rushing to her cheeks.

'Gran, it's so obvious; you work in tandem. You didn't show the least surprise when Tom said we could stay in his apartment. In fact, I wondered if you two had talked about it and reached a decision before we arrived.'

'Certainly not! Neither of us had ever met Bill Walsh or knew anything at all about him. He might have been a most unsuitable character.'

'You mean like some of the other men I've got entangled with in the past?'

Jenny bit her lip. She didn't want to start criticizing Karen. She felt far too happy to see her home again safe and sound and she had to admit that there was something very likeable about Bill Walsh.

'Does this mean that you two are planning a future together?' she asked quietly.

'It certainly does. We did think of tying the knot in Australia but then I thought I would like you to be there when we did.'

'What about Bill's family?'

'No problem there at all. Sadly, both his parents are dead; killed in a car crash three years ago – and he is an only child.'

'Heart whole and fancy free,' Jenny murmured.

Karen's eyebrows went up at the dubious note in Jenny's voice. 'Don't you believe me, Gran?'

'Of course I do, it's simply . . .' She stopped speaking. There were countless questions in her mind. Bill looked to be in his early thirties so why wasn't he married? Did he have a home of any kind. Where were they going to live?

As if in answer to her unspoken questions, Karen went on, 'Bill teaches at a boarding school and he has accommodation at the school. We are hoping that when we are married they will let him move into a larger flat or one of the houses in the school grounds. The new term doesn't start for a couple of weeks and Bill wants to go and check out what arrangements he can make.'

'In the meantime where are you staying?' Jenny asked.

'We are planning to spend the next couple of weeks down in Wiltshire in a hotel somewhere near the school,' Karen told her. 'If the school are unable to offer us the sort of accommodation we want then we will look for a flat or house in the area. For the next couple of nights we thought we'd stay in Wallasey because I was desperate to spend some time with you. I've told Bill so much about you that he wanted to meet you and get to know you as well.'

'We'd better smarten ourselves up, those two men will be back here any minute all eager to go and eat,' Jenny said, standing up.

'Yes, you're right,' Karen agreed, 'and I must freshen up first. I need to change. I've been wearing these jeans and this T-shirt ever since we left Australia. If I go and unpack some clean clothes can I bring them back here and have a quick shower?'

'Of course you can.'

'You are such a dear and so understanding I really don't deserve you, Gran,' Karen told her and gave Jenny a big hug and a kiss on both cheeks. 'I'll be back in two seconds.'

Thirty

The next day the marriage between Karen and Bill Walsh was fixed for Wallasey in early September.

'We could make it a double wedding if you like,' Karen murmured, turning to smile at Jenny and Tom as they all left the Wallasey Town Hall.

'That might be quite a good idea,' Tom agreed, squeezing Jenny's hand.

'That will do, Karen,' Jenny said sternly, but at the same time she returned Tom's squeeze.

'Gran, we both want you and Tom to be witnesses at our wedding,' Karen went on, looking anxiously from Jenny to Tom and back again. 'You will, won't you?'

'Of course we will,' Tom asserted before Jenny could respond. 'If you are here in Wallasey at all before the big day, remember you can stay in my flat if you wish. If you prefer to go somewhere else then I will quite understand.'

'No, no, we would love to stay with you,' Karen told him. 'It will give me a chance to spend some time with Gran and I will need all the help I can get from her to organize things – and being on the spot like that will be terrific.'

Although the next few days were chaotic, Jenny did manage to have some quiet moments with Karen. It was so very much like the old days when they had lived together in Warren Point that Jenny enjoyed every minute as they confided in each other and discussed the future optimistically.

Karen tried to explain the reason for her bad behaviour over the previous couple of years and to apologize for worrying Jenny so much.

'The past is behind us so let's forget what happened,' Jenny told her. 'Your future is all that matters and I am sure that with Bill it will be a happy one. He seems to be an extremely nice man, very capable and caring.'

'He is all those things and more besides,' Karen agreed fervently. 'I was fortunate to meet someone like him; I am also lucky that he was so understanding. I've told him everything; not only about Lionel but about Jimmy Martin and Hadyn Trimm as well.'

'That's very comforting to know,' Jenny told her. 'As long as you have done that then I think we should forget all about the past and never mention it again.'

Next day they went to Liverpool to look for wedding outfits. Jenny and Karen left Tom and Bill to organize details for the flowers; posies for Jenny and Karen and buttonholes for Tom and Bill. They also told Tom to order two separate cars to take them to the town hall and one to collect them after the ceremony.

'After that,' Jenny suggested, 'you had better go shopping for new suits for the wedding.'

Karen had no idea what sort of outfit she wanted but in the end she chose a very modest dress in pale blue silky fabric with tiny cap sleeves and a V-neckline. The waist was defined with a self-material belt that draped to one side. Although minidresses were all the rage Jenny was pleased that Karen insisted on her dress reaching her knees.

To wear over it she chose a classic-style coat in darker blue and, although it had the latest padded shoulders, it looked very attractive. To complete her outfit Karen selected a pale blue pillbox hat that was trimmed with a darker blue veiling.

Karen tried to persuade Jenny to buy a new outfit but Jenny refused. She did, however, buy a new cream hat and matching gloves that she said would liven up her plain green tweed dress and jacket, which was what she planned to wear.

Bill insisted on buying something sensible that would be suitable afterwards for work and chose a smartly tailored light grey three-piece suit and a self-striped white cotton shirt.

Karen decided to go shopping again to find some initialled cuff links for Bill so the two of them went to the jeweller's together and at the same time chose their wedding rings.

The night before the wedding Karen spent the evening with Jenny and slept on the sofa, determined that she and Bill wouldn't meet until they arrived at the register office.

It was a very quiet midday wedding on a perfect early autumn day with Tom and Jenny acting as witnesses. Afterwards the four of them were driven along the promenade for a very special meal at the Grand Hotel in New Brighton.

As they sat in the sumptuous lounge afterwards, looking out at the activity on the Mersey, of liners being towed out to the Bar by chugging little tug boats, Karen sighed deeply and exclaimed, 'I shall remember this day for the rest of my life.'

'I should hope you will,' Bill said, reaching for her hand and raising it to his lips and gently kissing her knuckles. 'It's not over yet, though. The best is yet to come.'

'Bill!' The colour rose in Karen's cheeks but her green eyes sparkled as they met his.

'Come on you two, finish your coffee, it's time we were heading for home if you want an early start in the morning.'

'What's the rush; we're only minutes away from Merseyside Mansions.'

'I know that but you've got to walk it,' Tom reminded them. 'I didn't think it was worth asking the car to come back for us for such a short journey. We can call a taxi if you wish,' he added hastily as he saw the look of surprise on their faces.

'No, it's a lovely evening, of course we can walk,' Karen and Jenny told him.

As the four of them strolled along the promenade they could see the moon in the far distance; a pale gold ball over the silhouetted tops of the Welsh mountains.

'It really is beautiful,' Karen breathed.

'Yes, a day to remember,' Jenny agreed.

As they entered Merseyside Mansions they found that the reception area had been decorated with dozens of silvery balloons and a banner with 'Congratulations Karen and Bill' emblazoned on it. A cheer went up and it seemed as if every resident in the place was assembled there to greet them.

There were tears in Karen's eyes as she listened to the babble of congratulations from all sides. People she'd never met before hugged her and patted Bill on the shoulder and wished them both happiness.

Inside the community lounge a trestle table had been set up in the centre of the room. It was laid out with a sumptuous array of sandwiches and cakes; in the very centre was a beautifully iced two-tier wedding cake.

Two waitresses were in attendance handing glasses of champagne to people as they came into the room and toasts were drunk wishing the newly married couple every happiness.

Throughout the evening the waitresses handed round the food and topped up glasses with wine. Cameras clicked, everyone eager to have a record of the event. When Dan and Mavis Grey exchanged anecdotes about their own wedding day they were quickly capped by stories from Ricky and Lorna Hill and then, to everyone's surprise, by a very amusing tale from Clare and Peter Green.

As Karen and Bill circulated, Jenny felt uneasy when she noticed that Jane Phillips had cornered Bill and engaged him in what appeared to be a very serious discussion. Whenever Bill tried to speak Jane held up a hand and shook her grey head and continued speaking in such an emphatic way that Jenny suspected she was relating gossip about Karen and Lionel.

Determined not to let her monopolize Bill or blacken Karen's name she walked over to where the two of them were.

'You have met Karen's new husband I see, Jane,' she said mildly. 'He's so charming that I know it is difficult to get away from him,' she added, lifting her eyebrows at Bill who looked rather puzzled by her flippant comment.

'Mrs Phillips has been telling me how well she knows Karen and how much everybody at Merseyside Mansions will miss her being here,' Bill explained.

'Really!' Jenny tried to keep the amusement out of her voice as she saw a pink stain appear on Jane's pallid cheeks. 'I hope she has been giving you a glowing report,' she added drily. 'Will you excuse us Jane.' She smiled, taking Bill's arm firmly. 'There's someone over here I particularly want him to meet.'

The rest of the evening went extremely well. The residents all wanted to know about Bill's job as a teacher and about where they would be living in Wiltshire.

It was almost midnight before Tom Fieldman brought the celebrations to a close. He thanked them all for making it such a special occasion and asked everyone to drink one final toast to the newly married couple.

'Perhaps we will all be buying new hats for another wedding soon,' Jane Phillips commented shrewdly as she left.

Jenny smiled but made no comment. She wondered exactly what Jane had told Bill and hoped she had managed to drag him away in time before she could say anything too derogatory about Karen.

She was so relieved and delighted that Karen seemed to have reverted to the granddaughter she had watched grow up and she wanted nothing to stand in the way of her future happiness.

Thirty-One

It was the school half term at the end of October before Jenny saw Karen and Bill again. In the meantime they spoke on the telephone and Jenny was pleased to hear that they had settled in to the two-bedroom house they'd been allocated in the school grounds.

'It's small but quite cosy,' Karen told her. 'It has two living rooms and a small kitchen downstairs and two bedrooms and a bathroom upstairs. There's no garden but we are surrounded by the school grounds so the outlook is quite pleasant.'

'It sounds ideal and should be easy to look after,' Jenny agreed.

'We hope you and Tom will come and visit us at half term,' Karen said, 'and then you can see it for yourselves.'

Jenny accepted the invitation but insisted that they would arrange to stay at a nearby hotel.

'Why don't you want to stay with us?' Karen asked.

'You said that you have only two bedrooms,' Jenny reminded her.

'I know, but there is a bed in the spare room; surely you wouldn't mind sharing with Tom?' Karen responded quickly. 'Or we could made up a bed for Tom on the settee.'

'No!' Jenny said very firmly. 'Leave it that we will come and visit you but we will be staying at a nearby hotel and in separate single rooms.'

She suspected that Karen was trying her hand at matchmaking, but although she was very fond of Tom she still wasn't sure that she wanted to encourage him by making such a commitment as sharing a bedroom with him.

It was a glorious late October day, mild and sunny, when they set off to visit Karen and Bill. The changing colours on the trees as they travelled south and the small, soft scudding clouds overhead made the journey very pleasant. They were both very relaxed and the occasional conversation between them was inconsequential and almost trivial.

They stopped at a country pub for a light lunch and then took a stroll around the picturesque village to stretch their legs before continuing on their way. Jenny felt both relaxed and happy and she was sure that Tom felt the same.

They reached their hotel shortly after four o'clock and before they were shown to their respective rooms they agreed to meet again at six o'clock.

'I'll telephone Karen and let her know that we'll drive to the school and collect her and Bill and take them out to dinner,' Jenny promised Tom as they went their separate ways.

Karen insisted that they came early so that they could see over the house before they went out for a meal and, because she seemed to be so excited about her seeing it, Jenny agreed.

It was a small house but delightful, almost like a doll's house when compared to the spacious home she and Karen had once shared. As Karen showed them the guest bedroom Jenny smiled inwardly, very pleased that she had declined Karen's invitation to stay with them. It was so small that there was only space for one bed.

When Tom and Jenny finally took their leave on the Sunday afternoon, they had enjoyed themselves so much that they readily accepted Karen and Bill's invitation to join them for Christmas.

'Bill's a really charming man isn't he,' Jenny said contentedly as they drove away.

'Very nice chap indeed,' Tom agreed. 'I'm so glad that things have worked out so well for Karen; it must be a load off your mind.'

'It certainly is. I really was despairing of her but let's hope all that is in the past. Bill has had such a steadying effect on her; she's like the girl I used to know,' she added with a relaxed smile.

'So now that she is safe and settled perhaps you can give some thought to your own future and to my proposal,' Tom said quietly.

'Oh, Tom!' Jenny laid a hand on his knee. 'I have treated you badly, haven't I.'

'You have, but I understand your reasons. Even I can see that Karen is a reformed character and I realize how upsetting her escapades must have been for you. As you say, that's all in the past, so now it's time to get on with your own life.'

'You're quite right and I fully intend to do that,' Jenny agreed in a serious voice.

'So what is your answer?'

Jenny was silent for several minutes before saying in a quiet but firm voice, 'I accept, Tom.'

Tom swerved to the side of the road and jammed on the car brakes. Before Jenny could ask what was wrong he had grabbed hold of her and kissed her long and hard on the mouth.

'I was beginning to think that I was never going to hear you say those wonderful words,' he breathed. 'You've no idea how happy you've made me.'

'I think we should keep the news to ourselves for the moment,' Jenny murmured cautiously.

'You mean until we have had time to talk about it at length and planned things in a sensible way?'

'Exactly!'

'Are you ready to name the day?' he asked eagerly. 'What about making it a Christmas wedding?'

'That's less than two months away.'

'How long do you need? I'd marry you tomorrow if it was at all possible.'

'Impetuous, aren't you,' Jenny said in a teasing voice.

'Well, at our age we haven't all that much time left to enjoy being together,' Tom reminded her.

'True, but I was thinking of the spring being a rather nice time for a wedding.'

'Next year!' Tom exclaimed in a shocked voice. 'I can't keep it secret for that length of time, not unless you move in with me until then.'

'We wouldn't be able to keep it secret for very long if I did that,' Jenny replied, laughing.

They talked about it for the rest of the journey home but failed to reach a decision and decided to sleep on it.

'The date is the most important,' Tom reminded Jenny as they reached Merseyside Mansions. 'Everything else will automatically fall into place.'

'You mean which flat we decide to live in or whether we should sell both of them and buy a small house?'

'Yes, even about that. The choice is very much up to you. I will do almost anything to meet your wishes,' Tom told her seriously.

'I'm sure we can compromise,' Jenny murmured.

'Whatever you want; your happiness is what is most important to me,' Tom assured her as he took her in his arms and held her close before kissing her goodnight.

As she relaxed into the comforting sensation of being pressed close to his big strong body, Jenny sighed contentedly. Now that she knew that Karen was so happily settled she felt as if all her worries were over and she revelled in the thought that at long last she would be able to concentrate on enjoying a life of her own. What was most important was that she wanted Tom to be part of that life and she marvelled at how fortunate she had been to meet him.

'Sleep on it and we'll sort all the details out in the morning,' he repeated as he released her and she went into her flat.

Although they met for coffee the next morning and went for a walk together in the afternoon, it was several days before they managed to finalize a programme of events.

They decided that they would be married on the Saturday before Christmas and in the evening hold a celebration party in the community lounge at Merseyside Mansions and invite all the residents.

They would ask Karen and Bill to be their witnesses and then ask them to stay on over Christmas. By then they should have started the Christmas school holidays so there would be no problem about them doing that.

They decided not to do anything about selling the flats or buying a house until the spring.

'Over Christmas Karen and Bill can stay in your flat and we can use mine, or the other way round,' Tom told her. 'It will also help us to make up our mind whether we want to stay here or move out to somewhere else.'

'Before we mention any of this to Karen and Bill we had better make sure that we can be married that Saturday,' Jenny murmured thoughtfully.

'Why do you say that? What do you mean?' Tom asked sharply with a worried frown. 'You're not having second thoughts about getting married?'

'Of course I'm not, nothing is further from my mind. The register office may be fully booked or they may not be working at all because it is so near to Christmas,' Jenny told him with a warm smile. 'You have no idea how much I am looking forward to it.'

'Then why wait? Why don't you move in with me right away. No one else need know.'

Jenny shook her head. 'Let's wait. It's not all that far away and we have the rest of our lives to be together. I will feel happier if it is all legal and above board before I start living with you.'

'Absolute nonsense, but I love you all the more for it,' Tom said with a dry chuckle.

'We've plenty of planning to do to fill in our time,' Jenny said rather primly.

'Yes, I know,' Tom agreed. 'To start with, when are we going to tell the people here?'

'As soon as we know for certain that we can be married on the Saturday before Christmas and we're certain that Bill and Karen can be here for that date. Anyway,' she added with a rueful smile, 'they'll probably find out whether we tell them or not.'

'True, but I would prefer that we make a public announcement so that it is out in the open and stop any silly rumours spreading,' Tom stated firmly.

They made a list of the tasks that lay ahead and as they managed to tick them off one by one Jenny began to feel as excited as any bride approaching her wedding.

It was more than thirty-five years since William had died so she felt in no way disloyal to his memory in marrying again. Eddy had also been dead for over seven years so she really did feel that she was embarking on a new life.

She was also supremely confident that her new life as Tom's wife was going to be a very happy and contented one. Tom had been a tower of strength ever since she had first met him and the feeling of being loved and protected by this strong, wonderful man had increased with each passing day.

She was also looking forward to no longer having to make important decisions about property and money matters on her own any more. The many years of doing so since William died had become a tremendous burden and she felt quietly relieved that in future she would be able to share them with Tom or even leave him to deal with them.

That wasn't her only reason for marrying Tom, she told herself with an inward chuckle. His sense of humour, the charisma and warmth of his character and, above all, the constant love and affection he showed towards her were something she rated highly because she had been starved of them for so long.

It was wonderful, she reflected, how everything was suddenly falling into place. Karen was happily married and settled in her new home and she was as free as a bird to enjoy whatever happiness her own future brought.

Thirty-Two

The fire broke out in Merseyside Mansions on the Thursday night, two days before Tom and Jenny were due to be married.

They had been in Jenny's flat going over all their arrangements when the fire alarm went off with a deafening screech that made conversing almost impossible.

'It's probably only a false alarm, it has happened before,' Tom said sanguinely as he took another sip of the brandy and soda Jenny had poured out for him.

'According to the fire drill we're supposed to assemble in the car park,' Jenny reminded him.

'You go out there if you want to but I'm staying here where it's warm and comfortable; it's freezing outside.'

'Yes, you're probably right,' Jenny agreed as they heard the loud clanging of a bell as the fire-engine drew up outside.

Almost at once there was a noisy hammering on the door of Jenny's flat and when she went to answer it a fireman was there demanding to know if she had been cooking that evening and asking to be allowed in to check the kitchen.

'You're clear,' he told them. 'The fire must be up on the next floor.'

'You haven't left anything cooking on the stove, Tom, have you?' Jenny asked.

'Not a thing,' he said quickly.

'Nevertheless, we'd like to check out your flat, sir,' the fireman told him.

'OK. I'll come up with you,' Tom said obligingly. 'I'll be right back, Jenny,' he added as he stood up and accompanied the fireman out of the room.

Twenty minutes later when Tom had still not returned Jenny went out into the passageway to find out what was happening. She found it full of people, all chattering excitedly.

'What's happened? Have they found out where the fire is?' she asked.

'On the next floor.'

'It's in old Mrs Parsons's flat and what's more it seems she's still in there.'

'You can hear her screaming.'

'Poor old soul; she's probably frightened to death.'

'How did the fire start in there?' Jenny asked.

'No one is sure, but apparently she was frying sausages.'

'She probably set fire to a newspaper left too near the cooker or to her own clothes while she was cooking.'

'It seems that her door is double locked and that she can't get to it to open it so they can't get in to her.'

'The fire brigade are going to put up a ladder outside and break in through the window.'

'They're too late,' Sandra Roberts interrupted. 'Her flat is next to mine and she has already been rescued. Someone has sent for an ambulance so that they can take her to hospital and have her checked over. She's in a right state.'

'Who was it that rescued her?' Dan and Mavis Grey asked in unison.

'Tom Fieldman. When he heard her screaming he put his shoulder to the door and burst the lock open and then he dashed in, grabbed Mrs Parsons up in his arms and brought her out on to the landing well away from her burning flat. He's still up there.'

'Let me pass, I must go to him,' Jenny said, pushing her way towards the stairs.

'I'm afraid not, ma'am.' A fireman stood at the foot of the staircase. 'No one can go up there, the fire is spreading.'

'I must; my friend Tom Fieldman has just this minute gone up there. And . . .'

'You mean the man who's rescued the old lady?'

'That's right.'

'Well, I'm sorry but you can't go up. Wait here and you might manage to have a quick word with him before they take him off to hospital.'

'Hospital? Why does he have to go to hospital?' Jenny asked, her voice shaking.

'His hands and arms are pretty badly burned,' he explained. 'He most certainly needs hospital attention.'

'Then I'll go with him,' Jenny stated. 'I'll go and collect my coat. I'll be back in a minute or two.'

'I'm not sure they will let you go in the ambulance,' the fireman warned, but Jenny wasn't listening. She was trembling and her knees felt like water as she rushed back to her flat, slipped on her coat and picked up a warm scarf and her handbag.

She locked the door to her flat and was back in reception just as two paramedics were passing through the reception area with a stretcher on which old Mrs Parsons lay huddled under a blanket. She was breathing noisily and with some difficulty as they made their way out to one of the ambulances parked outside.

Almost immediately two other paramedics brought Tom down the stairs and into the reception area. He was strapped into a chair and people moved aside to let them through.

Jenny's heart drummed in her chest as she saw how ashen his face was and noticed how very carefully the ambulance men carried him towards the door. Both his arms were covered by protective green cloth.

'No, you must let me come with you,' Jenny protested as one of the paramedics firmly moved her to one side. 'He needs me to be there with him.'

'Are you his wife?'

'Not yet, but I will be in two days' time,' she told them.

He hesitated, looking at his colleague for confirmation that it would be in order, and then telling her she could come with them when the other man nodded in agreement.

As they drove through the darkness to Liverpool Infirmary Jenny longed to be able to hold Tom's hand, but they were far too red and sore for her to do that. Enormous blisters had already formed on them and in between trying to speak to her he was making full use of the gas and air that the paramedic had offered him to help ease the pain.

The hospital was very busy and there were rows of people waiting to be attended to, but they were seen almost immediately. Tom was wheeled away by a porter and Jenny was left to give the man on the reception desk as much information as she could. When he had finished taking down Tom's name, address, age and as many other personal details as Jenny could provide, he told her where to sit and wait.

She felt sick with worry as she sat on the hard metal chair. The air was full of the smell of antiseptic. Her head was in a whirl because she had no idea how long it would be before she would be able to take Tom home.

She wasn't even sure how badly hurt he was because she hadn't really had an opportunity to talk to him since it happened, but she remembered the pain she'd been in only a short time ago when she'd scalded her hands.

Twice she went up to the desk and asked the middle-aged man sitting there booking in new arrivals if there was any news concerning Mr Fieldman.

'No, I'm afraid there isn't. Why don't you go and get yourself a cup of coffee, you look as though you need it.'

'I'm afraid to leave here in case he is discharged or there is a message from him for me.'

'Don't worry about that. I'll be here until six in the morning and I know where you are going so I'll send a porter to fetch you if there is any message for you or if you are needed.'

The coffee and a round of hot toast did much to restore Jenny's equilibrium. She realized that it was useless to worry; far better to plan how they were going to manage over the next couple of days. She wondered if Tom would be fit enough to go through with the wedding or whether they would have to cancel it.

Karen and Bill were due to arrive the following evening; at least she would have them there to support her, she thought thankfully. She'd do nothing about changing any of the wedding arrangements until she'd had a chance to talk things over with them both.

It was well after midnight when a nurse came to tell Jenny that Tom had been sedated, his burns dressed and that he was in a side ward.

'Can I see him?'

'He may not be fully conscious. As I told you, he had to be sedated so that his burns could be dressed. Why don't you go home and get some rest and come back tomorrow afternoon.'

'I'd like to see him now, before I go home,' Jenny persisted stubbornly.

The nurse frowned and peered at her fob watch. 'Only for a couple of minutes, and if he is asleep, then you must not waken him,' she said grudgingly.

'I promise,' Jenny told her.

Tom was in a small room in a single iron bed and was propped up into a half-sitting position with a mound of pillows. Both his arms and hands were encased in gauze and bandages right down to his fingertips. There were also blisters on his face and forehead and the front of his hair was singed.

He opened his eyes drowsily as she approached the bed and stared almost unseeingly.

'Oh, Tom, my darling, what have you done to yourself,' she whispered. 'You were so brave.'

His eyelids fluttered but it was as if they were too heavy for him to open them.

Remembering the nurse's instructions about not waking him she simply whispered his name again.

He managed a lopsided smile then drifted back into a deep sleep.

She wanted to kiss him before she left but was afraid to do so for fear of hurting him; she wanted to hold his hand but she could see that that was also impossible.

All she could do was repeat his name softly, over and over again before the nurse came and asked her to leave.

Thirty-Three

Jenny didn't tell Karen and Bill about the fire or what had happened to Tom until they arrived on the Friday, the day before the wedding was to take place.

'You should have telephoned and I would have come right away,' Karen told Jenny as she hugged her and sympathized with her. 'How dreadful that it should happen and that Tom is so badly hurt. I should have been here to help you deal with it. I feel terrible that you did it all on your own, Gran.'

'We're here now, so what can we do?' Bill cut in briskly. 'Can we go and visit Tom?'

'No, there's no point at the moment because they won't let you see him. He's still in intensive care. They only let me in for a few minutes and he wasn't awake while I was there. He's in terrible pain so they've sedated him.'

Bill nodded his head. 'I understand, but is there anything else we can do for you?'

'What you can do is help me decide what we are going to do about the party we planned to have here tomorrow night,' Jenny told him.

'You'll have to call the wedding off, won't you?' Karen mused.

'Oh yes, I know that. I phoned the registrar right away and let them know that our arrangement at the town hall had to be called off. They were most understanding and said to let them know when he was better and then we could fix a new date.'

'Well, that's one problem dealt with,' Karen said brightly. 'What's next?'

'I don't know whether to call off the party we'd planned to hold here or not,' Jenny said worriedly.

'If you do then there's going to be an awful lot of people disappointed,' Bill said thoughtfully.

'That's what I thought, but I don't really feel like the idea of partying at the moment, not with Tom lying so ill in hospital,' Jenny said with a deep sigh.

'It might help to take your mind off how badly hurt poor Tom is,' Karen told her. 'Come on, let's go ahead with it. We'll do all we can to help, Gran. That's right, isn't it, Bill?'

'Yes, of course we will, but I do understand what you mean, Jenny, about not feeling you want to do it.'

'Why not sleep on it and see how you feel in the morning,' Karen suggested.

'I know that's a good idea but it's not really fair on the residents here,' Jenny said thoughtfully. 'If we are not going ahead with the party then we should let everyone know so that they can make alternative arrangements if they wish.'

The three of them were silent for a few minutes, then Jenny squared her shoulders and stated firmly, 'We'll go ahead with it. I'm sure that's what Tom would want us to do.'

Karen said nothing but jumped up and hugged Jenny. Bill's handsome face broadened in a warm smile as he nodded his head in agreement.

'First thing tomorrow morning we'll go over all the details and I'll take over any of the jobs you were relying on Tom to do. We'll manage between the three of us. You're in charge, Jenny, so remember to delegate as much as you wish.'

The evening was a great success. The only person who made any deprecating comments was Jane Phillips.

'You and your family certainly seem to know how to draw attention to yourselves,' she commented in a sneering voice as she came into the community room and stared around at the decorations and lavish display of food and wine.

One or two other people expressed mild surprise that the party was still being held but Jenny noticed that like Jane they ate and drank their fill along with everybody else.

The room buzzed with chatter and laughter. Bill excelled at making sure that glasses were topped up and Karen did her share by handing around plates of food.

People seemed to welcome the opportunity to relate their own experiences of what happened on the night of the fire. One and all they were high in their praise of Tom's courage and bravery in rescuing old Mrs Parsons.

'She's not been badly burned because Tom shielded her with his body and he got her out so quickly. Even so, her family have decided that the time has come for her to have constant care of some kind,' Lorna Hill told them.

'I was told that one of her daughters was taking her to live with them until after Christmas to help her get over the shock of what happened. Then in the new year they would be making arrangements for her to go into a residential nursing home,' Mavis Grey added.

'She certainly won't be coming back to Merseyside Mansions,' Lorna Hill confirmed.

The evening ended shortly before midnight with Bill asking them all to drink a toast to Tom and send him best wishes for his speedy recovery.

Jenny felt exhausted but strangely happy at having kept their promise of giving a party and knowing that all those who attended had enjoyed the occasion.

Christmas celebrations a few days later were rather muted for Jenny, Karen and Bill. Tom was improving and was now allowed visitors, which meant they could see him each day. By Boxing Day he was so much better and obviously making such good progress that they asked him if he knew when he would be allowed home.

'They are going to do some plastic surgery on my arms before they let me come home,' he told them. 'I'll probably always have scars but other than that they will be as good as ever.'

Bill and Karen stayed on with Jenny until New Year's Eve, then they went back to their own home in Wiltshire. They wanted Jenny to go with them for a few days but were understanding when she refused because it would mean leaving Tom.

'Promise you'll phone if you need any help with nursing Tom when he comes home,' Karen insisted.

'I'm sure I'll be able to cope.' Jenny smiled. 'Thank you both so much for coming and for all your support. Thank you also for helping to make such a wonderful success of the party. I could never have managed it all on my own. I'll telephone and let you know the moment Tom comes out of hospital.'

It was the first week in January before Tom was allowed to come home. He looked thinner and he was rather pale, but he was in good spirits.

It was a bitterly cold day with a grey overcast sky and a threat of snow in the air. Jenny rushed him indoors and into his flat because she was fearful that after the warmth in the hospital he might catch a chill if he stood around talking to people.

The journey home had exhausted him and for the next couple of days Tom was content to be waited on and fussed over. He had looked thin so Jenny was determined to build him up with good nourishing meals.

Jenny telephoned Karen and Bill and assured them that she was managing quite well and that Tom was fine apart from the fact that he had lost so much weight that his clothes hung on him.

'I'm feeding him up so he'll soon put the weight back on,' she told Karen.

When she invited them to come for the weekend they declined saying that they'd had some heavy falls of snow and the roads nearby were so bad that unless they were really needed they would rather leave it for the moment and asked if Jenny and Tom would come to them at half term instead.

Jenny agreed that this would be best for all of them. Although Tom was making good progress he had not fully regained his strength. He tired easily and most days took a nap after his midday meal.

Later in the week when Tom suggested going out for a walk Jenny vetoed the idea. She was adamant that it was far too cold.

'You've only to look at the river and you can see that there's a gale blowing. If you tried to walk along the promenade you'd probably get blown away,' she told him.

'We don't have to go along the prom, we could walk up Victoria Road to the shops,' he suggested.

'Why? What do you need to buy? Tell me what it is and I'll get it for you.'

'Nothing except to get some flowers for you,' he told her mildly. 'It would be nice to have a walk and get some fresh air. I haven't been for a walk for weeks and I feel I need to stretch my legs.'

'You probably do, but not today,' she told him firmly. 'If you go out and catch a cold you'll be right back where you were when you came out of hospital.'

When they went to the coffee morning the following Wednesday Tom was welcomed back warmly by everybody there.

They were loud in their praise for what he had done in rescuing old Mrs Parsons and confirmed that she had now been moved permanently into a residential home where she could be looked after right around the clock.

They also expressed commiserations that all Jenny and Tom's plans for their wedding had had to be postponed.

'Yes, I'm afraid we will have to fix a new date for our wedding,' Tom said with a smile.

'We'll probably leave it until Easter now,' Jenny confirmed. 'Easter is very late this year, not until the middle of April, so it will be warmer by then,' she added.

'Perhaps you should take the fire as a warning,' Jane Phillips mused cryptically. 'We don't want to have another disaster at Merseyside Mansions and things do seem to go wrong for you and your family,' she added, her mouth pursing up into a tight grimace.

'Yes, Jenny, you are quite right. Easter is not until the twentieth April so you should get some sunshine by then,' Lorna Hill agreed quickly as if hoping no one would take any notice of Jane Phillips's rather pointed comment.

'So we can expect to have another party?' Jane commented in a rather acid tone.

'Party? What party?' Tom said, winking at Jenny and pretending to be surprised.

'Oh, didn't she tell you that while you were in hospital she went ahead and held the party you had planned for your wedding celebrations,' Jane said triumphantly.

'You did! You mean you partied without me!' Tom exclaimed in mock horror.

'That will teach you that you can't trust her; you never know what she will get up to,' said Jane with a disapproving sniff.

Several people jumped in to support Jenny's decision to hold the party and to say how well it had all been organized.

'Did you all have a good time?' Tom asked.

'That's all that matters then,' he said with a big smile when they all assured him that they had enjoyed it immensely.

'So does that mean we'll have another party then in April?' Clare Green's voice boomed.

'We'll certainly think about it,' Tom agreed. 'Let's fix a new date for our wedding first and then we'll go into the other details more thoroughly. A party here will be top priority I can assure you.'

Thirty-Four

Although they were planning on having an Easter wedding Tom and Jenny decided not to make any firm arrangements until they'd had a chance to talk to Karen and Bill. They wanted them to be witnesses so it was important that they found out first of all if they had already made plans for Easter.

Jenny thought they might be thinking of going away during the Easter holidays for a break and she didn't want to upset any of their arrangements.

'We'll talk it over with them when we go to see them at half term,' she told Tom.

'Good idea,' he agreed. 'We'll say no more about it until then and just hope people here drop the subject for the moment.'

The following Wednesday the residents present at coffee morning were agog with speculation about who was coming into old Mrs Parsons's flat. It had been newly decorated and snapped up the moment it went on the market.

Some people said it was a man, others stated it was a couple, but Jane, who always managed to know the very latest news, said that it was a woman.

'She's in her sixties and I understand she's an artist,' she pronounced.

'A woman! Hope she's a good-looking filly,' Major Mitchell boomed. 'I doubt if she'll be as handsome as your granddaughter, Jenny, but as long as she's young and fit she'll do!'

'You mean she'll be an asset and brighten the place up,' Tom commented.

'I'm hoping for more than that,' the Major chortled. 'I wouldn't have minded being in old Lionel's shoes last year. I mean, of course, when he got married not when he fell off his perch.'

'I didn't know you were looking for a bride,' Jane Phillips said archly. 'Bit long in the tooth for that though, aren't you?' she added waspishly.

'Never too old to be cared for and mollycoddled, always providing it's by the right person. If she's an artist and she's in her sixties she should have an interesting personality,' he added, removing his monocle and polishing it with the silk handkerchief he always sported in his breast pocket.

'Well, she's moving in this coming weekend so you will be able to judge for yourself,' Jane told him. 'I'll make sure she comes to our next coffee morning.'

The following Wednesday there was an exceptionally good attendance at the coffee morning. News of Major Mitchell's interest in the newcomer had spread and the residents were all eager to see his reaction when he met her for the first time.

'At least it's diverted attention from us and our future plans,' Tom said quietly to Jenny.

'Perhaps we'll be able to make it a double event,' she retorted with a low laugh.

Jane was as good as her word, bringing the newcomer to join them.

As they entered the room, Jane paused in the doorway until she knew she had everybody's attention, and in the expectant silence that followed introduced the new arrival as Isabel Harding.

There were murmured greetings from those present as they took stock of their newest resident.

She was of medium height, her grey hair cut into a straight sharp style that suited her bold features. She had bright turquoise blue eyes that were vivid and piercing as if they could see through to your innermost thoughts.

She was dressed in a striking purple two-piece wool suit and with it a double row of pale pink beads filling the low cut neck of the top. Her earrings were also pink; a cluster of pale pink beads that matched her necklace.

'By Jove, now there's an interesting filly,' the Major murmured. He removed his monocle, polished it and put it back in as if to see her even more clearly.

'Brings a spot of colour to the place and no mistake,' he chortled. 'A bird of paradise amongst a flock of sparrows.'

Rising to his feet, he squared his shoulders and strode across the room. 'Major John Mitchell, retired,' he boomed as he held out his hand to the newcomer.

There were some titters and amused looks as Jane took it upon herself to introduce him again.

With a smile Isabel stretched out her hand towards the Major who bowed over it and then gallantly raised it to his lips. He then took her elbow and guided her across the room to his chair and pulled up another alongside her for himself.

'Now, if you will tell me how you like your coffee I'll fetch you a cup,' he told her.

'No, you stay and talk to Isabel and I'll fetch the coffee,' Jane told him.

Although general conversation resumed everyone was straining to hear what the Major and Isabel Harding were saying to each other.

The Major wasted no time.

'I hear you are an artist,' he said. 'I regret I'm not familiar with your work.'

Isabel laughed, a deep rich sound. 'You wouldn't be,' she told him. 'I'm an artiste, not an artist.'

The Major looked slightly taken aback. 'An artiste?' he repeated, frowning questioningly.

'That's right. A circus artiste,' she explained, her blue eyes mesmerizing him.

'You mean you're a lion tamer,' John Mitchell chortled, amused by his own joke.

'Exactly. How very clever of you to know.'

'Good heavens!' The Major's eyebrows shot up. 'Are you serious? I was jesting, dear lady.'

Isabel looked amused. 'Well, you guessed correctly. I am retired now, of course,' she added with a deep sigh. 'I have appeared all over Great Britain and throughout Europe and my performances were even attended by Royalty.' Her eyes shone with pride. 'I can show you pictures and photographs that will make you gasp with surprise.'

'Indeed, dear lady. I shall very much enjoy seeing them,' the Major told her enthusiastically.

'I am still passionate about the circus world; it's in my blood. One of the joys of living here in New Brighton is that I will be able to visit the circus in the Tower grounds whenever I wish to do so.'

There were smiles on several faces as they overheard Isabel regaling the Major with details of her accomplishments, and it was noticed that the Major seemed to be completely overawed and, at times, he even appeared to be completely at a loss for words.

Tom and Jenny looked at each other. 'I don't think the Major is going to be the one who makes a conquest there,' Tom said quietly.

'No, I think that this time he's met his match,' Jenny agreed.

'Yes, it would be an interesting partnership.'

'So, do you think it will be a double event at Easter then?' Jenny queried as they exchanged smiles.

'Hard to say,' Tom prevaricated. 'We'll all have to wait and see.'

Confident that they could go ahead with their plans, they looked forward to asking Karen and Bill when they went to stay at half term if the dates suited them. But before they could do so, Karen had her own news to tell them.

'We're expecting a baby. Well, I am,' she confided with a giggle as she reached out and took Bill's hand. 'It's due at the end of May, isn't that wonderful?'

Tom and Jenny exchanged warning glances with each other as they both congratulated Karen.

'Where does that leave us over our wedding plans?' Tom asked as soon as they were on their own.

'I honestly don't know,' Jenny said in a bewildered voice. 'I did so much want it to be at Easter and I also wanted to make sure that Karen and Bill were there.'

'Karen won't really be up to all the travelling involved if it is at Easter, will she?' Tom frowned.

'I wouldn't think so,' Jenny agreed.

'In that case then perhaps we should bring it forward a week or two,' Tom suggested. 'What about making it the first week in April?'

'We could do that,' Jenny said thoughtfully. 'To some extent the date doesn't matter to us as long as it's not April the first.'

'It damn well does,' Tom said fiercely as he took her in his arms and kissed her. 'We've postponed it once and I don't want to have to do that again. I'd say let's get married tomorrow if we could arrange things at such short notice.'

'Stop being so impetuous,' Jenny said, laughing. 'Early April sounds fine. Shall we check the date with Bill and Karen to make sure that they are both quite sure they'll be able to attend?'

When they suggested it Bill looked rather doubtful but Karen was all in favour of the idea.

'It will be much better if you have your wedding then rather than after the baby is born. I might have difficulty in finding someone to look after it and you wouldn't want a baby crying its head off in the middle of the ceremony now, would you?'

'OK, let's see if we can fix things for the beginning of April,' Jenny affirmed. 'We'll let you know the exact date as soon as we have spoken to the Registrar and completed all the arrangements.'

'It will have to be at the weekend, on a Saturday, because I won't be able to take any time off so near to the school's Easter holidays,' Bill reminded them.

'Yes, I had thought of that,' Jenny told him.

'Have you also realized that I will probably be the size of a house by then?' Karen laughed, running her hands over her bulging figure.

'Is that important?' Jenny frowned. 'As long as you are feeling well enough that's all that matters.'

'I'm not sure that it's such a good idea,' Bill said worriedly. 'It will mean quite a lot of travelling from Wiltshire to here and then back home again the next day. It might be too much for Karen, she might not be feeling up to it.'

'You'll know nearer the date. If you think it will be too much for you, Karen, then let us know and we'll find two other people to be witnesses.'

'Oh no, I don't want you doing that,' Karen protested. 'I want to be there, Gran. Can't you arrange it a bit earlier? What about some time in March?'

'We'll see what we can do,' Tom promised. 'It can't be too soon as far as I'm concerned.'

Thirty-Five

As soon as they had arranged the first Saturday in April at the register office, Tom promised that he would rebook the cars and flowers and dinner for the four of them at the Grand Hotel.

'Do you still want to hold a party here at Merseyside Mansions afterwards?' he asked Jenny.

'Of course! They'd never forgive us if we didn't,' she said with a laugh. 'We'll phone Bill and Karen tonight and confirm the date.'

They were both delighted by the idea and Karen insisted that she'd be fine coming for the weekend. 'If I do feel exceptionally tired then I can stay on in Tom's flat for the rest of the week and Bill can come and pick me up the following weekend.'

'That sounds like a perfect solution,' Jenny agreed.

'Are you going to wear the same outfit as you had planned for last time?' Karen wanted to know.

'I don't think so,' Jenny told her. 'I'm not being superstitious but I feel I want to buy something new, something quite different.'

'Good for you, Gran. I wish I could come and help you choose it but I don't think Bill would agree to me doing that. He'd have me wrapped up in cotton wool and confined to bed if he had his way. He's even more excited about this baby than I am.' She giggled. 'He watches to make sure that I eat all the right foods, take vitamin pills and that I get the right amount of exercise and sleep.'

'Well, that's a relief. It means that there's no need for me to worry about you then,' Jenny said teasingly.

'There most certainly isn't, Gran. I'm the picture of health,' Karen said, laughing.

'Well, it looks as though we can go ahead with all our plans without any worries,' Jenny reported to Tom after she'd spoken to Karen.

'One thing we haven't checked on,' he said, frowning.

Jenny looked puzzled. 'What's that?'

'Whether or not it's going to be a double event.'

'You mean the Major and Isabel.' Jenny chuckled. 'I don't think we need worry about them, from all the rumours flying around I gather they are already an item.'

'Yes, so I've heard, but I wasn't sure exactly what to believe.'

'Jane keeps an eye on them and thoroughly disapproves of the fact that the Major is seen leaving Isabel's flat in the very early hours of the morning,' Jenny said with a smile.

'Really!' Tom's eyes widened. 'Lucky devil,' he muttered.

'I didn't know she'd taken your fancy as well,' Jenny said in surprise.

'She damn well hasn't. You know quite well what I mean. Still –' he heaved a deep sigh – 'it's not long now until March so let's hope nothing goes wrong this time.'

The run up to their wedding was so quiet that Jenny began to long for some excitement. She and Tom met up most days but their outings for meals or walks were relatively few; they both seemed to have put their life on hold.

They continued to go to the Wednesday coffee morning but even this social event had begun to pall. She sometimes wondered why they went on attending as she usually came away feeling disgruntled.

There was always so much disapproving gossip about what people were doing or discussions about the various changes in their own medication and the effect it was having on them. Apart from that there were the same old grumbles about the management committee and criticism about the way things were run.

Since the start of spring the way in which the garden was landscaped was another prominent topic. The gardeners were constantly being criticized either because the plants were behind schedule or because people didn't like the choice of bulbs and flowers or where they had been planted.

Jenny couldn't understand why these discussions became so heated and vitriolic. All residents had known when they moved into Merseyside Mansions that they were not allowed to do anything in the garden, so why not accept what was being done for them. She did. She was only too pleased not to have to maintain a garden any longer. Knowing how much hard work it entailed, she was more than delighted by the sight of snowdrops followed a few weeks later by daffodils and hyacinths when she looked out of her windows. She looked forward to enjoying a colourful display continuing throughout the summer without any effort on her part.

New Brighton itself was also slowly returning to life after the winter closures. Preparations were being made for the return of the circus in the tower grounds, the pier was being repainted and workmen were busy at the outdoor swimming pool in anticipation of an influx of summer visitors and day trippers.

The long promenade that ran from Seacombe to Wallasey Village, however, was practically deserted. High winds in early February had made a daily stroll along it out of the question and once the habit had been broken there seemed to be some reluctance in restarting.

Even the Mersey had been quieter than usual, with fewer liners waiting at the Bar to enter or leave the river and less commercial activity.

Jenny had been over to Liverpool shopping on her own several times. She had bought a new wedding outfit because she didn't think the one she'd chosen for December would look right at Easter.

Tom had rebooked the hotel meal and the cars for the new date they had chosen and had even placed a tentative order for the flowers, so it seemed there was nothing further to do until the actual day drew nearer.

They paid Karen and Bill a very short visit at half term and Jenny couldn't believe how well she looked. The talk had all been about the coming baby and the preparations they were making for its arrival. Karen delighted in showing them the nursery that she and Bill had decorated and the collection of baby clothes and all the other items they'd amassed ready for the new arrival.

Karen was now so large that the outfit she'd planned to wear at Jenny and Tom's wedding was no longer suitable because she couldn't get into it.

'I'll wait until the week before your wedding to decide what to buy just in case I get any bigger,' she told Jenny with a laugh.

'Would you like me to come for the weekend and go shopping with you?'

'No, there's no need for you to do that, Gran. I'll have to settle for whatever they have in stock that fits me,' she added with a laugh. 'I never dreamed I would be this big.'

'Well, you can always ring me if you change your mind, and I'll keep the next couple of Saturdays free just in case,' Jenny told her.

'She certainly is enormous,' Tom commented on their way home. 'Are you sure she isn't expecting twins?'

'I wouldn't think so. These days they have scans and know about these things in advance,' Jenny told him.

Nevertheless, she was concerned about Karen's size, but since she had very little to do with pregnant mothers she was sure that since Karen looked so well there was nothing to worry about.

Although it had been a long cold winter, the weather took a massive turn for the better in mid-March and promised to be warm, dry and sunny for their wedding.

The Saturday before the date fixed for their wedding was such a nice day that Tom suggested a walk along the prom to Harrison Drive and then they could have lunch in Wallasey Village and either walk home or catch the bus back to New Brighton.

They were just going out of the door when the phone rang.

'Leave it, probably nothing important,' Tom said quickly.

Jenny hesitated. 'I don't know. I did tell Karen that if she needed me to go and help her to choose her outfit for our wedding then I would go with her.'

'She's hardly likely to phone you today; it would be afternoon before you got down to Wiltshire and the shops would be closing by the time you got into the nearest town.'

'Yes, you're probably right,' Jenny agreed.

The phone was still ringing though as if the person on the other end had no intention of hanging up until it was answered.

'Oh, go on then, answer it,' Tom said resignedly. 'You won't rest until you know who it is, but be quick.'

When Jenny answered the call he could tell by the expression on her face that it was bad news. She was shaking as she tried to tell him who it was and what it was about but the words wouldn't come.

Tom took the phone from her trembling hand and his voice was curt as he asked: 'Yes, who is it? What is it you . . .'

Before he could finish speaking the voice on the other end cut in and the moment he recognized that it was Bill calling he listened in silence.

'Yes, I understand. We'll be there as soon as possible,' he promised before hanging up.

'Did you understand what Bill was saying?' he asked, looking at Jenny.

Jenny nodded then shook her head. 'I'm not too sure. I think I did.'

'Karen has gone into labour early and has been taken to hospital. The baby will be premature,' Tom told her.

She stared at him wide-eyed. 'We must go down there right away. Karen will need me to be there with her.'

'Yes, that is what I've told Bill we will do. Now can you pack an overnight bag for both of us. While you are doing that I'll go and put some petrol in the car and check the oil and make sure it is OK for the journey and then we'll be off.'

Jenny nodded, then she said in a worried voice, 'What about all our plans . . . our wedding day is only a week away.'

'There's plenty of time to sort that out,' Tom said as he picked up his keys and made to leave. 'We'll decide what to do about that when we know what the situation is with Karen. Let's get down there and see what we can do to help.'

Thirty-Six

They travelled most of the way to Wiltshire in silence, preoccupied with their own thoughts.

Jenny had never thought of herself as being superstitious but now she did wonder if, as seemed probable, they had to delay the ceremony yet again, this was some sort of warning that she was doing the wrong thing in contemplating marrying Tom.

She studied his profile. He was concentrating on his driving and his jaw was set in a firm, dominant line, his eyes fixed on the road ahead. He looked so determined that it was obvious that he was not a man to be trifled with and she began to wonder if she was foolish to be marrying a man who was such a strong character.

She had been independent for so many years that she would probably find that having to compel herself to consider someone else's opinion in everything she did for the rest of her life very restraining.

That was all nonsense she told herself; they thought about most things in the same way as each other; there was very little they disagreed about. When they did they always seemed to manage to reach a compromise.

Would that always be the case? Would there be a subtle change in their relationship when they were man and wife and living together or was she being unduly pessimistic?

At the moment they spent a considerable amount of time in their own apartments. She still felt free and independent and under no obligation to accept any of his views. Would it be different when they were married?

It was thirty-six years since William had died and, although she had lived with Eddy until eight years ago, because he was her son she had never felt restricted in the least by his opinions.

Subjugating herself to another person's ideas and way of doing things was going to be a learning curve that she wasn't sure she could swallow.

Tom was so quiet that she wondered if he was having similar misgivings. He had no family at all so he, too, had been free to make his own decisions and live as he wanted to do for a very long time. His wife, so he had told her, had died almost twenty years ago and she had been an invalid and in a nursing home for ten years before that. It had made him extremely self-sufficient; he did all his own shopping, cooking, cleaning, washing and ironing.

So what was the attraction that had drawn them together, Jenny wondered. Although they were both touching seventy neither of them was really lonely or looking for companionship. Was it because they had similar tastes; or was it some cosmic magnetism that they were unable to define, influence or even control.

'We've made very good time,' Tom commented, breaking their long silence as they crossed over the border into Wiltshire. 'I wonder what is the best thing for us to do? Should we simply drive to their home or would it be best to try and contact Bill by phone and find out if he is there or at the hospital?'

'Let's go straight to their home and if Bill isn't there then we can try the hospital,' Jenny told him.

She settled back into her seat, smiling complacently. Tom's mind, unlike hers, hadn't been dwelling on whether their forthcoming marriage was right for them or not but on the more immediate problem of Karen and Bill.

That was the sort of person Tom was, she thought gratefully. He was not only kind and loving but also extremely pragmatic. Why on earth did she need to confuse the issue by asking herself unnecessary questions about their relationship when she'd been lucky to find such a man.

Bill was at home when they arrived but on the point of leaving for the hospital. He looked worried and sounded very agitated as he greeted them.

'Karen was taken in early this morning but they sent me away and told me to come back later in the day,' he told them. 'I'm on my way now to find out how she is.'

'Right, then we'll come with you. Do you want to take your car or mine?' Tom asked.

'My car because I know the way,' Bill said immediately. 'I'll take your luggage upstairs and you bring your car on to the drive and lock it up and then we'll be off; that is, if it's OK with both of you? Would you like to freshen up or use the bathroom or anything?' he asked, looking from one to the other of them.

'No, let's be on our way. The sooner we have some news the better,' Jenny said quickly.

Ten minutes later they were in the hospital reception area waiting to hear how Karen was and whether or not they could see her.

They were asked to wait.

'The baby is very premature and the mother is extremely tired. She may still be sleeping,' a Sister informed them.

'Could you please check; I am her grandmother and I have come all the way from Merseyside to see her,' Jenny pleaded.

It was another quarter of an hour before someone came to tell them that they could see Karen for a few minutes. They were taken into a side ward where Karen lay. She looked very pale and exhausted but managed to smile weakly when she saw her visitors.

'I've messed up your wedding arrangements again, Gran,' she said with an apologetic sigh.

'Don't you worry about that, we can easily fix a new date when you feel up to it,' Tom told her quickly. He looked round expectantly, 'Where's the baby?'

'They've taken her away and put her in an incubator. I don't think they will let you see her. Not to worry, I'll be out in a couple of days' time and I'm hoping she will be strong enough by then for me to bring her home with me.'

The Sister returned to tell them that it was time for them to leave, interrupting their brief visit. Jenny and Tom immediately said goodbye to Karen and withdrew into the corridor, leaving Bill to have a few moments alone with Karen.

'It looks as though Karen is going to need your help for a couple of weeks at least,' Tom commented as they waited for Bill.

'I think you're right,' Jenny agreed.

'You are quite happy about us staying here to be with her?' Tom asked.

'It means changing all our wedding plans yet again,' Jenny warned.

'I know that but, as I said to Karen, we can always fix new dates when she is fit again.'

Jenny felt choked. She simply nodded her agreement and squeezed his hand.

'We'll take Bill for a meal and afterwards we'll let him know that is what we are planning to do,' Tom said as they waited for Bill to join them.

Tom was as good as his word. He kept up a light conversation throughout their meal but afterwards in the car going back to Bill's he assured Bill that they would both be staying to help look after Karen and the baby for as long as it was necessary for them to do so.

The discussion about the preparations they had made for the baby and what still had to be done continued well into the evening until Jenny said that she was so tired she would be falling asleep in the armchair if she didn't get to bed.

'I'm sorry,' Bill told her. 'I've been going over all the possibilities in my head ever since Karen was rushed into hospital and I am afraid I've taken advantage of you being here and talked my head off about it all. I can't tell you how relieved I am to know that you'll both be here when Karen comes home.'

'Well, I will have to nip back to Wallasey for a couple of days to cancel all the arrangements we have made for our wedding. I'll go first thing tomorrow but Jenny can stay here and help you get things ready for Karen coming home. I will be back down again as soon as I've sorted everything out up there,' Tom assured him.

'That sounds fine,' Bill agreed as they all stood up ready to go to bed.

Leaving the two men to tidy up downstairs, Jenny went on up to the spare bedroom. She was so tired that it wasn't until she had undressed and was stretched out under the duvet that she realized she would be sharing the bed with Tom.

Jenny remembered the protestations she had made about this the last time they had visited Karen but now somehow, it didn't seem to matter; in fact, it seemed right.

She stretched, sleepily aware that she was looking forward to the idea that Tom would soon be there in the bed beside her; it was so comforting to know that she would be sleeping in his arms.

Thirty-Seven

A week later Karen and the baby came home. She still looked pale and seemed nervous and ill at ease as she handled the baby. They hadn't yet decided on a name; Bill called her Beauty and Karen still referred to her as Baby.

At first they were all talking in whispers, tiptoeing around and shushing each other for fear of disturbing the sleeping scrap.

'This is nonsense,' Tom said with a laugh. 'We can't spend the rest of our lives like this. Keep the noise level low but surely we don't need to pussyfoot around like we are doing at the moment?'

'She's so very small,' Bill protested as he gently eased back the shawl from the tiny face it was half covering. 'She looks as though a puff of wind would blow her away.'

'You won't be saying that in a couple of months' time when she is bawling her head off in the middle of the night,' Tom said with a laugh.

Jenny was mildly surprised at how quickly her own skills in babycare returned. She was far more confident and adept at handling the new baby than Karen was. Privately, she thought she even enjoyed bathing and feeding the tiny scrap more than Karen did.

As the days passed Jenny was fully rewarded by seeing the new baby thrive. By the time she and Tom had decided to return to Wallasey, little Angela, as they had decided to call her, looked well and healthy and was feeding and sleeping without any problems.

Karen, too, had the colour back in her cheeks, her energy was once again at its peak and she had taken over complete control of looking after little Angela.

'I don't know how I would have managed without you, Gran,' she told Jenny gratefully as she kissed her goodbye.

It was the Tuesday after Easter and both Tom and Jenny had decided it was time for them to return to Merseyside Mansions.

'It's great being here but it will be good to be back in a child-free zone again,' Tom admitted. 'Everything seems to revolve around the baby's needs and routine.'

'They're besotted by her aren't they,' Jenny said happily. 'I think that the fact that she was premature has a great deal to do with it. Now she's as fit as any full-term baby. She's probably even healthier than most of them because she's been so protected ever since she was born.'

'Well, Karen and Bill will have a few weeks together before it's time for him to go back to school and by then Karen should be able to cope single-handed. If not, then she can always phone and let you know and I imagine you'll come running back.'

'I'm not too sure about that,' Jenny said in a thoughtful voice. 'You have been wonderful and I couldn't have done it without your help, but now I think it is time for us to attend to our own needs and happiness and for me to put you first.'

'You mean time to fix a new date for our wedding plans.'

'If that is what you still want,' Jenny agreed.

'Don't you?'

'Yes, but I'm not nearly so worried about it now as I was a few months ago. I'll be quite happy to simply live with you.'

'Heavens above woman, I never thought to hear you say those sort of things,' Tom said in a shocked voice.

Jenny bit her lip, wondering if she had upset him, or made him see her in a new light. The last few weeks had been trying for both of them and had put a strain on their relationship.

It was hardly fair on Tom to be expected to take on responsibilities concerning Karen, she thought uneasily.

'In fact, I thought you were so concerned about Karen and her welfare that you hadn't noticed that we've been sharing a bed together for the last few weeks, which is why I've not commented on it,' Tom said drily.

'Oh yes, I had noticed,' Jenny told him. She wanted to say more, to tell him how comforting she had found it to sleep with his arm around her, as if protecting her from the world and all its worries. It had seemed so right that she knew she was going to miss their closeness when life returned to normal once again.

If only she could be sure that he felt the same and could tell her that he needed her as much as she now knew she needed him.

'I suppose it's back to separate apartments when we reach Merseyside Mansions,' he said, almost as if voicing her thoughts aloud.

'If that's what you want,' Jenny said quietly and held her breath waiting for his reply.

When Tom didn't answer, Jenny felt a moment of panic. As she shot a sideways glance at him she saw his shoulders were shaking and his lips were tightly clenched and as their eyes met he exploded with laughter.

For a moment she felt irritated and close to tears. She had found looking after Karen and her new baby much more stressful than she had expected and now she felt completely exhausted.

Tom was quick to sense her mood. 'Sorry,' he said, grinning. 'How could you ever for a moment have had any doubts. Of course I want us to be together, night and day, and I do want us to be married because I realize that in your heart of hearts you think it is right and proper to make things legal, but there is no hurry. You look as though you need a rest, a holiday even. I feel whacked myself. I had no idea that broken nights could drain you so much. Let's put everything on hold for a couple of weeks and then start all our planning afresh.'

Although she agreed with him, Jenny found that settling back into the normal pattern at Merseyside Mansions was not as easy as she had anticipated. To her surprise she missed the baby's cries when its feeding time approached and she also found herself missing all the work attached to looking after it.

Tom had settled back into his old routine almost at once and seemed to prefer being in his own flat rather than in hers. He seemed to be quite happy sorting out his cupboards and getting rid of things he said were either no longer needed or duplicated items she already had in her flat.

Although they had not yet decided whether to stay on at Merseyside Mansions or to buy a small house or bungalow, he seemed to be intent on spring cleaning and decorating his own place.

'If I redecorate it right through then we can decide if we want to stay here in my flat or put it on the market. Either way it will be in good order. If we decide to stay on here then you can move your stuff in here and I can do a decorating job on your flat so that we can put that on the market.'

'If we decide to stay on here then would you sooner we moved into your flat rather than mine?' Jenny asked.

'Well, it is the larger of the two,' he pointed out. 'Things would be rather cramped in your flat when Bill and Karen and the baby come to stay, whereas in mine we do have the spare bedroom.'

'I wonder if they will want to come and stay though?' Jenny mused.

'You bet they will. Remember Bill gets quite long holidays; and they won't be able to afford to spend months at a time in hotels, so if they fancy a cheap seaside holiday then where would be better than here?'

Although Jenny knew quite well that what Tom was saying made sense, she felt reluctant to give up her cosy flat. For one thing, she had only to go a short distance to be out in the garden, whereas Tom had to walk along a passage and either take the lift or two flights of stairs to get outside the building.

Perhaps, she mused, it would be better to move away; to find a house or bungalow. One of the joys of being at Karen's house had been the sense of freedom it gave her to be able to open the kitchen door and step out into the garden; to be able to hang washing out of doors and wander through the garden whenever she felt the urge to do so, just as she had when she'd lived at Warren Point.

She didn't have to make up her mind right away, she told herself. In fact, they could even leave making a decision until after they were married. They had a roof over their heads, two in fact, so why not wait until they were both sure about what they wanted.

At present she was finding the gossip and unimportant chatter that went on at Merseyside Mansions extremely tedious and irritating. But Tom merely shrugged their fellow residents' remarks off or completely ignored them.

'You'd probably find the isolation and lack of friendly faces even more difficult to contend with if we moved away,' he warned, and she wondered if he was right.

She was also well aware that there were other things to be considered. At present they had no worries about outside decorating or maintenance. Even the garden was attended to without them having to make a decision about it.

Thirty-Eight

They heard the telephone ringing as they approached Jenny's flat on returning from a walk along the promenade. As Tom unlocked the door Jenny hurried to answer it, saying with a smile, 'Whoever it is they're determined that I'll answer it.'

When she lifted the receiver she was surprised to hear Bill's voice say, 'Hello, is that you, Jenny?'

'Hello, Bill, is something the matter? You sound worried.'

'There's nothing wrong, well, not really, but I'm trying to speak to you before Karen comes back from the clinic.'

'So there is something wrong . . . is it to do with the baby?'

'No, no; nothing like that; she's only paying a routine visit, the baby is fine, thriving in fact.'

'So what is wrong, then?'

'Well . . .' He hesitated and Jenny heard him take a deep breath. 'It's just that I have a problem that's all.'

'Go on.' Jenny held her breath, wondering what was the matter. She could hear Tom moving about in the kitchen filling the kettle and switching it on, then the rattle of the cups as he laid them out on a tray ready to make tea the moment the kettle boiled.

'Well, it's like this,' Bill explained. 'I have to go away next week, school trip to Belgium. I'd like to get out of it but it's not possible and, well, the truth is I'm worried about Karen. I don't like leaving her to cope with the baby for a whole week on her own.'

Jenny was on the verge of pointing out that during the war mothers had been left to cope on their own for far longer than a week when their husbands went off to fight. But she knew that would be no comfort to Bill so she kept silent.

'What I'm really trying to say, Jenny, is would you and Tom come and stay down here for the week while I'm away. I know it's only a couple of weeks since you were here and that you probably want to get back to your normal commitments but . . .'

'Oh, Bill, don't sound so worried and apologetic,' Jenny interrupted. 'Of course we'll come and stay for the week, no problem at all.'

'You will?'

The relief in his voice was so great that Jenny couldn't help laughing.

'You don't have to sound like a condemned man reprieved right at the last minute,' she said with a laugh.

'Well, I can't help feeling that it is rather an imposition to ask such a favour of you. Can you come next Friday? We leave early on Saturday morning and we don't return until the following Sunday.'

'Of course we will. Don't give it another thought. Simply tell Karen of the arrangement,' Jenny told him.

Tom frowned when she conveyed Bill's message and told him that she had agreed that they would go down and stay for the week with Karen.

'What's wrong? Why don't you want to do it?'

'I'm happy to help Bill out but at the moment it is rather inconvenient.'

'What on earth do you mean?'

'You seem to have forgotten that I'm in the middle of decorating my flat.'

'Yes, I know you are but there's no urgency is there?'

'Well, yes. I want to complete it while I'm still in the mood for decorating.'

'Surely a week won't matter?'

'It will to me. I want to get it finished and then do your flat. Anyway, it's not a week, it's ten days if we have to be there for Friday night and we don't come home again until the Sunday.'

He paused, then his face brightened. 'I tell you what, why don't you go and stay with Karen for the week and that will leave me free to devote all the time I want to finishing my painting job here. With any luck,' he went on enthusiastically, 'I can do your flat as well while you're away and then we'll have everything spruced up and we can go ahead and plan the date for our wedding.'

'OK, I'm agreeable to that; in fact it sounds a splendid idea,' Jenny agreed. 'I'll make enquiries about train times and let them know what time to expect me on Friday.'

'There's no need to do that. I'll drive you down and then come straight back,' Tom told her.

The thought of spending a week alone with Karen and baby Angela pleased Jenny immensely. They really would have time to talk, take little walks together and go shopping. It would be so much more intimate than when Bill and Tom were there as well.

They travelled down on Friday morning, deciding to make a day of it and stop somewhere for lunch. It was a glorious late spring day and Jenny felt excited and as light-hearted as if she was going on holiday.

Well, she told herself, it would be a holiday in a way. Certainly it was something quite different. Secretly she was glad to be away from the upheaval the redecorating was causing. Everything seemed to be untidy and topsy-turvy and it made her feel irritable even though she did her best to conceal the fact from Tom.

In truth she didn't want her flat decorated; as far as she was concerned it was all right as it was. She knew Tom was being practical and that it meant that if they decided to stay on at Merseyside Mansions then whichever flat they elected to live in would be in pristine condition and so would the one they decided to sell. It also meant that if they agreed they wanted a bungalow then both flats could be out straight on to the market.

Spending a week with Karen in her house, Jenny thought, would also give her a chance to decide if she really wanted to take on the responsibility of a house again.

If they chose a bungalow there would be no stairs to contend with but there was bound to be a garden. Tom liked decorating and doing things around the flat but she wasn't too sure that he was keen about gardening. He'd certainly never said that he missed having a garden.

Perhaps a garden meant more to a woman than to a man, she mused. It was so lovely to peg out the washing and watch it blowing in the wind and then a few hours later gather in armfuls of fresh-smelling dry clothes rather than simply fish them out of a tumble dryer.

It was also so invigorating to simply open the door and step outside and breath in fresh air first thing in the morning or on a hot close day.

Strangely enough, she thought, Karen, like most of her generation, didn't really appreciate this. There was no daily fluttering of white terry-towel nappies because she used disposable nappies for the baby and all the tiny baby clothes usually went into the washing machine not out on to the clothesline.

They arrived at Karen's just after three o'clock. Bill had not yet come home from the school but Tom said he wouldn't stay as he wanted to get back.

'I know your time will be taken up getting Bill on his way when he comes in and I'm busy decorating,' he told Karen. 'I'll come back a week on Sunday to collect Jenny. You two enjoy yourselves next week.'

Bill came home almost the moment Tom had left. He said he was sorry to have missed him but he was only in the house for about half an hour before he, too, left for his journey to Belgium. Along with the help of two other teachers he was taking a party of twenty boys and since it was the first time they had participated in such a venture it needed a great deal of supervision.

As soon as they were alone Karen put the kettle on and they settled down to a cup of tea and to make plans for what they wanted to do in the coming week.

'We have the car so we can get out and about and I can take you to see some of the local beauty spots or to visit some of the local National Trust places,' Karen told her.

'With the baby?'

'Why not? I can put her in the back in the special carrycot I have for her that fits on to the back seat of the car. We unfasten it and simply take it out of the car with her still in it when we reach our destination. It's so simple.'

'So different, too,' Jenny remarked with a smile. 'I remember I used to have to walk everywhere with you when you were very tiny because your pram was too big to take on a bus or train.'

'Well, her pram is too big for trips of that kind, but in a few months' time when she can go in a pushchair I shall get one that folds up and then we will take it in the car or on a bus with no problem at all. At the moment she is so light that this carrycot is perfect, so let's start planning where you want to go and what you want to see.'

'Sounds admirable, but of course we will only be able to do short trips,' Jenny commented.

'No, we can go out for the entire day if we want to. All Angela's paraphernalia can be packed in a bag and taken with us. She needn't be any trouble at all.'

Thirty-Nine

Jenny and Karen had a wonderful week together. Jenny felt as if things were almost the same as they'd been when Karen was a lively schoolgirl, enthusiastic about everything they said or did. It was as if all the traumas during the intervening years had been wiped out and there had never been all the worries and upsets they'd endured.

Jenny found baby Angela a real delight. She was now almost two months old and a bundle of joy. Jenny felt almost as proud as Karen when people stopped to admire her and say that she looked like a lovely little doll in the pretty pale pink layette that Jenny had knitted for her.

'I don't know what it is about babies but they really seem to bring the best out in people,' Karen said, smiling happily.

'Probably the trusting way they stare up at you or because they look so fresh and innocent,' murmured Jenny as she looked over her shoulder at Angela, who was asleep in her carrycot, firmly anchored on to the back seat of the car.

They were driving home after a day spent on the coast in Weston Super Mare and Jenny deemed it was a good opportunity to sound Karen out about the plans she had formulated in her own mind for a new wedding date.

'I thought early in June,' Jenny told her. 'Or perhaps about the middle of June, say a month from now. Tom will have finished decorating both flats by then and with any luck we will have made up our minds about whether we are going to move or stay put.'

'Why do you want to move? I thought you were quite settled there, Gran,' Karen said in surprise.

'Well, yes I am. I do like my flat very much but Tom wants us to move into his because it is larger and has a second bedroom.'

'Do you need two bedrooms?' Karen mused.

'Well, yes, we do for when you and Bill come to stay.'

'We could always put up in a hotel, there's certainly plenty of those in New Brighton so that would not be a problem.'

'If you and Bill are coming to visit us then I would sooner you stayed under our roof than someone else's,' Jenny said firmly.

'You are still missing having a house and a garden?' Karen murmured.

'A house or perhaps a bungalow.'

'Is Tom in agreement?'

'Well, yes, but I don't think he would want a garden, leastways not a very big one.'

'If it's only a small one then you have neighbours living so close to you that you haven't any real privacy,' Karen pointed out.

'That's true! We could always employ a gardener but you know what it's like – they never do things quite the way you want them done.'

'I think Tom's idea is the best then, and you should stay on at Merseyside Mansions. There are plenty of shops close by in Victoria Road, you can always take a walk on the promenade and you are only half an hour or so from Liverpool. Why not give it a try and if you don't like it and still feel you want a house or a bungalow then move later on.'

'That is one solution,' Jenny agreed, 'but we are getting older and the longer we put off moving the more difficult we will find it is to do so later on. We are no spring chickens you know,' Jenny reminded her.

'Rubbish. These days moving house is so simple. The removal men come in, pack everything for you and put it exactly where you want it to be in your new home.'

'Anyway,' she went on when Jenny remained silent, 'Bill and I would always come and help you.'

'You make it all sound so simple and easy that it looks as though I'm making a fuss over nothing.' Jenny sighed.

'Let's get back to fixing this new wedding date,' Karen suggested, adroitly changing the subject.

'Well, I thought if we made it when Bill has his half term then you and Bill can be there and we won't have to try and do everything over a weekend. We could even spend a few days together afterwards. So when is Bill's half term?'

'It's now. That's why he's taking these boys on this holiday trip to Belgium. They do it now so that it doesn't interfere with their term's work and gives them a break before they have to sit exams.'

'Oh, dear. I didn't realize that.'

Jenny sounded so crestfallen that Karen quickly said that it wasn't really any problem. They would make the time to come as long as it wasn't when Bill had to organize exams.

For the rest of the journey they talked about what they would wear and the hundred and one other things that would have to be planned in advance.

As they pulled up outside Karen's house they could hear the telephone ringing. 'Stay here in the car with Angela while I dash to answer it, will you,' Karen said as she took her keys out of the car. 'It's probably Bill,' she called over her shoulder as she hurried towards the front door.

When she reappeared a few minutes later she came over and opened the passenger door. 'It's for you, Gran; it's Jane and she said it was important.'

'Jane, Jane Phillips? What does she want?'

'I don't know, Gran. She simply said she wanted to speak to you urgently because it was very important.'

'Really!' Jenny's tone was scathing. 'She's a trouble-making old witch. Probably seen Tom talking to another woman or going into my flat and she thinks it's a juicy bit of gossip to pass on to me,' she grumbled as she got out of the car and headed for the house.

Two minutes later when Karen followed with baby Angela she found Jenny white-faced and shaken, holding the receiver in her hand.

'Is something wrong, Gran? Have you had bad news?' Karen asked, taking the phone from her hand and putting it back into its cradle.

Jenny nodded. 'Yes. It was about Tom. He . . . he's had an accident.'

'Oh, no! What sort of an accident?'

'He fell off a ladder while painting the ceiling in my flat and he's been taken to hospital in Liverpool. Jane said they think he has a broken femur. I'll have to get back right away, Karen.'

'Yes, of course. I understand.' Karen put an arm around Jenny's shoulders and gave her a reassuring hug.

'Do you think you will be all right here on your own Karen? I promised Bill I'd stay until he got home.'

'Of course I'll be all right. He'll be home in a couple of days' time. Don't worry about me,' Karen told her quickly.

'Can you run me to the nearest railway station or shall I phone for a taxi?'

'Slow down, slow down or you'll be having a heart attack,' Karen said worriedly.

'I'm all right. Don't fuss, Karen. I must get back as quickly as possible. I'll go and get my things together.'

'Come and sit down in an armchair for a minute or two. If Tom is in hospital then he's in good hands and there is not a lot you can do so do sit down for five minutes.'

'Come on,' Karen urged when Jenny looked uncertain.

'I'll make a pot of tea and you can think through what is the best thing to do,' she said, leading Jenny over to one of the armchairs and making her sit down in it.

'Gran, will you look after Angela for me for a minute or two,' she said quickly, picking the baby up out of its carrycot and passing her to Jenny.

'Stay in that armchair and don't move. I don't want you dropping her,' she added with a forced laugh as she went into the kitchen to make the tea.

Jenny had calmed down a little by the time Karen returned with the tea.

'I hate leaving you in the lurch like this and I know there may not be very much I can do for Tom if he is in hospital but I do feel I ought to be there,' Jenny explained as she sipped the hot tea.

'Of course you do, and don't worry about me,' Karen told her, leaning forward and squeezing Jenny's hand.

'As soon as I've drunk this tea I'll go up and pack my case. If I leave anything behind then you can let me have it next time we see you.'

'Don't worry if you leave things behind, I'll take care of them,' Karen assured her.

'Right,' Jenny placed her cup down on the side table. 'While I go and do that could you look up the train times for me and then send for a taxi.'

She stood up and made for the door, then paused and looked back at Karen. 'Now are you quite sure you will be able to manage on your own?'

'Of course I can; now stop worrying,' Karen told her as she picked up her own cup and Jenny's and carried them through to the kitchen.

When Jenny came back down ten minutes later, Karen was putting the baby into her carrycot ready to put her in the car.

'You're not driving me to the station; I told you to order a taxi.'

'When did I ever do what you told me,' Karen replied teasingly. 'Come on; stop wasting precious time. I'm driving you.'

It wasn't until ten minutes later, after they'd left the house, that Jenny realized that Karen wasn't driving in the direction of the railway station.

'Where are you taking me?' she asked in a worried tone.

'Home to Wallasey, of course. I wouldn't trust you on a train, not in the state you are in. I've phoned Bill so he knows what is happening and he will come to Merseyside Mansions when he gets back home.'

'Karen, I don't want you to do that,' Jenny complained.

'No arguing, Gran! You didn't seem to be very sure that I could manage on my own, remember? Well I'm not sure that you can either so this way we can support each other.'

Forty

It was almost dark when they arrived at Merseyside Mansions. Angela was fretful and hungry, Karen tired after the long drive and Jenny was apprehensive and concerned because she knew it was too late to visit Tom in hospital that night.

They had broken the journey for a meal so they were not hungry, but both of them felt they needed a cup of tea and they were longing for their bed.

'You make the tea while I feed Angela,' Karen said as she unstrapped the carrycot from the back seat and locked the car up.

She handed Jenny the carrier bag that held milk as well as a loaf of bread, bacon and eggs for their breakfast the next morning that they had bought en route.

Apart from the security lights, which were left on all night in the corridors, the place seemed to be darkness. Jenny fumbled with her keys, opened the door to her flat and switched on the light. The sight that met their eyes made both women gasp in dismay.

The furniture had all been moved as close to the walls as possible and white dust sheets covered everything in the room including the floor. An overturned stepladder stood in the centre of the room. There was a large tin of paint overturned beside it lying in a thick white gooey mess.

'We certainly can't stay here tonight, we'd better go up to Tom's flat; it can't be in a worse mess than it is down here,' Jenny said as she stepped back, switched off the light and locked the door.

Tom's flat was in perfect order and showed obvious signs of having recently been decorated. Everything looked pristine clean and fresh.

'Thank heaven for that,' Karen murmured. 'I was afraid he might have been working on both flats at the same time, you know how disorganized men can be sometimes.'

'Not Tom,' Jenny said firmly. 'He always finishes one job before starting the next. He's very methodical.'

'Yes, he's even washed up and put away whatever dishes he was using for his last meal,' Karen commented as she went into the kitchen to put the kettle on and prepare a bottle for Angela.

An hour later the three of them were in bed and asleep. Jenny had thought she would toss and turn all night, she had so many thoughts and questions buzzing around in her head, but the moment her head touched the pillow she was asleep.

When she awoke next morning she couldn't for a moment remember where she was. Then, in a flash, it all came rushing back and she was up making a cup of tea for herself and Karen and wondering how early they could go to the hospital to see Tom.

'I think we ought to phone first and ask them if we can visit,' Karen advised. 'No point in us all going over there and then spending hours hanging around if they will only let us visit at certain times.'

'But this is an emergency,' Jenny said heatedly.

'To us it may be but to them it is routine, Gran. They won't change their rules simply to please us. Why don't you speak to Jane Phillips first and see what news she has now.'

'No!' Jenny shook her head. 'I'll have a word with the concierge and see what news she has.'

'Very well, but let's have breakfast first and you can do that while I am bathing Angela and feeding her.'

The concierge had not heard any fresh news from the hospital but while Jenny was talking to her Jane Phillips came into the reception area and spotted her there.

'Ah, so you are home, Jenny. Have you seen Tom or heard any news about how he is now?'

'No, I was just asking if there had been any message from the hospital.'

'Well it's hardly likely that they would ring here again because I told them you were on holiday and we had no idea when you would be coming home.'

'You didn't give them Karen's number?'

'How could I when I didn't know it?'

'Yes, you did, Tom gave it to you and you phoned it to let me know what had happened.'

'Well, I didn't know if you wanted them to have it or not. You are always so secretive about your affairs. Anyway, Tom knew it and obviously told them, so they would have rung you if they thought he was in any danger. Or perhaps they have tried ringing you and not got an answer since you're not there,' Jane said sharply.

Jenny bit her lip to stop herself saying anything that might antagonize Jane. She wasn't in the mood for wasting time bantering with her while several other people were standing nearby and constantly interrupting to ask her about Tom.

'I suppose you don't know what the visiting hours are at the hospital?' she asked, looking round hopefully.

'Try phoning them, I'm sure they will be able to tell you,' Jane said sarcastically.

'Yes, that is what I am going to do,' Jenny said and turned and hurried back to the flat.

It was mid-afternoon before they saw Tom. He was propped up in bed halfway down a ten-bed ward looking very fed up but otherwise not really much the worse for his ordeal.

His face lit up when he saw them and he raised a hand in welcome.

'They say I can come out in a couple of days,' he told them as soon as their greetings were over and he had the time to comment on how well baby Angela was doing. 'In fact, I think they would like me out by Sunday.'

'It's Friday today, how on earth are we going to cope? You won't be able to walk will you?' Jenny said worriedly.

'No, but they will be supplying me with crutches when I come out so once I get used to using those I'll be able to get around.'

'You'll have to be very careful,' Jenny admonished.

'True, and I won't be able to finish off the decorating, not for a couple of weeks at any rate,' Tom agreed gloomily.

'You're not going up a ladder again in a hurry,' Jenny told him firmly.

'I wasn't on a ladder only on a set of steps,' Tom protested.

'Well, that's the same thing, so exactly what happened? How did you come to fall off then? Did some of the rungs break or something?'

'No, they didn't break and the accident was my own fault,' Tom explained. 'Instead of getting down and moving the steps I overreached and they went over sideways and took me with them. I tried to save myself and somehow my leg was underneath the steps and that was how my femur was broken.'

'So how long were you lying there?'

'Not very long, thank goodness, because it was very painful.'

'Someone heard you fall did they?' Karen asked.

'No, not exactly. Jane Phillips was doing one of her inspection walkabouts, you know what she's like, and she heard me yelling. The next thing I knew she was in the flat and had found me lying there. She wanted to try and move the steps off me and to help me to get up but I was pretty sure that I had broken my leg so I told her to leave me where I was and to go and phone for an ambulance.'

'Well, I suppose we should be thankful that she is such a busybody because you could have been lying there for hours or days before you were found,' Jenny admitted grudgingly.

'Yes, the ambulance people were great. The paramedics knew exactly what to do and they gave me something for the pain while they lifted the steps clear and then put me on a stretcher.'

'And Jane was still hanging around?'

'Of course, so I gave her Karen's telephone number and asked her to phone and let you know what had happened,' Tom explained.

'She probably enjoyed doing that,' Jenny murmured with a tight smile.

'So you can come home on Sunday,' Karen interrupted. 'How do you get home? Will you be able to get into my car or would a taxi be a better bet?'

'I think they are prepared to send me home in an ambulance because I have been told I mustn't bend the leg for a couple of weeks because there is some damage to the patella, that's the knee cap.'

'Perhaps we had better speak to the Sister and make sure this is what is going to happen and what time we can expect you home,' Karen suggested.

The Sister confirmed everything Tom had said. 'He will have to come back in six weeks' time for a check up and probably need a course of physiotherapy afterwards,' she added. 'However, don't worry about that now. You will be notified when he has to attend. By then he should be able to travel in the normal way,' she added. We will notify your own doctor but if you follow the advice in the instruction sheet we will give you when you leave here there should be no complications.'

'So what time on Sunday can we expect him home?' Karen asked as the Sister turned to leave them.

'It will probably be in the morning, some time between ten o'clock and midday as soon as a doctor has seen him and discharged him. It all depends on how busy we are.'

Forty-One

Tom arrived home shortly after midday on Sunday. He looked gaunt and seemed to have difficulty in balancing himself on the crutches the hospital had provided. His right leg was in plaster and he had a large black leather splint from just above the knee to the ankle that made it impossible for him to bend his leg at all.

The ambulance men helped him into the reception area of Merseyside Mansions and then left him with Jenny and Karen who were waiting there for him.

It was a beautiful warm spring day and the reception area was very busy with people arriving home either from a walk along the promenade or from church. Others were passing through on their way to have lunch at one of the nearby restaurants.

They all stopped to speak to Tom and said how sorry they were about his mishap and how pleased they were to see him home again and wished him a speedy recovery.

It was well after one o'clock before they were able to get back to his apartment and by that time Tom was almost too exhausted to enjoy the meal of salad and cold meats that Jenny had prepared in readiness for their return.

As soon as they had finished eating Tom wanted to go and look at Jenny's flat and decide what they should do about finishing off the decorating, but both Jenny and Karen insisted that he should have a rest first.

Although he seemed rather annoyed about this he admitted that he did feel rather exhausted and that he had been awake most of the night anticipating his homecoming.

'Sit down in your armchair for a few minutes,' Jenny suggested. 'I'll make some coffee and when we've drunk that we'll all go and take a look.'

Before the coffee was ready, Tom was asleep.

'He looks absolutely worn out,' Jenny murmured as she fetched a rug and wrapped it round him. 'I'm sure his hair is a lot greyer than it was.'

'Probably because of all the pain he has been in,' Karen murmured sympathetically.

Tom was still sleeping when Bill arrived.

'I came straight here. I haven't washed or unpacked my things, just dumped them in the hallway at home,' he told them. 'When I checked the times of the trains I found there's not a full service on a Sunday so I had to make a dash in order to get one right away.'

He listened attentively as Jenny told him about the accident and agreed wholeheartedly that Karen had done the right thing in driving her home.

'If you'd like her to stay on then I can catch an early morning train home tomorrow,' he told Jenny. 'I have to be back at school tomorrow otherwise I would stay on as well and give you a hand.'

'No, really there is no need for that,' Jenny said quickly. 'Tom has crutches so he can get around and we won't be doing anything of importance for the next couple of weeks.'

'What about if he has to go to the hospital for treatment or a check-up?'

'We can always get a taxi.'

Although they kept their voices low Tom seemed to sense that there was someone else there and stirred and opened his eyes.

'Hello Bill, what are you doing here?'

'I came to collect Karen and take her home. How are you feeling?'

Tom grimaced as he tried to pull himself upright in the chair. 'Not too good. Give me a couple of weeks though and I'll be back to decorating.'

'Do you think that is wise?' Bill laughed. 'I'd give it a miss if I were you. Take that tumble as a warning that it's time you stopped doing such strenuous work.'

'Are you suggesting that I'm too old to do DIY jobs?' Tom scowled.

'You're getting that way by the look of things,' Bill joked back.

'Got to finish what I started. Have you seen the room? Come on,' he said abruptly before Bill could answer, 'I'll take you and let you see it.'

Jenny held her breath as Tom struggled painfully to his feet and then swayed as he put out a hand to get his crutches that were just out of reach.

No one said a word as Bill grabbed at his arm and Jenny thrust the crutches towards him. Karen raised her eyebrows at Jenny who pressed a finger to her lips.

'Shall we wait here or go with them?' Karen whispered as the two men reached the door.

'Perhaps we should stay here,' Jenny murmured.

'It's Tom's first walk since he came home from hospital – what if he stumbles or falls over?'

'Leave it to Bill. Tom will probably be less nervous without an audience. Let's make a meal while they're out. Bill must be starving and then you will want to get on the road as it's quite a long drive home.'

Tom was not a good patient. He resented not being able to do things and became tetchy and irritable. They had plenty of visitors during the first week. Jane Phillips called in most days to ask how he was – unless she had seen him out in the passageway first and stopped him there to interrogate him about his progress.

The Major brought him some books to read and a bottle of whisky, warning him to have a nip only before bedtime, not during the day, because he didn't want to be held responsible if Tom fell over again. He invited them to go to his flat for a snifter and to meet Isabel. Jenny thanked him and promised they would do so when Tom was a little more mobile.

'Who is Isabel?' Tom asked after the major had moved away.

'Isabel is his new girlfriend. Surely you remember her. She's quite flamboyant and caused quite a stir when she first arrived. He thought she was an artist but she explained she was an artiste; not a painter as he'd thought but a lion tamer.'

'Heavens! She should have some tales to tell. We'll have to take the Major up on that invitation.'

Sandra Roberts and Beryl Willis saw Tom in reception and wished him a speedy recovery. Dan Grey called at Tom's flat to wish him well and reminded Jenny that if he or Mavis could help in any way she had only to get in touch.

Despite all the offers of help and assistance Jenny found the first week that Tom was home was something of a nightmare. He was not very adept at using his crutches and seemed to be continually catching them in things.

He blamed it on the smallness of the flat. Jenny took up all the rugs because she was afraid that if he caught one of his crutches in the corner of one of them he might have another fall. She moved the furniture around so that as far as possible he could walk freely across from the door to his chair without having to negotiate any obstacles.

At night he seemed to have considerable difficulty in settling down in bed. The enormous splint on his leg made it impossible for him to lie on his side.

From the spare room where she was sleeping, Jenny could hear the upheaval and groaning as he tried to get comfortable. Once or twice she went in to see if he would like a hot drink but he was so cross because he had disturbed her that after that she tried to ignore the noises coming from his room.

Instead she found a small bell and put it on his bedside table and made him promise that he would ring it if he needed help during the night.

Although he promised that he would use it Jenny was pretty sure that he wouldn't and she spent a great many sleepless hours listening to him groaning out loud as he tried to get comfortable.

After the first few days, because the weather had broken and it was raining non-stop, Jenny encouraged him to walk up and down the passageway outside his flat.

'It will give you some exercise and help you to get used to using your crutches,' she told him.

At first he was reluctant to do so because he kept meeting other residents who wanted to know how he was and questioning him about how it had happened and precisely what he had broken.

'Perhaps I should put up a notice on the desk in reception giving them all the details,' Tom grumbled. 'They make me feel like a prize idiot.'

'Never mind, as soon as the weather is better we'll go for short walks on the prom,' Jenny promised.

She was quite annoyed when one morning Jane stopped her and told her that she had just seen Tom going into her flat.

'I thought you should know, Jenny, because with those dust sheets all over the floor he could easily get those crutch things caught up in the folds of cloth and have another fall,' Jane told her.

'What on earth do you think you were doing,' Jenny asked him crossly when he came back to his own flat.

'Looking to see what work still remained to be done,' he explained rather sheepishly.

'Really! I thought perhaps you were going to try and do it today,' she told him sarcastically.

'I'm worried about how long it will be before I can finish it. It's one hell of a mess at the moment.'

'There's no point in brooding about it,' she told him. 'Rest until that leg is better and you can walk again and then we'll decide what to do about my flat. We can always pay someone to come in and finish it.'

'No, I want to do it myself. I started it so I'll finish it,' he stated firmly. 'I don't want a professional criticizing my efforts. He'd probably insist on doing it all over again and that would cost us a mint of money.'

'As you wish,' Jenny compromised, 'only don't take risks and don't try and do it too soon.'

'Until that is finished we can't get on with our wedding plans,' Tom pointed out.

'Until your leg is better and you can walk again we can't get married anyway. I'm not walking down the aisle with a man on crutches,' she told him.

'I wasn't thinking of a big slap up do,' Tom said with a sigh. 'That doesn't seem to work for us, it always ends up that we have to cancel. This time I thought of a quiet register office wedding with just Karen and Bill there and then the four of us going for a meal afterwards. Nothing else; no big party here next time.'

'That suits me perfectly,' Jenny agreed. 'As soon as you can walk without crutches then we'll go ahead,' she told him firmly.

Forty-Two

Jenny spent the worst week she could ever remember after Karen, Bill and baby Angela left. She had never known Tom to be so irritable or short-tempered.

He complained all the time that he was bored, and nothing she did seemed to please him. He said that his leg was hurting and that he couldn't get comfortable in his armchair or in bed, but he wouldn't take the painkillers the hospital had prescribed.

'I don't believe in them,' he stated. 'You take pills for one thing and you then have to take some other pills to counteract what the first lot did. I'd sooner grin and bear it.'

'Well then, I wish you would try grinning,' Jenny told him. 'At the moment you are scowling all the time like some old gargoyle.'

Tom gave her a withering look. 'Thank you for being so understanding.'

'I do understand and I know you must be in pain and discomfort with that splint contraption on your leg. That's the reason the hospital recommended those painkillers. They will help to reduce the inflammation as well as make the pain more bearable,' she added as she took away the pills and glass of water she'd brought for him.

Even though he was in pain Tom was restless. He couldn't sit still for a minute and mooched round the flat picking things up and putting them down and constantly dropping one of his crutches in the process. Often he was unable to pick it up again for fear of overbalancing so Jenny had to stop what she was doing to go and help him.

On Tuesday the weather improved. The rain had stopped and the sun was shining from a clear blue sky so Jenny suggested a walk.

'How do you think I can go for a walk with this lot,' he said, struggling to lift up his leg encased in its splints.

'Well, I thought we could take a short stroll along the promenade, sit in one of the shelters and watch what is happening on the river.'

Although he scoffed at the idea, after they'd had lunch he said he thought a walk along the prom might be a good plan.

Their walks became a regular feature of their day.

Sometimes they took them in the morning, sometimes later in the day. A lot depended on what Tom wanted to do. His confidence about walking improved rapidly and by the end of the week they were taking some really long walks along the promenade and his mood was slightly improved.

When they returned on Friday morning, Jenny opened the door to Tom's flat and saw that someone had slipped a note under the door.

She waited until Tom had flopped down into his armchair before going into the kitchen to switch the kettle on and read it.

To her astonishment it was from Bill.

'I'm in your flat finishing off the decorating,' it said. 'Don't let Tom know. Pop along when you can manage to do so.'

She wanted to rush and see him right away but an inner caution made her carry on as if nothing had happened. She had left their midday meal in the oven and, as soon as she had cleared away after they had eaten, she went along to her own flat on the pretext of taking the rubbish out to the bin.

Tom was so tired after their walk and a good meal that he only grunted. He had switched on the television and was engrossed in one of his favourite programmes.

Jenny gasped when she let herself into her flat. All the dust sheets had disappeared and the steps from which Tom had fallen were leaning against one wall. The ceiling had been freshly coated and there was a strong smell of emulsion paint.

She found Bill in the kitchen making a cup of coffee.

'Bill, this is a tremendous surprise. How did you manage to get in?'

He grinned as he gave her a bear hug and a kiss on the cheek. 'I used Karen's keys.'

'Why didn't you let us know you were coming? I would have had a meal waiting for you. Are you on your own? What on earth made you come? Are Karen and baby Angela all right?'

Jenny's questions tumbled out in such quick-fire succession that Bill had no chance to answer any of them.

'Coffee?' he asked.

'Well, yes, why not.'

'Why not indeed. After all it is your coffee. I'm afraid you'll have to drink it black because there's no milk.'

'If you wait a minute I can pop back to Tom's flat and get some,' Jenny said, moving towards the door.

'No, don't do that. I don't want Tom to know I'm here, leastways not for the moment. I don't want him to discover I'm finishing off the job he started until it's all completed, in case he starts to protest and make a fuss.'

'He probably will make a fuss,' Jenny said ruefully.

'By the time he finds out it will be too late for him to do anything about it though,' Bill said, smiling. 'I take it he's dozing at the moment?' he added.

'Either that or he's engrossed in something on TV, but he won't be for long if he finds me missing.'

'Well, you get back to his flat and make sure you keep him occupied. I'm planning on getting everything down here completed and all cleaned up by tomorrow evening.'

'You mean you are staying the night?'

'I am and what's more I'm sleeping in your bed, so I hope you don't mind.'

'Not at all. What about food and everything?' she asked.

'Don't worry about me. I brought sandwiches with me and I intend to pick up some milk when I go out for a pub meal this evening.'

'That hardly seems right,' Jenny protested. 'At least let me feed you.'

'If you do that then Tom will know I'm here and we both know he will protest strongly about me working on your flat.'

'So you are going to sneak off tomorrow as soon as you've finished and leave me to face the music are you?' Jenny said with a laugh.

'Not a bit of it. When I've finished I'll let Tom know I'm here and keep my fingers crossed that when he sees the results he'll be so pleased that it's all finished that he won't be annoyed.'

'Well, I suppose there's not much I can do in that case except say thank you, Bill. One thing I must insist on though is that I go out and shop for you tomorrow morning.'

'I see. You don't want me wasting any precious time on such frivolities as eating or shopping.'

'You are quite right,' she agreed, her eyes twinkling. 'Don't worry,' she added as she moved towards the door. 'I'll be very discreet and I won't let on to Tom what you are doing. I'll leave you to tell him when you're finished.'

She was still smiling to herself as she went back to Tom's flat. It was such a relief to know that the work on her place was being finished and that there would be no need to argue with Tom about who was going to do it. She couldn't get over the fact that Bill had made his way into the building and been in her flat since early in the morning without her ever knowing.

By mid-afternoon the following day Bill had finished his self-imposed task and knocked on their door. Jenny had been waiting for this moment all day and her heart pounded when she heard him there.

'Finished?' she whispered as Tom called out to ask who it was when she went to answer it.

Bill nodded.

'We have a visitor, look who's here,' Jenny said as she brought Bill into the sitting room.

'Bill? Good grief, what are you doing here? Where's Karen and the baby?'

'Oh, they're at home. I popped up on my own to see how you were,' Bill said, grinning broadly as he shook hands with Tom.

'Well, sit down and Jenny will make some tea; that is unless you'd sooner have a beer or a tot of whisky.'

'No, no, tea will be fine. I'm driving so I won't have anything stronger.'

'A long way to come just for a cup of tea,' Tom commented. 'Did you have some other business in this area?'

'Yes, I did as a matter of fact,' Bill said as he sank into an armchair facing Tom. 'I had a bit of tidying up to do.'

'Oh?' Tom looked mildly interested and waited for him to go on.

'Yes, a flat that needed finishing off.'

'Oh yes.' For a moment Tom didn't seem to understand what Bill was telling him. Then he frowned. 'You don't mean Jenny's flat do you?'

'The very same,' Bill agreed as he took the cup of tea from Jenny and ladled two spoonfuls of sugar into it.

'You knew about this?' Tom pushed aside the tea that Jenny proffered to him and stared at her angrily.

'Not until it was too late to do anything about it,' she said mildly. 'Isn't it wonderful though to know that it is all finished and that the flat is all cleaned up.'

Tom didn't answer, but his scowl deepened and Jenny tried to move on to other topics. She could see that he was angry and she wanted to divert his mind from what had happened. She began to make enquiries about the baby but Tom cut across her conversation almost as if she wasn't there.

'So Jenny asked you to come and do it and let you in and didn't say a word about it to me,' he said in an angry voice.

'No, it had nothing to do with Jenny. It was Karen's idea and when she put it to me I agreed with her wholeheartedly that it was the least we could do to help. I came up very early yesterday morning . . .'

'Yesterday morning! You mean you've been here for almost two whole days and never once thought to come and ask me what my opinion was or what I had planned on doing in that flat.'

'Well, it was obvious what you were planning to do,' Bill said with a laugh.

'Really?'

'You were putting emulsion on the walls and ceiling and freshening up the paintwork. Not that it really needed doing because it was very clean.'

'It needed doing,' Tom said assertively.

'I always think it's a waste of time decorating before you sell because the new people always want to put their own stamp on the place and usually their ideas are different from yours.'

'Probably your ideas about how it should be done are different to mine,' Tom grumbled.

'I think it was very kind of Bill to give up his weekend and do this for us,' Jenny intervened, hoping to pour oil on troubled waters.

'Well, you would, seeing as you asked him to come and kept the entire arrangement secret from me,' Tom retorted.

'No, Jenny didn't ask me,' Bill said firmly. 'In fact when she found me in the flat working she was very surprised and wanted to come straight away and tell you but I persuaded her not to. I was hoping that it would be a pleasant surprise for you and that you would feel relieved because it wasn't hanging over your head that it needed to be finished.'

Forty-Three

Tom's bad mood continued. Long after Bill had left he sat in a sullen brooding silence, not even reading the newspaper or watching television.

'If you are feeling annoyed and have something to say then say it,' Jenny stated when she asked him if he wanted a cup of tea and he didn't even answer her.

'What does it matter what I think or what I feel about things since you completely ignore my wishes,' he retorted. 'You knew damn well that I wanted to finish that decorating myself and yet you cajole Bill to come and do it without even a word to me.'

'I also knew that you couldn't do it and that you were worried about it. As a matter of fact, it was exactly as Bill told you. I didn't ask him to come and I was astonished when I found him in my flat and realized he'd been working there practically all day.'

'A likely story,' Tom said in a scathing voice. 'Anyway, if it is true then why the hell didn't you come straight back up and tell me that he was here and what he was planning on doing.'

'Bill asked me not to do that. He wanted to finish the decorating and then tell you. He thought it would be a lovely surprise for you.'

'It was a surprise all right! What does he know about decorating? I bet it's one hell of a mess down there.'

'No, he's finished everything off beautifully. Why don't you come and look for yourself?'

'Not much point if it is all done,' Tom said tetchily. 'It's too late now to make any changes. We'll just have to hope that nobody notices how amateurish the painting is.'

Jenny bit her lip and said nothing. She could see that it was pointless arguing with Tom. He was obviously hurt and annoyed by what had happened even though she and Bill had intended it to be for the best.

It was almost a week before Tom finally agreed to go and look at the flat. They had been for a walk along the promenade and for the first time in days held a normal conversation.

As usual he had tired fairly quickly and they had sat down for a while in one of the shelters out of the hot sun.

There had been plenty of activity on the river to watch as well as children playing on the shore and paddling in the water. It was so hot that she helped Tom to remove his linen jacket and then offered to go down on to the shore, where there was an ice-cream van parked, and get them each a cone.

She had expected him to refuse but to her surprise he had seemed to be keen for her to do so.

When she returned with it he thanked her and seemed to be more relaxed than he had been since he came home from hospital. As they sat there enjoying the activity going on all around them, Tom talked about things in general and then finally about the flat.

'We'll go and check it over when we get back,' he pronounced, 'make sure it's ready to go on the market.'

'On the market?' Jenny looked at him in a rather puzzled way.

'That's our next step, isn't it, since my flat is preferable to yours because of the second bedroom.'

'Well, that's quite true but there's no hurry to get rid of mine immediately, is there?'

'No point in wasting money paying maintenance charges on both,' he said decisively.

Tom was strongly in favour of putting Jenny's flat on the market as soon as possible, but she was reluctant to do this. During the past week she had spent as much time as she could in it, usually when Tom was sleeping, and her fondness for it increased and she wasn't at all sure that she wanted to sell it.

She had liked it from the first moment she'd moved in there and now it seemed like a haven of peace after the unpleasant atmosphere in Tom's flat. Furthermore, it contained all her own possessions, which she kept rearranging to make the most of the space and appearance of the flat.

However, to humour Tom, she agreed they should take a look on their return from their walk. He glanced round critically and Jenny waited for some adverse comment about Bill's work but there was none. Instead he seemed to be summing up as many of the good aspects of the flat as possible. He commented on the lightness of the rooms, the view from the window and so on.

When they went back to his flat he immediately found a pen

and paper and while she was making them a cup of tea he was busy concocting an advert to go into the local newspaper.

'I think we should put this in the *Liverpool Daily Post* and some of the national newspapers such as the *Observer* or *The Times* and perhaps the *Manchester Guardian*,' he told her as he passed it over to her so that she could read what he had written.

'It's fine but there's no hurry to do anything at the moment is there,' she murmured in a non-committal voice as she handed it back to him.

'It's about the only thing we can do at the moment since you refuse to go ahead with our wedding plans while I'm on crutches,' he said brusquely.

'That wasn't quite what I said,' she retorted quietly. 'I do think it would be better to wait until you are able to walk without them though. It is only a matter of a couple more weeks now,' she added in as bright a voice as she could manage.

'How do you know that? My leg is still so damn painful that they may decide I need further surgery or something.'

Jenny said nothing. Indeed, her thoughts were not so much on Tom and the delay in fixing their forthcoming wedding date as on forfeiting her flat. She hadn't dreamed that she would feel like this; it wasn't possessiveness so much as realizing what a wonderful haven it was from the rest of the world and one she didn't want to lose.

'Let's fix a price for the flat. I think we should ask the same as you paid for it or perhaps a bit more?'

'I'll think about it,' Jenny promised.

'There's nothing to think about,' Tom said tetchily. 'Let's settle it now and then you can take the advert along to the newsagents in the morning when you go shopping. I'll note down the newspapers we want it to go in and then if you ask the newsagent he will contact them all for you, so tell him you want three insertions in each of them. That should bring it to the attention of a good number of people and we'll wait and see what happens.'

Jenny felt herself growing angry. It was her flat so surely it should be her decision about when they sold. After all, there was no hurry and once it was gone she would have nowhere to live even if she needed it. True, she was moving in with Tom, but his flat was in his name and he hadn't said a word about making the ownership a joint one. Where would she stand if something happened to him or if they should decide to part company?

She wanted to talk this through with Tom but she was afraid that while he was in such an antagonistic frame of mind he wouldn't be prepared to be reasonable. Come to that, she reflected, she wasn't in the mood herself to discuss such a delicate subject.

Taking the sheet of paper from him she folded it over and placed it in her handbag.

'We haven't agreed on the price,' he pointed out.

'No, I'll think about it and put a figure on it in the morning,' she prevaricated.

All she wanted to do at the moment was to end this conversation so that she could give herself time to think and decide whether or not she actually wanted to sell her flat. There really was no hurry. They didn't need the money.

'It's a very good time for us to sell,' Tom went on as if determined to pursue the matter. 'I can always be here to show prospective buyers around and talk over any points they raise; it won't interfere with anything you might be doing like shopping or going to the hairdressers or anything else.'

Jenny didn't answer. If she had to sell the flat then she'd prefer to deal with any potential buyers herself but she suspected the truth was she didn't want to sell it.

She toyed with the idea of asking such a high price for the flat that no one would even consider coming to look at it. But that would only prolong things because as soon as Tom saw the advert in the paper he would argue that she was being ridiculous and telephone the newspapers and ask them to correct the asking price.

There must be some other way, she reasoned, and wondered if it would be better to rent it out as a furnished flat. If she did that on a fairly short-term lease then she would know that it was always there for her should she ever want to move back in.

It was an alternative, although she had to admit that she didn't like the idea of other people, complete strangers, living in her flat and using all her equipment and even sleeping in her bed.

The only other ruse was to say she had put the adverts in the papers even though she'd not done so. Tom would find out eventually, of course, but it would give her time to decide what she really wanted to do.

Forty-Four

Tom was incensed when he discovered that the reason why the adverts had not appeared in any of the newspapers he'd selected was because Jenny hadn't inserted them.

'You defied me!' he raged, his face red and angry.

He looked so menacing that Jenny felt a frisson of fear run through her. Then she made matters worse by shrugging her shoulders.

'What's that supposed to mean?' Tom asked, his eyes flashing angrily.

'I'm not ready to sell, that's what it means,' she replied defiantly.

'That's too bad. I say that it is better that we sell while the market is buoyant. This is the best time of the year to sell; it's when people are thinking of moving home. Leave it until August or later and people will put off making such decisions until next year.'

'So, why can't we leave it until then? I'm not in any hurry.'

'We need to get our financial situation tidied up. I've had plenty of time to sit and think about these things over the last couple of weeks and I can see that there'll be a lot of unnecessary expense incurred by hanging on to that flat.'

'I'm the one meeting all the costs not you,' Jenny pointed out.

'You are at the moment but you won't be when we are married,' Tom argued.

'Why do you say that? I'll still have my own pension and money from investments,' Jenny pointed out stubbornly.

'Yes, and that's another matter that needs dealing with. Everything should be in our joint names and we should have a joint bank account so that we know precisely how much money we have coming in and what we are spending.'

'Are you proposing that we have a set amount for housekeeping and then perhaps you give me an allowance; some pocket money each week so that I can go to the hairdressers and buy some new stockings if I need them? If I want money for anything else, will I have to ask you for it?' Jenny asked in a scathing tone.

Tom's colour heightened. 'That's the way most married couples balance their budgets,' he blustered.

'That might have been the case in your parents' day, or even in yours when you were married, but not now. No, I am happy to pay my fair share of everything we spend including all the running costs of the house and on our food, but I keep my own money and spend it how I see fit. If I want to buy something for Karen or baby Angela I don't intend asking permission from you first to find out if I can do so.'

'You're being totally unreasonable and building this into a stupid argument,' Tom said angrily. 'I had no idea you could be so wilful. I should have guessed, of course, the moment I found out that you hadn't placed those adverts in the newspapers like I told you to do.'

'Is that so!' Jenny's voice was icy. 'Until this moment I had no idea that you could be such a chauvinist. I'm coming to the conclusion that it's not a wife you are looking for but a slave; someone to be at your beck and call and accept your judgement in everything. You are certainly not the man I thought you were.'

'Is that so,' he repeated, mimicking Jenny's words. 'I thought you were in love with me and would do whatever I wanted, yet ever since my accident, which was caused by doing something to please you, you have given me the cold shoulder completely. What happened to those cuddles and all that sweet talk about how much I meant to you during those nights in bed together?'

'You are forgetting that at the moment you have one leg encased in plaster almost from hip to ankle.'

'It might stop us making love but it doesn't prevent you from sleeping in my bed and comforting me,' he railed, his eyes flashing with anger.

'Tom, it's out of the question so let's cool it until after we are married.' She smiled and tried to keep her voice light. 'It won't be long now. As soon as you've had the plaster off we can set a new date.'

'I've done that already,' he told her with a sneer. 'I got tired of you messing around and prevaricating first for one reason and then another. I like my life to be ordered so I phoned the register office and told them we were now ready to make a new date. They were most understanding. It's all fixed for next Tuesday.'

'Next Tuesday! That's only four days away. Karen and Bill won't be able to come because Bill can't take any more time off work as they are in the middle of important exams.'

'We can get married without them being there,' he said brusquely.

'I want them to be there though, they're the only family we have.'

'You can see them afterwards, we'll go and spend a few days with them as soon as we are married if that is what you want.'

'It's all so rushed though. Who will we have as witnesses?'

'That's the last thing you need to worry about. The registrar said they'd find someone in the office. Hell's bells, woman, stop making such a fuss about it. It's only a piece of paper and if you weren't so bothered about it all being legal I wouldn't have taken the trouble to go through all this rigmarole at all,' he said angrily.

As he spoke he reached out and grabbed her by the arm, twisting it so that a sharp pain ran from her elbow up into her shoulder.

'Let go of my arm, Tom, you're hurting me,' she begged, tears in her eyes.

In response he frogmarched her through to the bedroom. 'Get on the bed,' he said hoarsely. 'I'll soon show you if having my leg in plaster stops me from making love to you.'

His assault was both vicious and unfeeling. She sensed he was trying to establish his dominance over her and she didn't like it. She lay passive, realizing that he was so much stronger than her that there was little point in fighting him.

When he was satiated and rolled off her exhausted she gingerly edged her way off the bed and then, not even stopping to put on her shoes, fled back to her own flat.

She lay on the bed, her face buried in a pillow, sobbing. For several minutes her mind was utterly blank; she was unable to think or reason. Then, very slowly, her sobs subsided and she sat up and dried her eyes and went into the kitchen and poured herself a strong drink.

She was too old to change her ways, she decided. She studied her reflection in her dressing table mirror as she combed her hair and renewed her lipstick. She was beginning to look old; there were wrinkles not simply laughter lines around her eyes and her hair was practically grey all over.

Taking a deep breath, she began to take stock of her life. Her hair might be turning grey and she might have a few wrinkles but she still had good health and plenty of energy, she thought gratefully.

Tom coming into her life had been like a breath of fresh air. She had been grateful when he sprang to her defence over the criticism levelled at Karen when she'd married Lionel Bostock. She not only liked Tom as a friend and companion but in so many ways she had come to depend on him, so would she be happy if that all ended, she asked herself.

She listed the positive attributes in her life. She was financially independent and was competent about making her own decisions. She enjoyed the freedom of living at Merseyside Mansions and being able to come and go as she pleased. She loved her flat and took pleasure from having it furnished the way she wanted it to be. Living on her own she was able to indulge in the sort of meals she enjoyed and eat when it suited her. Living alone meant that she was not regimentally tied to the clock or a strict routine.

She no longer felt responsible for Karen now that she was happily married to Bill and had an adorable baby daughter.

She had been flattered and excited when Tom became interested in her and, in that first phase of happiness, she had overlooked these details. It had been almost like a courtship where at first each person was trying to please the other or else didn't notice the other person's faults.

If Tom wanted to be her friend, even to be her lover, she would be happy to concede as long as she remained free and untrammelled and, above all, retain her own flat.

The accident had changed him. She'd had no idea that he could be so bad-tempered and aggressive. He was far too dominant. He expected her to fall in with his wishes whether they suited her or not and that was something she didn't intend to do.

Now that he was sure of her, or at least thought that he was, his true colours were revealed and she was no longer besotted by him. He had feet of clay after all and he wasn't a hero on a pedestal as she had seen him in those first hazy months.

He could be charming but he had a temper, he could be extremely grouchy, he wanted his own way in everything from which TV programme they would watch to controlling how they spent their money.

Becoming someone's wife only to be in thrall to their moods and under their tight financial control was not for her she decided.

She looked round her flat; this was her very own haven; it offered her an escape from the world as well as her freedom and she intended to keep it that way.

Having taken stock of the situation she decided that it was time to move on yet again. Her mind was made up; from now on she was absolutely determined to live the kind of life she wanted and not be beholden to anyone.